THE
OF Pleasure
PANIC
JORDAN'S GAME

HUSS

JORDAN'S GAME
BOOK TWO

Copyright © 2018 by JA Huss
ISBN: 978-1-944475-39-0

Edited by RJ Locksley
Cover Design by JA Huss

DEDICATI✳N

For all you fuckers out there who refuse to use an asterisk.

JA HUSS

PROLOGUE

J*RDAN

The many ways in which people find sexual pleasure will never stop fascinating me, but those who enter my world typically fit into a few neat little packages.

You've got your standard whips-and-handcuffs people. Some like it soft, some like it hard, some stay right in the middle. But the one thing they all get off on is pain. The threat of pain, I should clarify.

Because then you've got your standard fighters. Lovers who like all the extremes in every direction. Anger and bliss. Honesty and lies. Loyalty and cheating. It doesn't matter what the two extremes are, it is always black and white. They get off on pain too, but it's mental anguish that lights their fire.

There's a third category. The ones who crave drama outside the relationship. They're adrenaline junkies, addicted to the portrait they paint—of themselves, of others, of the world—and how they can make people react. They like the rush that comes from unfortunate circumstance.

Then you've got your mind-fuckers. It's pretty much an all-of-the-above kinda worldview. Physical pain that becomes pleasure, that becomes mental pain, that becomes pleasure, that becomes panic, that becomes pleasure.

I might be a mind-fucker.

But I don't play the games, I just run them. So it doesn't matter.

There are as many types of games as there are people who play them.

There are simple games, there are elaborate games, there are boring games—but who am I to judge?—and then there are games *within* games.

I'm sitting at the table overlooking the now-defunct lobby thinking about this next game, while Darrel Jameson, my full-time investigator since he quit the FBI and came to town to help find a lost girl for my friends, looks over the file in front of him. It's pretty interesting if you know how to read between the lines. I do, and so does he. That's why I use him.

"Huh," he says.

"Right?"

"I don't know what to think about this one."

"So don't think. Just get me what I need."

"We're gonna make waves."

"I'll ride them."

"We're gonna piss people off."

"When don't we?"

Darrel and I chuckle and do a fake *cheers* with the cut-crystal glasses we're drinking from. There was still whiskey behind the fucking bar. Good whiskey.

"OK." He sighs, then tips the rest of the amber liquid in his glass down his throat. He enjoys the burn for a few seconds before adding, "If you say so. I'm just the hired help."

"Yeah, right." I laugh. "I need it by Wednesday. This shit needs to happen on V-day, got me?"

"Got ya, boss." And then he gets up, tips an imaginary hat, walks across the room, and disappears down the stairs with the file clutched in his hand.

I drink the rest of my Scotch, thinking about how this one might go down as I trace my target's name in the construction dust that's settled on the table.

I'm sitting in the old Turning Point Club. I broke in. Couldn't fuckin' take it anymore. I had to see what the hell was going on in here.

Which is a big, fat nothing. Just a lot of plastic over the tables and chairs downstairs, a lot of dust up here, and a lot of darkness, since the security shutters are all closed and the revolving door has been boarded up.

A whole lot of... emptiness.

Back when I used to play games, I came here. I fucked a lot of willing, deviant men and women here. But it was sold over a year ago now and it's been sitting idle ever since. It's driving me crazy. I'm on the brink of distraction wondering what will become of it.

I gotta get this under control.

So many things are happening in my life right now.

This new game I'm playing is risky, no doubt.

Never done anything like this before.

Probably won't ever do it again.

So I better make it count.

CHAPTER ONE

*ISSY

"Say it with me!" I'm yelling that to the ladies in my women's empowerment masterclass.

"GO FUCK YOURSELF!" they all yell back.

"One more time!" I urge.

"GO FUCK YOURSELF!"

"What are you gonna do from now on?"

"BE IN CONTROL!"

"And how ya gonna do that?"

"TAKE NAMES!"

"And what are you gonna do with those names?"

"KICK SOME FUCKIN' ASS!"

I smile, fold my hands in front of me, and admire my clients one at a time. I always do this at the end of my masterclass. I acknowledge every one of them, hold their gaze for exactly two seconds as I picture how much stronger they are now than when they came here, and then repeat that until I've given everyone in the room their due.

"You," I say, walking the circle, pointing to them one at a time as I pass, "are not the woman you were when you first came here, are you?"

"No," they say. This time they don't yell. Two of them are crying, one is holding it in, but doing a horrible job, and the other three are taking deep breaths as they look skyward with their eyes closed. Just the way I taught them.

"You are brave," I say, touching each of them on the shoulder as I continue to walk around the circle. "You are strong," I say. "And your past does not define you."

They stare at me. All of them are crying now. But it's not a sad cry. It's not desperate and confused. That was who they were when they came through my doors two months ago on day one.

Who they are now, at the end of day sixty, bears no resemblance to who they were then.

"Ladies," I say, stopping to smile. "I pronounce you graduates of Issy Grey's Go Fuck Yourself Masterclass." My assistant, Suzanne, hands out their certificates and I shake their hands, keeping the affirmations going.

I am proud of each and every one of them. All of them are changed.

I did that.

Well, *they* did that. But I definitely helped.

It's a fulfilling feeling. To help. To make others your priority. To take them in all broken and sad and give them the tools they need to succeed.

This job isn't a job. It's a calling. And when I'm doing it, I am complete. I need nothing else.

Thirty minutes later the office has cleared out, Suzanne is cleaning up after our final exam—which started with kickboxing and ended with wine—and I'm peeking out the window in the door, watching Chella Baldwin as she looks both ways, crosses the street, and then bustles into my storefront, bringing the cold and snow with her.

"Whew!" she exclaims. "Stupid cold out there tonight. I saw your grads leave, congrats!" She holds out one of her cute pale yellow takeaway teacups that say Chella's Tea Room on them in swirly black calligraphy. She also has a pale yellow box tied with black string which I know contains one or two of her delicious lemon tarts.

"Thanks," I say. To all of it. The tea, the tarts, and the praise. "What's going on over there?" I nod my head to her shop. "You're so busy tonight."

Chella cocks her head at me with one of those are-you-fucking-kidding-me looks she gives me often.

"What?"

"It's Valentine's Day," she says.

"Oh." I'm so not interested in thinking about that right now. So I start shuffling papers on Suzanne's desk to make that clear.

"You're coming over."

I smile at her. Because she's Chella and she's sweet, and smart, and beautiful, and so that's what everyone does when she tries to butt into their lives for what she feels is a very good reason. She's old-money rich. Her father is a senator. Walcott is his name. Senator Walcott. He's been in DC for like thirty years. Which makes him powerful. Very powerful. I've never met him, so maybe my opinion of him is off, but on TV, when he's standing up there preaching to people about morals and ethics, all I see is… lies.

And that's what I expected when I heard his daughter owned the tea shop across the street. But that's not what I got once she came over to introduce herself.

She is nothing like her father. I almost can't even imagine her sweet face next to his sour one. I brought him up once to try to feel her out, see what kind of relationship she has with him, because she's never mentioned him. Not once. But she just said, "Smith and the baby are my family now."

"I am not going over there." I say it with firm conviction. That's what I do. That's who I am. Issy Grey, life coach extraordinaire. Filled up with the firmest of convictions.

"You are," Chella says. "Remember that game I told you about?"

"Oh, God, not this again. Come on, Chella. You know I'm not interested in that stuff. Just let it go."

"Listen," she says, leaning into my ear like she's gonna whisper a secret. "I have the game master over there. He almost never takes meetings with clients. It's almost always done anonymously. But for you, he made an exception."

"Am I supposed to be impressed that some man has made time for me?" I almost snort.

"This isn't any man, this is the *game master*."

"My answer is no, Chella. I'm not interested in a fantasy fulfillment game. Especially"—I do snort this time—"if it's sexual. I can think of nothing I'd like less than that."

She wraps her hands around my arm and leans in again. "That's because you haven't tried it yet." And then she winks. "I played," she says. "Couple years ago."

"You did?" I'm surprised at this. Not that I should be, I guess. Considering who her friends are. Who her husband is. But Chella? She's so sweet, and smart, and put-together. What in the world was she thinking?

"Mmmmmhmmm," she coos. "It's how I met Smith."

"Real-*ly*?" I drawl, more than a little curious now.

"Yup. And let me tell you, it was the most fun I've ever had in my life. Plus, you know"—she wiggles her diamond at me—"I got marriage and a baby on the way out of it. Not to mention a bunch of cool friends."

Elias Bricman. Quin Foster. Yeah, those are some friends, all right. They're well known around town, but not for the things one typically wants to be known for. Kinky sex games, secret clubs, masculine power.

"Just come over and talk to him about it."

"Who?" I ask. "Smith?"

"No, silly. The master. I can't tell you his name. He tries to keep all this stuff on the down low because of his day job. But you already know him, so…"

"I know him?" I ask, blinking at her. Because despite my resolve to get away from her as quickly as possible so I can go home and just take a long, hot bath alone, I'm so very, *very* curious now.

"Yes. Personally."

"Are you fucking with me right now?"

"No," she insists. "Come over and see. Otherwise this little secret will eat away at you, Issy Grey. Forever. You'll be kicking yourself tomorrow if you don't satisfy your curiosity. And I know you," she says, poking her finger into the fleshy part of my upper arm. "Your curiosity is insatiable. Just two weeks ago I mentioned a woman I know from the Denver Women's Tea Brigade who found out her husband was cheating on her and emptied their bank accounts to get ready to bail, and you—"

"I found her," I finish before she can. "And helped her. That's all."

Chella gives me one of those knowing looks, the kind with the raised eyebrow and a smirky grin that says, *That's all, huh?*

I hesitate, my resolve faltering. Because I am insanely curious about who this stupid game master is. Especially if I know him. I look around, thinking about who it could be.

"Come on. You've got nothing to lose. You can say no and that's that. Game over. But at least you get to know something practically no one else knows."

I think about this for a second. "Why would he out himself to me?"

"Because, like I said, you already know him. And he trusts you."

God, I'm dying now. He trusts me? Who the hell? And Chella knows I'm dying because she says, "Get your coat and walk over with me. Have a cup of tea, enjoy the festive atmosphere, and have a nice conversation with a handsome man about sex. It's Valentine's Day." She winks. "And your plans involve a date with your bathtub."

"How do *you* know?" I ask, defensive.

"Because you've been my best friend for almost a year now, Issy. Ever since you moved into this office last spring. It's my job as Denver's premier busybody to know what you're up to."

I can't stop the smile. Or the laugh. "Fine," I say, giving in. "But just one cup of tea. And I'm not playing this game. I'm only going to see who this mastermind is."

"Perfect," Chella sings. "Get your coat.

The Tea Shop is right next door to the old Turning Point Club, which went out of business a little over a year ago and no one ever reopened it. Which is surprising, since it's prime real estate. But I'm not looking to have the business I run associated with a sex club, so the building next door to Chella's shop being empty was actually one of the reasons I decided to rent space here. I mean, yeah, the name of my business *is* Go Fuck Yourself, but that's badass. And the women who come in afraid, desperate, and sad leave feeling empowered.

I do good here. The name has nothing to do with it. I'm not gonna apologize to anyone for the name, even though the city tried to make me change the sign and served me with an injunction three days after we opened. But that's another story. And I won that case anyway. In many different ways.

"Pfffft," I say to myself as we cross the snowy street.

"What are you huffing about?" Chella asks.

"Nothing," I say. "So what kind of game does this master mastermind?"

She looks over her shoulder as she reaches for the handle of her shop door and smiles. "Just wait. You'll see."

We go inside and there's like a bazillion couples having romantic... dinner? Afternoon tea? Wine? It's some combination of the three, I think. But the whole place smells wonderful. Like your grandma's kitchen at Christmas and a French bread shop all mixed together. "Mmm," I say, taking in the scents. "What's on the menu? That's not just cookies and cakes."

"I've got one set up for you and your date. So you'll see soon enough." She winks at me.

"My date? This is a meeting, Chella. Not a freaking date." And why is she winking at me? It's like she's got some secret plan going on here. And not just this sex game she's trying to rope me into, either. Something else. Is she trying to set me up with this guy?

"Where are we going?" But she doesn't respond, just leads me through a maze of tables to the private room in the back. "OK. Look, I'm gonna need some more—"

But before I can get the rest of my objection out, she opens the double doors and waves me in.

"Jordan?" I say.

Jordan stands, buttons his suit coat, and then walks towards me with his hands outstretched. He leans in to kiss my cheek and gives me a friendly hug. Says, "Nice to see you again, Issy. How's business going?"

"You?" I ask, pulling back, dumbfounded. "You're the… the… *sex master*?"

"Surprised?" he asks, arms out wide as if to say, *This is me.*

"But you're… you're a lawyer," I stammer. "Not just any lawyer, *my* lawyer."

"Not true," he says, waving me over to the table. I oblige him and sit. Mostly because he pulls out my chair and nods his head, but also because I'm eyeballing that bottle of wine on the table and sitting means I'm one step closer to drinking. "I was your first contact at the firm, but technically, Stratford was your legal counsel. How'd that all turn out, anyway?"

All that is in reference to the legal battle I had with the city over the word 'fuck' in my storefront sign. "I won," I say, lifting my chin. Because technically, I did.

"I heard you settled." He's pouring us both a glass of wine. "And the sign above your store says *Go F*ck Yourself.* With an asterisk." He winks.

Fuckin' winkers. Why is everyone winking at me today?

"I did settle, but I still won. Glenn Stratford gave me some good advice and I took it. It was the best possible outcome. And if you already knew this, why are you asking?"

"Just filling the empty spaces, Miss Grey."

"They paid me to change the sign. Almost ten thousand dollars. And," I stress, "they paid my legal fees too. It would've been counterproductive to continue the fight. I won."

Jordan smiles. He's one of those dashing men. Tall, square jaw, nice suit, expensive watch and shoes. Always put together. Brimming with confidence. Old money. "Indeed you did, Issy." He lifts his glass in a toast. I clink it, more to get that first swallow of wine down than to celebrate. I don't know what it is about Jordan Wells, but he's always made me nervous.

If I were one of my clients I'd say it's probably because he's so handsome. So bold. So self-assured. And even though I sell bold self-assurance right along with kickboxing and jujitsu classes, it's a show. It's always a show. People are people, and ain't no one figured out how to be in control all of the time. They just learned how to fake it better than most.

I'm an excellent faker. So no, that's not it. His looks and arrogance aren't what make me nervous.

"Anyway," Jordan says, cracking open a briefcase sitting on the empty chair next to him. "Business, huh?" He takes out a tablet and starts tapping on it.

"What's that?" I ask.

"Your application."

"I didn't apply."

"Chella did that for you." He looks at me over the top of his tablet. "You know that. That's why you're here with me on Valentine's Day and not out with... who would you be out with if you weren't here?"

17

"Fuck you," I mumble, then take a long gulp of wine. Jordan just chuckles to himself.

Why am I even bothering?

You're bothering, Issy Grey, because you really don't have plans tonight. And at least you're out somewhere. And there's wine. And a handsome man to look at across the table, even if you do want to punch him in the face right now. And Chella will bring us dinner.

And all that sounds a whole lot better than going home and binging Netflix while I drink wine in the bathtub tonight.

"OK." He sighs, like my application might be giving him a headache. "Let's just go through the questions to see if you're a good candidate for a game."

I blink at him. Three times. Slowly. To exaggerate the fact that this whole thing is ridiculous. "I never said I wanted to play a game. Chella did."

"But you're here," he says. "And you sat down. And you're drinking my wine and, presumably, going to eat dinner with me. So… you're interested." He pauses for a beat. "Correct?"

"I'm curious," I say, feeling defensive. "Possibly intrigued. That's it."

"Am I wasting my time?"

"Jesus Christ, Jordan. Just get on with it, OK? I'm not gonna play a game with you at this table. I'm tired. If you've got something interesting for me, something that might put a new spark into my life, then let's fuckin' hear it."

He looks back down at his tablet, smiling.

I roll my eyes and sigh. Loudly.

"So you're interested in our Panic Game Package?" He's still looking down at his tablet.

"What? What the hell is a panic game?"

"You know," he says, tapping away on his tablet like this is no big deal. "You need to be pulled out of your comfort zone." He raises his eyes to meet mine. "Choking. Strangulation. Domination. Stuff like that."

"What? No!" I actually laugh. "Who the hell—"

"Lots of people, Issy. It's nothing to be ashamed of."

"I'm not ashamed. I'm aghast at how you could've gotten me so… wrong!"

"Oh," Jordan says. "Well, this wasn't me, remember? This was Chella."

"Chella actually thought I needed a choking game?" I'm… perplexed. To say the least. Chella knows more about me than anyone these days. Which isn't saying much, since I've kept most of my past hidden. I'm not ashamed of it—I just don't feel it's productive to wave my mistakes around like a banner. Plus, my entire career was built on the premise that I fix people like me, not *am* people like me.

Which I do. I mean, I fixed *me*, right?

"No. Chella thought you needed a panic game. Perhaps I misinterpreted her request for you. Shall we ask her?"

"No," I say. "Just… no. I don't—"

"OK, maybe I got it wrong. Panic can mean a lot of things, but mostly it is about control. And let's face it, Issy. You're a superstar control freak. It's pretty normal to crave a little submission."

I open my mouth to object again. But he hushes me with a raised finger. "Just let me finish. Panic can just mean you need a little…" He takes a deep breath as he thinks. "A little spontaneity in your life. A little chaos. Or a little bit of danger, maybe? Not everyone wants the danger part, so ignore that if that's not what you're after.

I'm just explaining all the ways a panic game can go, that's all."

I've got nothing for that. Before this conversation the words 'panic' and 'game' never went together.

"So... which one is you?"

"None of them." I laugh. "I mean, I'm a control freak for a reason. I like a predictable life. I love order, and neatness, and clean lines, if you want my interior design taste. I have two God-given talents. Martial arts and the ability to make people believe the things I tell them. I'm satisfied with those two talents. I'm satisfied with what I have and I'm not looking for a panic game, OK? I'm not looking for any game. I only came because Chella talked me into it."

"That's it?" Jordan asks. "You only came over here to discuss a sexual fantasy fulfillment game with me because your friend... what? Offered it up?"

"Yeah," I say, again feeling defensive.

"So you have no interest in this?" Jordan raises an eyebrow at me. "Be honest, Issy. I mean, I'm just here to make you happy, OK? That's my only job. So if you're interested in this at all, just tell me. I can find you something you'd enjoy."

I start to answer, but he holds up a finger again.

"Think hard," he says. "You won't get another chance to play. I'll have to blacklist you. That's just the rules."

I huff out a frustrated breath of air. "OK, then hold on. Let me wrap my head around this."

"Take your time," Jordan says, sipping his wine.

"I mean... I guess I could use some kind of game. I'm just not sure what. Do you have like... a menu? Or something?"

Jordan laughs. "A menu?"

"You know what I mean. Like a list of what you offer. What kind of games are there?"

"It's your fantasy, Issy. Not mine. They're all custom. You already said you don't want to submit to anyone. So perhaps you'd like to be the top? Hmm? Is dominating a man your fantasy?"

"God, no." I laugh.

"OK, how about ménage?"

I make a face and shake my head. "No, I don't think so. Sounds so... messy."

He huffs out a laugh at that, then mumbles something that might be, "You're telling me." He tabs a few things on his tablet and says, "Why don't you just tell me what you like, Issy? No need to be embarrassed, OK? I'm a professional. This is my job."

"You're a lawyer," I say, frustrated that I'm being cajoled into having a sex conversation with a man I hardly know.

"Which means you can trust me to keep anything you say confidential. I mean, I'm a man of my word, but if it makes you feel safer, we can sign an NDA." He shrugs. "That way we can't talk about it and we can forget about the part where other people find out."

"Do you have one of those with you?" I laugh.

"Of course," he says, pulling out a contract from his briefcase. "I sign them all the time. What you're feeling is pretty typical." He hands it to me. I take it and the pen he offers. "It's really basic. We put the date, time, and place on there. Then we both sign. And that means we're legally obligated to keep this just between us. If I breach, you can sue me. How's that?"

It is a pretty straightforward contract. And that is all it says.

So I sign. Because I actually do have a fantasy. And fuck it, right? I think Chella did this as a friend. She means well. So why not? I pass it back and he signs his, then folds it up and places it in his briefcase.

"OK," Jordan says, smiling at me as he leans back in his chair and takes a sip of wine. "Hit me, Issy. What's your fantasy? And I'll see if I can help."

"Well... I have always..." I cringe, not sure if I should actually say it.

"Go on, you're almost there."

"Well." I sigh. "Ever since I moved in across the street I've sorta had a secret fantasy about the club."

"Club?" Jordan asks.

"You know," I say, nodding my head in the direction of next door. "That place."

"Turning Point?" he asks. "It's closed. And I don't have a sex club on my roster of games, so..."

"I know it's closed. It's not really the sex club part, but the... scene part."

"Scene?" he asks, blinking, as if he's confused.

Which just makes me heat up with anger. I want to slap him right now. "Are you or are you not a sex game master? Why are you acting like you have no clue what I'm talking about?"

"I just need specifics, Issy. Tell me what you mean by *scene*."

"You know. People... watching. Lots of people. Like a whole crowd of people."

"Public sex?"

"No," I say quickly. "No, not public. Private, but in a place with lots of people."

"A bar?"

"No. That's not private."

"So a sex club." He laughs.

"Whatever. I guess so. I dunno. Sex with…" I think about what he was telling me about panic a few minutes ago. "With chaos. Yes. I think you got that part right. I want some safe chaos. That's the fantasy I think about most. So can you make a game about that?"

He grimaces. Then sighs. Then looks up at the ceiling. Then stands up and buttons his suit coat. "Ya know, Issy, I don't think you're really a good candidate for this after all."

"What?"

"Yeah, let's forget the whole thing. I'll let Chella know it didn't work out, OK? You go ahead and enjoy the dinner. I hear it's delicious."

And then he puts on his coat, grabs his briefcase, and walks out.

"What the fuck?" I get up and go after him, but he's already making his way through the tables of people, and it's either let him leave or make a scene, so…

So I just watch him go.

"What the hell happened?" Chella says, coming towards me holding a tray of silver-domed dishes. "I was just bringing dinner."

I take a deep breath. Deep. Count to ten.

"Issy!" Chella whisper-yells so the people all round us don't hear. "Did he just walk out on you?"

"Yup," I finally answer. "Said I wasn't right for this or some bullshit like that."

"Come in here and sit down," Chella says, bumping her hip into mine to indicate I should retreat back into the little private tea room.

23

I do. But only because I left my purse in there and need to go fetch it. But by the time I walk those ten steps to the table two seconds later, I feel exhausted and just plop back into the chair.

Chella sets the food on the table and takes the place of Jordan across from me. "What do you mean? Like he turned you *down*?"

"Yes," I say, both annoyed and defensive about the way she stressed the word 'down.' "Apparently I'm not a good candidate for his stupid game."

"That's ridiculous," Chella says. "Let me go talk to him—"

But I reach over the table and grab her by the shirt sleeve before she can fully stand up. "No. You will do no such thing. I didn't want to play, remember? It's just… he was kind of a dick about it. So just fuck him."

"Jesus, Issy. I'm so sorry. This is all my fault. I didn't mean for it to make you feel bad."

"I know." I sigh, forcing myself to move on by lifting up the silver dome on the plate. "What's this? Can we still eat?"

"It's parmesan risotto with roasted shrimp. And yes, I insist you stay. I'm taking a break right now, so I'll take that jerk's place." She lifts the dome off the other plate and starts spreading her napkin in her lap.

I do the same, but… fuck. This whole feeling of… I dunno… failure washes over me and I can't shake it. "God, I hate him now. He was so rude, Chella."

"Forget him, OK? I'm really sorry. And believe me, he won't be getting any referrals from me again." She takes a bite of risotto and then feigns orgasmic pleasure.

Which makes me smile, then laugh. And when I take a bite, I try to outdo her. Pretty soon we're making so much noise, servers are poking their heads into the private tea room to see what's going on.

"Don't mind us," Chella calls to them. "We're just a couple of girls getting off on food!"

After that, we quiet down and just eat, drinking our wine. Well, I drink wine. Lots of wine, actually. But Chella is eight months pregnant, so she's got sparkling cider. By the time dessert is served I'm pretty tipsy. It's a beautiful, decadent strawberry tart with whipped cream on top. And believe me, the risotto was just foreplay compared to this treat.

"So," Chella says, her lips wrapping around a spoonful of strawberries and whipped cream. "Did you... tell him your fantasy?"

I scowl. "I don't want to talk about it. I'm feeling better about it now, so let's just let it go."

Chella takes another bite of tart and presses her lips into the spoon to get all the cream as she withdraws it. If you were a man watching her do that you'd probably mistake it for something sensual. And it does come off that way a little, if you're a man and don't know her. But I do know her. And I know that move. She does that at tea all the time when she's got an opinion about something that differs from mine.

"What?" I ask. "Just say it."

"Nope," she says. "Moving on."

"Chella," I growl. "Just tell me what you're thinking, for fuck's sake."

"Well..." She smooths her napkin in her lap. And now I really know she's got something to say, but doesn't want to. "Just..." She looks up at me. "Was it a really weird fantasy?"

I think about this for a moment. "No. I mean, I'm pretty sure it's common."

"What is it?"

"I'm not telling you."

"Come on, Issy! I've seen and heard it all. I used to go to Turning Point, you know."

I make a face, unsure.

"Is it a ménage? Because that was mine and it was"— she laughs—"pret-*ty* fun."

"No. Nothing so bold. I mean, all I asked for was a... scene. You know?"

Chella cocks her head at me. "A scene? As in drama?"

"No." I huff. "Like a sex club scene. You know, where tons of people watch and you get off, and it's safe, and a little bit anonymous."

"Mmmm," Chella says, smiling. "I had you pegged for a panic girl, but what do I know about people's sexual fantasies?"

I'm about to protest her assumption about me, but then decide I can see her point. I can be a control freak. And it's pretty common to assume a control freak wants control because they lost it once and never want to feel that way again.

Which, in my case, would be accurate. So I shut up.

But then she says, "I did that too."

"What? A panic game?" Because that's what's still on my mind.

"No, the scene thing."

"Jesus. Really? I thought you said Smith never let you do anything in the club?"

"We didn't really. Well, one time he took me down there to watch. And we"—she cups her hand around her mouth and whispers—"fucked in front of a whole bunch of people."

"Yes," I breathe. "Like that. That's what I was thinking. It's not weird, is it?"

She shrugs. "A little."

I narrow my eyes at her. "You never know when you should lie, do you? You're supposed to say, No, Issy. It's not weird at all."

She laughs. "It's not weird if you understand why you want it." She stares at me for a few seconds. "Do you know why?"

It's my turn to shrug. "It's just... kinda sexy, that's all."

She inhales, exhales, then nods. "So... I've heard that when Turning Point was in full swing, Bric—he ran the place, so this was his thing, I guess—used to place his game player naked in the center of the lobby during private parties, blindfolded. Anyone at the party was allowed to touch her. Stimulate her," Chella says with a knowing nod of her head. "So she had no idea whose touch it was. Was it male? Female? Never found out. Because Bric would take her upstairs and fuck her afterward. He was the only one allowed to fuck her, I guess."

"Holy fuck." That wasn't what I was thinking, like at all. But it does sound kinda sexy if you're in a safe place. And you trust the guy. But I don't say that to Chella. Because what kind of empowered woman wants that, right? It would be the height of hypocrisy to tell my clients to be powerful and then in private willingly give up all power. To a *man*.

"Right?" Chella says. "Like, if I had known that was an option on the menu when I was playing the game, I might've requested it."

I laugh. Loudly. Then look around to see if anyone heard me. "Wait, you're saying that was a game? Like this really happened?"

Chella shrugs. "I've heard Smith and Bric talking. So yeah, I think that was real. But it wasn't me." She sighs. "Unfortunately."

"So what I asked for was not so weird, right? Why was Jordan so freaked out about it?"

Chella takes a bite of her dessert and thinks about this for a few seconds. "I think Jordan misses the Club. And maybe what you're asking requires him to put something Club-like back together. And maybe he's worried if he does that, he'll just say fuck it and reopen it under a new name."

"Did someone buy the building next door?"

"Long time ago," Chella says. "But they just started doing work in there a few weeks ago. I have no idea who owns it now. Or what they're gonna turn it into. But I think Jordan regrets not buying the building. Regrets not keeping the Club open. And your request probably hit him close to home, ya know? So don't take it personally. He just reacted like... well, a man. That's all."

"Yeah." I sigh. "Makes sense. And I'm glad I stuck around and had dinner with you. Somehow you put everything into perspective. Have you ever thought about being a life coach?"

Chella almost spits out her tart. She covers her mouth with her napkin, swallows, then takes a deep breath and says, "Hell, no! Are you crazy? I'm a mess! I can't be telling other people what to do."

28

"You're the most put-together mess I've ever met, Mrs. Baldwin. But OK. I get it. And I won't bring it up again. But if you do ever want to get into the life-coach business, you call me first, understand?"

"Deal," she says. "Should we call it a night? Or do you want to finish the wine?"

"Wine," I say, laughing.

So I do. Chella sips her sparkling cider and we talk. And laugh. And it's probably the best night out I've had in ages.

By the time the Tea Room is ready to close, it's quiet and nearly empty. I put on my coat and make my way through to the front of the restaurant to pay.

Chella waves me off, saying I was her date tonight and dinner's on her. And so I head to the front door, ready to go back to the office to get some work, in case I can't sleep tonight, and then go home to my small, hundred-year-old house and just... decompress from all this introspective thinking.

But that's when I see the flashing red and blue lights.

That's when I notice the street has been shut down and there are dozens of cops and men in suits, and...

"What the fuck is going on?" Chella asks, coming over to stand next to me.

"Dunno," one of her servers says. "They came in here about forty minutes ago, said no emergency, but they were shutting down the street to traffic, so if anyone had a car parked outside, they should go get it now. About a third of the people cleared out immediately."

"What? Why didn't you tell me?"

The server smiles, then shrugs. "He said nothing to worry about. And you were having fun."

"But..." I stutter. "But they're in my *office!*"

I push through the door, cross the street, and even though at least four people try to stop me with a mad grab at my coat sleeve, I yank free and continue walking until I'm stepping right up to the man in a suit who seems to be in charge. "Just what the fuck is going on here?"

He looks down at me. He's a tall guy, mid-thirties, maybe. Dark hair and dark eyes. His suit says high-ranking government asshole. But his mouth says, "I'm afraid someone was pranking you, Miss—"

"Grey," I say. "What do you mean, pranking me?"

"We got an anonymous tip that there was a meth operation being run out of this office."

"What?"

"And then we got a search warrant, so we went inside."

"You didn't even call me?"

"Not sure if you understand what a search warrant is, but it gives us permission to—"

"Don't mansplain to me! I know what a fuckin' search warrant is!"

"Good," he says, opening up a small notebook and writing something down. "Then you understand why we didn't try to get your permission first."

I look at my office. There are dogs in there. Cops everywhere. Guys in special uniforms I don't even recognize.

"Special Agent Ivers?" a man with a giant German Shepherd says, snapping my attention back to the guy who seems to be in charge.

"Yes," Ivers says.

"We found something. You better come have a look at this."

CHAPTER TWO

FINN✳

My father died on a Tuesday.

It was a dark day. Late last fall when the trees around DC were turning gold, and red, and brown, and the city air was nothing but a mean, cold wind that sliced through you like a knife. The funeral was short and small.

He was the rock of my world for most of my life. A guy with big ideas, and the nerve to see them through, and the gall to take what he wanted if no one gave way.

And even though there were a lot of things I didn't like about my father, he didn't deserve to go out the way he did.

I take a drink of my whiskey-laced coffee, not caring that I'm working. My boss has been giving me light days ever since I landed here at the FBI satellite office in Denver, so I'm expecting this to be another one of those. Boring, meaningless hours that add up to twenty-four and then start all over again.

"Hey, Finn," the waitress—Darla—says as she positions a pot of coffee, ready to refill my cup. I put a flat hand over the cup to stop her. Don't need the whiskey watered down any more than it is or it might lose its kick. "Need the check then?" she asks.

"Sure," I say, not looking her in the eyes. Not looking at her at all. Just staring out the window at the approaching night.

"You doin' OK these days?"

"What?" I ask, forcing myself to stop looking outside and focus on her instead.

"You seem so... distracted lately. Everything all right?"

"Sure," I say. "What could be wrong?"

She offers me a small smile. We had something once. Maybe. But it's gone now. At least that's how I see it. But she's nice. She's always nice. So I rein in that dark part of me that wants to tell her to go fuck off and leave me alone, and instead channel my father. Say something he'd say. "Thanks for the coffee." He always was polite. Right up until the end.

"No problem," she says. Another smile as she writes something on the check and sets it on the table. And then, thankfully, she's gone and I'm alone again.

I like the alone.

The door opens, a bell jingling, which draws my attention to the front of the diner where Declan Ivers stands, looking around for a few seconds before he spies me. I can't hear it over the din of conversation, but then again, I don't need to hear it. The long sigh he lets out once he spots me is something you can *see*. And then he's heading my direction.

"Fuck, Murphy," he says, sliding into the booth across from me. "I've been calling you for hours. Why the hell didn't you pick up?"

I don't even bother mustering up a shrug. Just hold my coffee cup in both hands, twirling it on the table.

"Look, I got a job for you tonight, OK? You need to get your shit together."

I lift the cup, take another sip of my Irish coffee, and meet his gaze. He's wearing a dark suit just like mine, only it's a few steps up in the quality department.

I don't wear cheap suits, but this asshole, you know the kind. They dress to impress. Cuff links, and silk ties, and shoes that cost a fortune. All accentuated with the status-symbol watch on the wrist and the haircut that never seems to change. I just take the fucking suit out of the closet, put it on every morning like I'm supposed to, and call it good. Though I do have a nice watch.

I can't decide if I like Declan Ivers or not. I mean, he's not what I'd call good-natured, but he's not really an asshole, either. So I'm just waiting him out.

I don't have to like him. I just need to get along with him.

"What kind of job?" I ask, uninterested. I only have one job here and that's... well, drinking this whiskey.

"The kind you do," he says, looking me in the eyes.

We stare at each other for a few seconds, his gaze sorta challenging, mine sorta apathetic.

"OK."

Declan pulls out his phone, starts stabbing at it, and then there's a little whoosh sound that says he's sending a message. My phone lights up on the table, the sound off, so there's no incoming ding, but I glance down at it anyway.

It's a picture of a woman. She's got blue eyes, long, dark hair, and an expression that's something between a scowl and a smile.

"Who's this?" I ask, suddenly more interested as I pick up the phone and tab the message open from the home screen so it won't disappear.

"Issy Grey. She's one of those life coaches. Motivational speakers or whatever."

"OK," I say, looking up at him, trying to put the pieces together. "So what's the job?"

"We think she's involved in something pretty big."

I wait for more, but he stops. Like I'm supposed to ask another question. I close my eyes and count to three because I hate this game he plays. Fuckin' Declan is all drama all the time. How he's still in the FBI, I'll never understand. I open them, making myself breathe slowly, and oblige. "What kind of something?"

"Well"—Declan sighs—"we got a tip earlier today that there's some kind of meth operation happening in the office space she rents."

"Meth?" I groan. "Again?"

"Somebody's got to clean it up," Declan says. "Today that's us. We're waiting on the warrant now, then we're gonna meet up with DEA and head over there to take a look. So let's go."

I stay where I am, wondering if I should get up and leave. Not leave with him, but leave this whole fuckin' town. I mean… I guess it would be bad if I didn't just toe the line. Shit would go off the rails, I'd be asked a bunch of questions, things would get messy.

But then again, it always gets messy.

"Look," Declan says, lowering his voice as he leans over the table towards me. "I get it. He was your father. So losing him was a blow. He was one of us, and I liked him too. But he's gone, Finn. And it's not like he didn't fucking deserve it. So pull your shit together and do your fucking job."

The anger inside me swirls like a wind whipping up a storm. But I hold it together, straighten my tie and pull out my wallet. I throw down a twenty, force myself to stand up, putting on my coat at the same time, and wait for Declan to follow.

"We're good then?" he asks, getting to his feet. But what he means is, *You're good?*

"Sure," I say. Because why not?

"I'll text you the address. Meet me over there. And Finn," he says, holding onto my arm as I start to move away. I stare down at his fingers on my coat sleeve, then raise my eyes to meet his. He lets go of my arm. "Don't fuck this up. It's important."

"Sure thing," I say, rolling my shoulders a little to get rid of the building tension. "Just tell me what to do."

"Good man," Declan says, shooting me a smile as he pats me on the shoulder.

I watch him walk off. Keep watching as he smiles at Darla and heads out the door.

She doesn't smile back. He doesn't notice.

There are a lot of things Declan Ivers doesn't notice these days. Which is ironic, since he's FBI, just like me.

But then again, he's nothing like me.

Whatever.

I follow, passing Darla, smiling as I go, and say, "See ya later, Darla," because I think that's what she needs tonight. A nice goodbye from me.

"You too, Finn. Have a nice Valentine's Day."

I stop, look over my shoulder at her as I reach for the door handle. "What?"

She's smiling back at me. Cute girl, especially in her pink Cookie's Diner waitress uniform. Kinda short and tiny. Red hair—little bit wavy—and blue eyes. "You didn't even know, did you?"

I shake my head.

"So glad I gave up on you ages ago. You'd just break my heart, Finn."

"Yeah." I shoot her another smile, a better smile. "Breaking shit is my specialty."

Outside it's cold and the fading light is gone. There's a little bit of wind, which I relish as I make my way down the street to my government-issued car, because the diner was kinda stuffy. When I get in and slam the door closed, the cold lingers. It lingers even after I start up the car, blast the heat, and start picking my way through the heavy traffic of downtown Denver.

I check my phone, find Declan's text, and press it to make the map app pull up. Then I reluctantly turn the ringer back on because... yeah. Gotta deal with reality, I guess. Which is a joke, of course.

Go F*ck Yourself is located near the Capitol building. The sign is lit up white and the letters are bold and black. And for a moment I wonder what kind of woman names a business something like that.

Apparently Issy Grey.

The streets are still open when I park my car—Declan and crew still a few minutes away according to a new text—and I get lucky with a spot right out front. I wait there, car engine off, darkness all around me, and look across the street at a busy little place called the Tea Room.

Inside there's tables filled with couples, no doubt celebrating the most fake holiday on record like it actually means something. All smiles, holding hands, gazing into each other's eyes like dumbasses as they wait for some equally stupid romantic dinner to appear in front of them.

I bet some of those guys have diamond rings hidden in the food. I bet some of those guys will be asking that all-important question every woman seems to wait her whole life for. I bet some of those guys will end this day more miserable than when it started.

A knock on my window draws my attention away from the Tea Room and back to the job. Declan is standing on the passenger side of my car making one of those roll-your-window-down gestures that actually has no meaning in modern times, since windows don't roll down anymore. They slide down, as mine does when a button is pushed.

"DEA and dogs are on their way."

"Sure," I say, getting out of the car and joining him on the sidewalk.

"We're meeting them out back to keep this shit quiet a little longer," he says, nodding his head across the street at the Tea Room. I narrow my eyes, trying to get his meaning. He says, "Grey is over there having dinner. Gonna keep this low-key as long as we can. "

"Ah," I say, tugging my coat closed to keep the chill out. Well, called that one, right? Whatever poor asshole is having dinner with her tonight will most definitely be going home miserable.

We slip into a narrow space between her building and the one next door and come out into a small parking lot off an alley. There's a whole team of FBI guys at the door already, wearing black vests with large yellow letters on the front and back. The guy in front is holding a battering ram, poised in position, while the two behind him have guns drawn.

I yawn. Declan sees me, closes his eyes for a second, misses the actual ramming of the door, and then opens them, still looking at me. "Be present," he says. "This shit is no joke."

"I'm here," I say.

The three guys with guns go in first, battering ram set aside now, and Declan and I wait it out as they search the place. TV makes our job look a lot more exciting than it really is. I mean, I haven't ever had to go inside a building alone like Fox fucking Mulder and take my chances. You send in the real team first to do your dirty work, then guys like me go in after it's all clear.

By the time it is clear, the DEA has shown up with dogs, and Declan and I enter behind them.

There's no one inside so I just stand there, looking around.

Lots of smaller rooms in the back. Like little offices, but with no computers or anything. Just tables. Maybe consultation rooms or something. There are motivational posters hanging on the walls. Posters that say things like, "There are no traffic jams on the extra mile," and, "Success is not a destination, it's a journey."

The front room is huge. Tall, industrial ceiling with open ductwork. One side has mats and punching bags hanging from the ceiling, like they practice kicking men in the balls over there. The other side is set up with low tables and big overstuffed chairs and it barely takes any imagination on my part to picture small groups of sad women sitting around them drinking coffee as they lament what their lives have become.

Declan disappears out the front door. I stay behind, hidden in the shadows, and watch as a small woman with long, dark hair and fiery eyes comes running across the street, forcing her way through several Denver cops who try to stop her with a mad grab at her coat.

Issy Grey.

But she makes it and stands toe to toe with Declan, who is at least a whole foot taller, as they talk. Or, more accurately, she yells at him, her arms flailing as the whole what-the-fuck-do-you-think-you're-doing act plays out.

A guy with a dog brushes past me, goes through the front door, and stands next to Declan, waiting to be seen. I push past people after him, wanting to hear this part, and end up standing next to the dog as it pants, looking up at me with a wide dog-faced grin.

I actually smile at him because... dogs.

"Finn," Declan says. "Take Miss Grey down to Lakewood for questioning."

"What?" the woman says. People have her by the arm now. Two men. Two big men.

And then shit just goes... *awry*.

Her body twists, her arms and legs also in motion. She's got one restraining arm bent behind the guy's back and he drops to the ground crying out in pain. The other one gets a chop to the throat that leaves him gasping for breath and even though I'm the agent and she's the suspect, I find myself rooting for her to take out Declan too.

It's not personal or anything. I just like to root for the underdog.

She doesn't. Take him out, that is. A massive show of force has her face down on the pavement, her cheek pressed into the sidewalk, as she spits threats about lawsuits and unreasonable violence.

Seconds later she's led away, wrists zip-tied behind her back, and shoved in the back of my car under Declan's orders.

I just stand there, watching the entire scene play out with my usual level of indifference.

"Finn!" Declan yells right up in my face. "For fuck's sake, get your shit together! Take her to Lakewood and put her in a room!"

So I do. Because that's my job.

I get in the car, start it up, and make my way slowly through downtown and over to Colfax, deciding against the freeway, since there's only one freeway route over to Lakewood anyway and it looks packed with traffic as I pass by. I drive slow, not in a hurry, and look at the woman in my back seat from the rear-view mirror.

She stares back, daring me to speak to her.

But I don't.

Because I just don't care enough about what's happening to put forth the effort.

Almost an hour later she's in a dimly-lit room, hands cuffed to the table, ankles shackled, screaming threats at the camera and two-way mirror that would make a biker blush.

I'm standing on the other side of the mirror in a room filled with monitors, holding a bag of Mrs. Fields' Chocolate Chip Cookies I got from the vending machine, feeding them into my mouth one at a time, watching her.

She's tiny. Everything about her is small. But fierce. Nothing about her is weak.

The door bursts open and Declan walks in, slamming it closed behind him. Issy Grey hears it—the room isn't completely soundproof because of the mirror—and stops spewing threats to tilt her head and listen.

"Did you talk to her?" Declan asks, slumping into one of two chairs.

"Nope," I say, shoving the last cookie into my mouth, bunching up the empty bag, and tossing it towards the trash can. I miss, but don't pick it up. "I have no clue what's going on, so just waiting on you. Where the fuck have you been?"

Declan looks at me with an expression that says, *Watch your mouth, son,* but doesn't bother to say the words out loud. Doesn't have to. We both know who's boss here and it sure as fuck isn't me.

He pulls up a screen on one of the many monitors stationed around the observation area, which displays a dossier of Ms. Grey. Three others contain footage of the raid. One is a live image of a chest cam on an officer still on the scene, two are looping different discoveries found in her back rooms, and the last three are trained on her, inside the interrogation room.

"OK, so this is where we're at. We got an anonymous tip this afternoon that there was a meth lab over at Go Fuck Yourself—"

I laugh at the name because I sorta love it. Issy Grey is totally the kind of person who names a business Go Fuck Yourself.

Declan just continues. "Upon arrival it was clear the tip was bogus, but during the search the dogs sniffed out a sizable amount of C4 explosive."

"What?" I say, pulling out the chair next to Declan and taking a seat. "Her?" I flick my thumb over my shoulder at the two-way.

"Like a lot of it, Finn."

I laugh. "Bullshit. She's an elf-sized demon, sure. But no one would be that aggressive and call that much attention to themselves if they're holding C4 explosives in their back room."

"Obviously"—Declan sighs, rubbing his temples with two fingertips—"something's going on here. So let's go in there and get to the bottom of it."

"Wait," I say, placing a hand on his shoulder to prevent him from standing. "You think she's... what? Using her little women's empowerment classes as a front for terrorists?"

"Maybe," Declan says.

I laugh. "Really?"

"I follow the evidence, Finn. If you know anything about me by now, it should be that. And this woman had five hundred pounds of C4 in her back storeroom. So let's go talk to her and see what the deal is. I'm Bob, you're Joe."

"Fuck that," I say. "I'm Bob and you're Joe."

"Whatever," Declan says, standing up.

Bob is good cop and Joe is bad cop. Declan always plays good cop-bad cop during interrogations. It's cliché, but it works. Usually. I've only been working with the Lakewood office for about three months, but Declan has already proven himself to be a powerful interrogator, so I generally just follow his lead.

Besides, being bad cop requires a lot of effort and I'm just not into that kind of investment tonight.

We exit the observation room, enter the hallway, then open the door that leads to the interrogation room, go inside, and close the door behind us. No one is watching on the other side of the glass now, but she doesn't know that. And the whole thing is being recorded, so it hardly matters.

"'Bout fucking time," the demon-girl spits. "I want my phone call and my lawyer. If you think I'm gonna—"

"Issy," I say, because I'm good cop, and he always goes first and he always uses first names. "You're not under arrest. We're just here to question you."

"Then set me free. Unchain me and let me go. I've got nothing to say."

"What my partner *meant* to say," Declan adds in his most unfriendly FBI agent tone, "was that you're not under arrest *yet*. If you want a lawyer, you will be. So think very carefully about that request, Ms. Grey."

"Lawyer," she says.

"Issy, listen—"

"Lawyer," she repeats. "His name is Jordan Wells. I'm not saying anything until he gets here."

Declan looks at me, almost smiling, which makes me squint my eyes at him for a moment. "Jordan Wells, huh? You got that guy on retainer?"

"Lawyer," she says one more time.

I take a deep breath and walk over to the table, taking a seat across from her. I have no idea who Jordan Wells is, but obviously Declan does. I've only been here three months and his name hasn't come up before, so I'm just gonna roll with it.

"Look," I say. "It's obvious that someone is fucking with you, OK? Even I can see that. So all you gotta do is help us out. Tell us who you're in trouble with. We'll get all the information we need and you'll go home tonight and sleep in your own bed. How's that sound?"

She's already opening her mouth to protest while I'm still talking, but then she gets a confused look on her face, shuts her mouth, and turns her head.

"What?" I ask. "What was that?"

She shakes her head, but I'm not sure if she's telling me to go fuck myself—which kinda makes me happy if she is—or if she's trying to convince herself that whatever idea just popped into her head can't be true.

Declan takes over. "Look, Ms. Grey, we already know you're involved with some bad people. But what we don't know, and what we need to know, and what we will know before you ever leave this room, is the name of the organization and the person you report to. So let's all save ourselves some time and just button this up real quick."

She doesn't take the bait. Just chews her lip and stares at the bland, grey cinderblock wall.

"Issy," I say. "It only gets worse if you refuse to cooperate."

"Lawyer," she repeats one more time. "I want to see Jordan Wells and I want to see him right the fuck now."

"Well then." Declan sighs. "We're gonna do this the hard way then." He leaves the room without further comment, which means it's my turn to take over and convince her the lawyer is a bad idea.

I lean back in my chair, trying to appear unaffected and casual.

Issy Grey sneers at me.

"Nice Valentine's Day, huh?"

"I'm not talking to you, so save your breath."

"I mean, you were over at the tea place, right? Having dinner with your boyfriend before all this happened?"

She rolls her eyes at me.

"Oh, I get it," I say, laughing. "No boyfriend, then? You were there with all your single-girl friends? Trying to forget all about this day? Trying to make it go away? Trying to—"

"I'm not going to fall for it." She squints her eyes at me, her gaze lingering on my chest, like she's looking for a badge. But of course, there is no badge. I'm in a suit, not a uniform.

When her eyes meet mine I say, "Finn Murphy. Special Agent Finn Murphy."

She shrugs like it hardly matters.

Declan comes back into the room, slams the door behind him, walks over to the table, plants both hands on the hard, stainless-steel surface, and says, "Got a backup lawyer? Because it appears Jordan Wells is out of town and unreachable."

"Bullshit!" Issy says, her voice high-pitched and agitated. "I just saw him a couple hours ago. We were going to have dinner!"

"Ah," I say, snapping my fingers and pointing at her. "So that's why you didn't want to talk about it. He broke up with you, didn't he? And on V-day too! Jesus, what a dick."

But she doesn't take the bait. Just looks down at the table, like she's having some sort of private revelation.

Finally, after several long, silent seconds, she says, "Then call his partner, Glenn Stratford."

"Can't," Declan says. Which has me curious as to what he's playing here.

"Why the hell not?" Issy yells.

"Because the whole office is shut down for the mid-winter holiday."

She scrunches up her nose. It's a nice nose. Small, with just a slight upturn to the end of it. Which, I have to admit, is kinda cute on her. "What?" she breathes.

Declan shrugs. "That's what the answering service told me. On mid-winter holiday for the next week."

"But that makes no sense," Issy whispers under her breath.

"Why not?" I ask.

"Because," she says, "it... he... we were... never fucking mind why, OK? It just doesn't. There's no such thing as a mid-winter holiday!"

Declan and I exchange a glance. He picks it up from there. "So... you can either find another law firm and spend the night being booked and violated as your internal cavities are searched for drugs while we get another warrant and seize the contents of your house"—he stops to smile and spread his hands wide, like he's about to offer a gift—"or you can just make this easy. Make it all go away by being cooperative."

I chuckle, mostly at the aghast look on Issy Grey's face at the mention of a cavity search. But also because Declan plays bad cop pretty well.

A knock at the door makes all three of us look at it. Declan walks over, has a whispered conversation with whoever is on the other side, and then nods and takes a file folder from the visitor. He turns back to us and closes the door behind him.

"Well, this might be your lucky day, Ms. Grey. Seems like we've picked up some chatter about your case. Come with me, Finn. We've got news."

I take one more look at Issy Grey, whose wide blue eyes are darting back and forth between us with equal parts curiosity and fear, and leave the room with my partner.

Back inside the observation room I say, "What the hell was that?"

"For real," Declan says, easing himself into the chair in front of the monitors. "We've got chatter. Seems like she might be telling the truth. The DC office just sent us an alert about a terror cell using unsuspecting female-owned businesses as fronts for a massive campaign."

I can't stop the laugh that bursts forth. "You're joking, right?"

"Why would I joke?" Declan asks.

"Because that's… a little convenient, don't you think?"

He shrugs. "I'm just doing my job, Finn."

"So we're just gonna let her go?"

"No," he says. "No. You're going to take her up to the Silver Springs safe house and keep her there until we figure out what's going on."

"Is that legal?"

Declan smiles. "It is if she agrees to go. Just make her agree."

"And how the fuck am I supposed to do that?"

"I'm sure you'll figure something out. Go on, I'll text you directions to the safe house and meet you up there later. And don't underestimate this one." He slaps the file onto the desk, opens it up, and points to something.

I read the paragraph and yet another guffaw comes out in response. This tiny woman might be the most interesting thing to happen to me since I came to Denver. Because Issy Grey has the rank of seventh-degree black belt in Jujitsu. That's like ten years of serious, disciplined study.

"Who the fuck is this chick?" I ask.

"That's what we need to find out," Declan says. "She might not be a terrorist, but I'll bet you a hundred bucks right now she's not who she says she is. Find out, Finn. And then call me. Because DC is all up in our shit about this new threat and we need to figure out her connection quick or lots of people might get hurt."

He leaves me there to figure things out. I study her file a little more. Mother was a veterinary technician, no father listed on the birth certificate, no college education, an assortment of odd jobs since age eighteen—including a Burger King in Waco, Texas, one Nate's Auto Repair in Escondido, California, Hialeah Racetrack in Florida, and then a short stint as a cab driver in New York City.

All of which is weird in and of itself. Her job history reads like a classic runaway, except she was already eighteen… so not a runaway. At least not an underage one. But the really curious thing is that her juvenile record was sealed. Not just sealed, but absolutely sealed. Meaning even the FBI can't see it without a court appearance and permission from a judge.

Which is unusual.

You have to read between the lines a little to get it. You have to know what the empty spaces mean. You'd have to've been there yourself.

Issy Grey isn't who she says she is.

Issy Grey is lying.

CHAPTER THREE

✳ISSY

Finn Murphy is lying.

I'm not quite sure about what, but I know men, it's my job to know men, and I know when a man is lying.

First he and his partner came in here blustering about terror cells, threatening me with a cavity search if I didn't waive my rights. Then some file got delivered, they disappear, and only Finn Murphy returns, this time trying to sweet-talk me into believing I'm one sleepy judge away from having the entire contents of my juvenile record unsealed and my house seized in a search warrant.

And then he said I was in danger. Someone was looking for me, someone whose identity he wasn't at liberty to divulge, someone who would hurt me badly if I was found.

And that's the only part of those threats that hit home.

"So which is it, Issy? Easy way? Or hard way?"

"How about my way?" I say.

"Sorry, darlin'. Not an option. 'Fraid it's this way or the highway."

I consider everything he's told me so far. It's a scary scenario. I mean, you tell anyone that a dangerous person is looking for them, especially after they were just set up and hauled down to the local FBI satellite office for questioning, they tend to believe you.

I just don't believe him. I've been too careful. I've been free for a long time. And the only asshole I need to fear is already in prison.

"I'll take the highway," I say, smiling up at him as the words come out. "I'm grateful for your offer of *protection*"—I have to control myself when I say that word to avoid rolling my eyes—"but I can take care of myself, thank you. So I'll just be going." I jingle the cuffs, which are still attached to the table.

He pauses, thinking, then offers me a very fake smile and says, "OK," as he reaches into his pocket to reveal a key.

Too easy. So I'm still on high alert. But it's all fake, so I play along.

This is about Jordan's Game, and as soon as the thought manifests in my head, I have to stifle a laugh. What a dick. He turned me down and then the game started.

But I have to hand it to him, that dick is good at this. Because this shit is seriously real.

"Something funny?" Finn asks.

"Nothing you need to worry about," I say, rubbing my wrists once he removes my cuffs. "Don't forget the feet," I say, nodding my head at the shackles around my ankles.

Finn releases those and backs off, like he wants to keep his distance from me.

I find that interesting. Because it means he has some idea of what I'm capable of.

Would he know that if this was just Jordan's way of starting the game he insisted I would never be playing?

I shrug it off as diligence. Stand and stretch languidly. Like I have no cares whatsoever.

Which is a lie. I'm a champion liar.

I'm thoroughly intrigued by Special Agent Finn Murphy for two reasons. He's either the man Jordan has assigned to me and is playing along like this performance will win him an Oscar, or—and honestly, I find this far more interesting—he's got no idea he's playing the game.

I decide to find out.

"Can I have my personal belongings back now? I need my phone so I can call an Uber."

He laughs, a loud, incredulous burst of joy that echoes off the ceiling. "I can take you home, Issy."

"Fine," I say, feigning surrender. Take me home means sexual fulfillment fantasy, right? Why else would he make that offer? "Let's go then. It's late and I have to be up early to prepare for my next Go Fuck Yourself seminar at noon tomorrow."

He studies me a little longer, his hazel eyes searching mine, darting up and down my body with what might be a look of fascination.

Men react to me in one of three ways. One—they find me annoyingly aggressive. Two—they find me inexplicably mysterious. And three—they ignore me completely.

If I didn't start this evening out with that meeting with Jordan Wells, I'd have chosen number three for good old Finn here. But we *are* in that game, he *is* the man I'm playing with, and as far as game pieces go—well, let's just say… having Special Agent Finn Murphy fuck me in a sex club is probably gonna be the highlight of my life.

He's tall, a foot taller than me at least. His sandy brown hair is cropped short on the sides, but has some length on the top. Enough length to give him a bed-head look. You know the one, the just-woke-up-after-fucking-all-night kinda style. And his eyes are hazel. Not brown, not green, but both.

He opens the door to the interrogation room by punching a sequence of numbers on a keypad, which he doesn't even try to hide from me—yet another clue that this whole thing is bullshit. I wonder how he got his people to play along?

Ah, but that would be Jordan's job, right?

Fuckin' Jordan. Mid-winter holiday? Really? That's all he could come up with?

Then again, it was all that was needed, wasn't it? Why bother with details that won't matter? I called for him, his office gave me a plausible excuse, I accepted it, and we've moved on to phase two of the game now.

Playing.

Which is the best part, right?

Finn waves me forward, through the door, into the hall, where I wait for him to lead me out of here. I'm ashamed to say I wasn't paying attention when they brought me in, so I don't remember the way. A slip in protocol, I admit. And if this wasn't all bullshit just to set up the sex that will surely be happening tonight, I'd be harder on myself for the lapse.

I just follow him instead.

We pick up my stuff from a woman behind glass at a counter. My purse is returned in a large, clear, plastic bag. And once all that is settled, we make our way to the garage where his car is parked.

He opens the rear door and smiles again. "I'm afraid you'll have to sit in back, Issy. Civilians aren't allowed to ride shotgun."

I shrug, giving in again. I really do have a seminar tomorrow and I like to be up early to prepare. It's already getting late, so we need to wrap up the deviant sex game quick so I can get some shut-eye before dawn.

I sit behind him, then scoot over to the passenger side so I can study him better as we drive. We're at the Federal Building, all the way over in Lakewood, so the drive into downtown will take at least twenty minutes. I sit back and enjoy my view as he starts the car and makes his way out of the garage.

"So... I got a glimpse of your file, Issy."

"Yeah," I say, my mind on the shape of his lips as he speaks. They're nice lips. Kinda full, but not too full. I bet they would feel wonderful between my legs.

"See something you like?" he asks.

It's only then I realize he's looking at me in the rear-view mirror. "I'm just curious, is all."

"About?"

"You, of course. You know, how you got mixed up in all this."

He frowns in the mirror. Squints his eyes at me. "Mixed up in all what?"

Oops. He must take this game stuff more seriously than I do. I guess I need to stay in character.

"Wait," I say, putting my actress hat back on. "What file do you have on me?"

He glances in the rear-view, but only for a moment as we get on the 6th Avenue Freeway back towards Denver. "Same file we have on everyone once they get our attention."

"So you just put it together today?"

"I didn't, the department did. That's what they handed to Declan when we got interrupted."

"Yeah, right before you guys decided to let me go. So what'd it say? To make you change your minds?"

"It's not the file that made us change our minds."

"Then what?"

"The news that came with it."

"Which was?" Jesus. Am I gonna have to lead this guy into participating in a decent conversation now too? I mean, shit. You'd think banter would be included in the sex game package, right?

"Chatter, Issy. Chatter about what happened to you tonight."

For a second I think he's referring to my conversation with Jordan. There are several silent seconds of me irrationally picturing these guys listening in on that.

"Were you guys spying on me while I was at Chella's?"

"Who's Chella?"

"The tea shop, you idiot! Did you have bugs over there? Did you hear—"

"Whoa, whoa, whoa," he says. "Calm down, ninja. We didn't have bugs over there." He glances at me in the rear-view again, cocks his head slightly as he squints his eyes. "Why, you hiding something? What was really going on over there?"

I take a few moments to consider if he's lying. I can't imagine Jordan bugging the tea room. Like… this whole thing is about discretion, right?

"Issy?" Finn prompts. "You got something you need to share with me?"

I huff out a laugh. As if. I laugh again. As *if* I'm going to be the one to initiate the game play. Nope. If I wanted to ask a man to fuck me in front of strangers, I wouldn't bother playing Jordan's Game and letting all these people in on it, now would I?

"You know there's a confidentiality agreement, right?"

"What?" he asks.

"Between me and Jordan. I signed it, he signed it, and that means he can't talk to you about shit."

"Yeah," Finn says, getting off the freeway and easing onto Colfax. "That's typically what lawyers do."

"So did he talk to you? Did he tell you anything?"

"Who?"

"For fuck's sake," I yell. "Jordan!"

"He's out of town, remember?"

I cross my arms and lean back into the seat. "Right."

We're quiet after that, but I catch him stealing glances at me in the mirror. I don't tell him where I live, but he finds it anyway—must've been in my file—and parks right out front of the fixer-upper I bought when I first came to town. It's an old house that needed a lot of work, so I got it for the amazingly cheap price of just over a million dollars.

It's also the only single-family home within three blocks of the Capitol building and there were several developers interested in the property, if only to knock it down and sandwich another apartment building between all the other apartment buildings that have sprung up in this neighborhood over the past decade. There's two tall, brick buildings flanking the long front yard on either side, and neither of them have windows facing me, so it's unusually private for the city.

Lucky me. I am the proud owner of one total piece of shit house. Because it needs everything. New roof, new windows, new floors, new plumbing, new electrical… you name it. It needs it. I have plenty of money to do all that, but time is something else altogether. You can't buy time and that's something I never have enough of these days.

So I just live with it. And I don't even mind all the noises the boiler makes, or the way the water takes forever to get hot, or how none of the electrical sockets work on the second floor and I have to run extension cords up the stairs to get light.

After living there for almost a year, I find I actually love the place. Even though it's practically falling down, it felt like home immediately. I love walking inside after a long day and just falling into the couch cushions and looking around at the mess.

And I love the front yard. There's no back yard to speak of. Just a cement slab in between the house and the detached garage. But the front yard… those tall buildings on either side… they make me feel walled in and safe.

I am a control freak about everything but this house. It's like… it's like the imperfections are perfect, ya know? So many people have lived here before me and each one of them is ingrained into what makes this place a home. It's chaos, but not. Because it's history.

I check my watch. Almost nine thirty. This guy better have a sex club in mind if we want to get this show on the road. I refuse to show up for a seminar on no sleep, no matter how good the promise of sex sounds, but I'm willing to play along for a few hours if it'll get this whole fantasy game over with.

"So…" Finn starts. Like he wants to ask me something but he's not sure how. Like he's not sure what to do next. Jesus Christ. Fucking amateurs.

"So you wanna come in?" I finish for him. "I mean, you *do* want to come in, right?"

He chuckles a little. I can still see him in the rear-view mirror. "Are you propositioning me?"

"Yes," I say. "So open the damn door and let me out already. I can't open it from the inside, remember."

Our eyes meet in the mirror. Hold each other's gaze for the count of three. Then he laughs, and I laugh, and he gets out and opens my door. I get out, taking his offered hand to help me, and it's... normal.

It's normal. I don't know why and I can't say how it happened, but it is. Maybe it's the game? Maybe it's because we both know we're playing. We both know why we're together tonight, we both know what's gonna happen next, and we both need it.

I'm not sure.

But I like it, I realize. I like the certainty of how things will now play out. I like the prearranged scenario.

I like him, too. Sorta. In that new possibilities kind of way.

I think he's got potential and I don't know how or where he's planning on fucking me in front of other people tonight—hell, maybe this is just a practice run or something? Maybe the game goes on for more than one night? I have no idea—but it's OK.

We're gonna fuck, and then he's gonna say something like, *Hey, I know this place we should go*, and I'm gonna say, *OK, let's do that*, and then we're gonna make those plans, and yeah...

I haven't had sex in almost six months and I'm way too close to scoring to back out now.

We walk up the front walkway, which is made of those old cement blocks from like the nineteen forties. You know the ones. They're all tilted and uneven, so far away from the flat surface they used to be. I've tripped over them several times coming home from the corner bar since I moved in. I joked with my homeowners' insurance chick, Miranda, that they should count as a security system, they're so dangerous. We had a good laugh at that, but she didn't give me the discount.

Then there's the trees. They are old, and tall, and sturdy, just like the windowless brick walls that surround them. Their trunks are easily four feet in diameter. And the roots…. Jesus, the roots. They are poking up from the earth in all directions. Gnarled, and twisted, and amazing. I'm pretty sure the trees are what killed the walkway. Probably why my plumbing sucks too.

But I don't care. I love them.

In the spring they're like an umbrella. It rains, and rains, and rains, and almost nothing gets past their jungle-like canopy. It's a shitty yard for growing anything because there's no sun. And my front lawn—if you can call some spotty patches of grass a lawn—is a mess, just like the house.

But it's a beautiful yard for sitting in the shade and that's really all I expect of it.

When I get to the door I turn and smile at him, appreciating him a little more now that I'm no longer handcuffed, as I unlock it.

"What?" he asks. "Changing your mind? We don't have to do this, ya know."

I grab his tie and pull him towards me. He's so much taller than me I figure the logistics of kissing will be comical, at best.

But the kiss isn't comical at all. There's no awkward nose-bumping, no *Which way do I turn my head?*, no teeth crashing.

He simply bows his head and... there he is. His mouth finds mine, his full lips covering me, then he nips my lip, making me gasp in surprise. I open my eyes to look up at him. Normally I keep my eyes closed for kissing, but the unexpected pain associated with the pleasure of the kiss knocks me off my game.

Did I enjoy that?

He doesn't give me time to decide because he takes my face in both his hands and knocks me sideways as he crushes me with his lips.

My legs almost buckle for a moment. My heart either speeds up or stops altogether, I'm not sure. My mind spins—maybe from the wine at dinner, but maybe not.

I think I... *swoon.*

CHAPTER FOUR

FINN✳

I shouldn't be doing this. I'm gonna lose my job. I'm gonna get a black mark I can't afford to have. I'm gonna…

Fuck it.

Her mouth is delicious. She tastes like dessert and sweet wine. She tastes like Valentine's Day. I kiss her harder after that thought, threading my fingers into her hair, then grabbing fistfuls to hold her close and keep her from pulling back, because it's been way too long since I had a date on Valentine's Day and even though she's probably a criminal and a liar who's gonna end up in prison before this is all said and done… I can't help myself. I just react.

The tie grab was unexpected. Shit, who am I kidding—this whole fucking thing was unexpected. But it was the tie grab that got my full attention. Little fucking wannabe dominatrix, that's what she is.

Newsflash, Issy Grey. Headline reads: *Not Gonna Happen.*

I guide her through the open door, making sure she doesn't trip over the rug, and kick it closed behind me as I continue my punishing kiss.

"Upstairs or on the couch?" she asks, still kissing me.

I don't answer, just push her up against the foyer wall and drag her coat down her shoulders. She's wearing a blazer underneath. Something completely professional. It comes off with the coat and they drop to the floor in a heap.

Her hands automatically go to my coat, but I grab her wrists and tilt my head at her.

"What?" she whispers, breathing heavy from the instant passion and heat we've created.

"Don't touch," I say. It's not a request, either.

"What?" she asks again. A small chuckle escapes with her question.

"You heard me," I say, undoing the top button of her white blouse. It's a feminine blouse, low-cut with a tiny ruffle running down the seams on either side of the small, gemstone buttons sparkling in the light coming in from the windows on either side of the door.

A crooked smile appears on her face. We're not kissing anymore, but that's OK. We've got time for more of that later. She huffs out another tiny laugh, but this time it's laced with cynicism. "Is that how you like to play?"

"Sure," I say. "My time, my game, my rules. You want me to leave, Issy Grey, owner-operator of one Go Fuck Yourself empowerment establishment? Just say the word and I'm out."

She stares at me, still smiling.

"But if you want me to stay, we do it my way."

"Fine," she says. "But it had better be worth it."

"Had it?" I ask. "Or what?"

"Or I'll quit," she says, back up, pressing her body against the wall. "And stop playing. So if you fancy yourself a top, you better know what you're doing."

I laugh. Like… I think this might be the truest moment of pure joy I've had since my father died. "I know what I'm doing."

"Good," she says, bowing her head slightly so she can look up at me through her long, thick eyelashes. Her blue eyes are wide and calm. "Because I do too."

I rip her fucking blouse open. The tiny fake gemstone buttons go flying, skittering across the hardwood floor. And then I rip her fucking bra open too. The front-closing clasp breaks and Issy lets out a small gasp. "Do you have any idea how much I paid for this fucking bra?"

"I'll buy you another one," I say, dragging the blouse and the bra away from her body so she's forced to present herself to me, naked from the waist up.

My hands grab her tits automatically, taking what is now mine. Her eyes are still wide, but no longer calm. They're teeming with shock, excitement, and a healthy side of desire as I fondle her, pinching her nipples hard enough to make her close her eyes and hiss out a breath.

"Be careful," she growls. "I have a very fine line, Agent Murphy. And if you cross it, you're gonna find out where my boundaries are immediately."

Yeah. Pure joy. I kiss her mouth again, my tongue pressing against hers, my hands still busy playing with her breasts. "A less experienced man," I whisper into her mouth, "might take that as a threat, Ms. Grey."

"It's a promise," she whispers back, her words still laced with dessert and wine. "Not a threat."

"But I take it," I say, ignoring her, "as a challenge. Fair warning of the rules over with, you will now stop talking and just listen."

Another small, incredulous laugh escapes.

But it's cut short when my hand slides up her breast and lands on the side of her neck. I don't squeeze. She doesn't need that extra embellishment to understand what that signal means.

Her throat muscles move as she swallows down whatever it is she's feeling. Fear? Probably not. She's far too capable in a fight for fear to be her first reaction.

No, that hard swallow was... desire.

My other hand slips into her slacks. They're not tight around her waist—kinda loose, actually. Riding low, like her hips are the only thing keeping them up. Like these pants might be left over from a time when she was heavier, but she keeps them around to wear on days she wants to be comfortable at work.

Or—and this second thought is far more likely—she wears them loose in case she needs to use one of those kickboxing moves she tried on the cops back at her work tonight.

But who cares?

I find her wet between her legs and decide I was right. Desire.

"I know your type," I say, leaning in to whisper the words into her ear. She sucks in a breath of air and a chill spreads across her neck, making her skin prickle up. The tiny, soft hairs just below her hairline are standing on end. "You're a control freak. You took martial arts to maintain that facade. You run that women's empowerment class to spread your brand of control to others. And to be a leader. You like to lead, don't you?"

She stays silent, which pleases me immensely, because it means she took my command seriously.

"Don't you?" I ask again.

And again, she reads me correctly. Because she answers. "I just know my place in the world, that's all."

"And what is your place in this world, huh?" I ask, taking my hand away from her neck so I can tenderly stroke her cheek with my fingertips. "The one we live in tonight."

She stares up at me, her eyes wide again. Still filled with desire, no fear. "To play your game until one of us wins."

"Really? Are you sure you wanna play? I'm a formidable opponent."

"Very. Fucking. Sure," she says. And now her eyes are slitted, almost closed. And it's not with desire. It's with clear defiance.

Which almost makes me laugh. Because she gave in and challenged me back in the same breath.

I like that, I realize. I like it a lot.

I have no clue how we got here or why we're doing this, but whatever. It's fun. So I don't really care about the how or the why. I only care about what comes next.

I take both her hands and place them near the button of my pants.

She doesn't require clarification and she pops the button open without comment, her eyes never leaving mine as she unzips me, reaches inside to grab my cock, and begins to massage it until I feel myself grow under her touch.

I close my eyes. Barely a blink, but I allow myself to enjoy the moment.

She stays quiet. At least with her voice. Her eyes, her expression, the movement of her hands—those all speak to me in a way that doesn't require speech.

I fondle her tits again, this time gently, and smile at her. There's no need for dominance and submission roles when partners are playing the same game.

I don't even need to encourage her further. She lowers herself to her knees, pulling my cock out as she descends, her eyes on mine, and opens her mouth.

I'm fully hard by this time. She's… I sigh… perfect. Like fucking perfect. Like she's done this before. Like she knows how to control a man by giving in.

Is she controlling me?

But I don't have time to think about it, because just as that question pops into my head, she swipes her tongue across the tip of my cock.

I long-blink again, smile as I enjoy one more moment of pleasure, then open my eyes just in time to see her take my cock fully into her mouth.

Words aren't necessary. It's something I've learned over the years through practice with other women. When two people are living in the same world, playing the same game by the same rules, you only need to react.

Which is what I do next when I grab her by the hair and give her the encouragement she needs to take me deep into her throat. She opens her mouth wide, gags a little, which makes me react again, easing up on my demand. But she doesn't pull back. Instead she reacts to *my* submission, sucks in a deep breath of air, grabs my thighs with both her hands, and presses herself up into my groin until my balls are pressing against her chin.

Jesus.

Now that is what I call control.

She pulls back, saliva spilling down her chin, and starts pumping my cock with both hands, using her own spit as lubrication.

Looking up at me, she smiles.

I smile back. "You," I say, "are not how I saw this day ending, Issy."

She shrugs, smirking. "It's a good game. So far."

"Oh, Ms. Grey. We haven't even begun yet."

She stands up, her hands still busy on my cock. But then she pulls away, and her slick hands find her own breasts and begin to massage them. She lifts one breast up towards her mouth, her lips parting, bringing her nipple closer, closer until…

I almost come just watching her tongue sweep across the peaked bit of flesh and swirl around the small, slightly darker circle of skin that surrounds it.

I can't stop myself. I grab her tits and lift them both to my face, burying myself between them.

Her hands slip behind my neck, her long fingernails scraping against skin, sending a chill through my entire body.

"I think I need you naked," I say, looking down at her. "Now."

Her fingertips find the waistband of her trousers and one small jiggle later, they find their way over her curves and drop to the floor. She steps out of them, kicking them aside as she kicks off her shoes. And now she stands before me wearing only thigh-high stockings attached to a sexy garter belt. No panties. Just the belt.

"Jesus." I say it out loud this time. "What the fuck?"

She smiles. Knowingly. Coyly. "You like? Or not?"

"Oh, I like," I say. "I like very much. I just…"

"Didn't expect me to be… what? Seductive underneath all that control?"

"Did you wear this for Jordan?" I ask.

"What?" She looks confused, which is cute on her.

I touch her hair, unable to resist feeling her softness. Such a surprise. "Jordan Wells. I mean, it's Valentine's Day. And hey"—I throw up my hands—"I'm not usually a guy who takes advantage of a woman after a crushing breakup, especially when said breakup occurs on V-day, ya know? But fuck it. I don't give a shit. His loss, man."

"You think I'm dating *Jordan*?"

"Well, you're obviously dating someone. And you had dinner with him tonight. At the very sexy little tea room across from your work. So…"

"So what? That means I'm fucking him? He's my lawyer."

"OK," I say, hands in the air. "But if you didn't wear this for him, then who?"

"Well, I'm with you, aren't I?"

Avoidance. Which annoys me. So I say, "Hey," taking her chin in between my thumb and forefinger to tip her head up to me. "No-talking rule is still in effect."

She shrugs. Which is her silent way of saying, *You're the one who brought it up, asshole.*

I forgive her attitude. I mean, obviously she's lying. She might be willing to play this little game with me tonight, but emotions are off limits. And I'm one hundred percent on board with that.

I started this day with too many emotions, filled with dread and an overwhelming desire to be alone. Wondering if I had any purpose at all. Wondering if coming to Denver was a mistake. Wondering if my whole *life* was a mistake.

But this woman brings something worth experiencing to the table. Her background is mysterious and seductive. Her small, curvy body is tantalizing. And the things she can do with her mouth… overwhelmingly entertaining.

I say, "Just so you understand. The kind of sexual ride I like to take comes with a dark underbelly. I like to lose control a little. I like to walk the edge. I like to push limits and create havoc."

She stares up at me, blank. Then a coy smile creeps across her face. A smirk, like she knows things. She says—breaking the rules—"Is that a warning, Special Agent Murphy?"

"Take it any way you want. I'm just letting you know… there's no point to pleasure without a little panic."

CHAPTER FIVE

*ISSY

"So you're what? An adrenaline freak? A risk-taker? You thrive on fight-or-flight options? You like stormy waters and calm winds drive you crazy?"

"Don't psychoanalyze me. And stop talking."

"Hey, you're the one who opened up this whole line of questioning." I'm acutely aware that I'm standing in front of him wearing sexy stockings and pretty much nothing else. I'm also acutely aware that his cock is spilling out of his open zipper, hard and straight, the tip red and swollen from me sucking on it, and glistening in the dim light coming in from my front windows. "And you're obviously worried about the kind of freak flag you fly, because you figure I deserve a warning before we go any further, is that about right?"

His eye twitches. Most people would miss it. I'm not most people.

"Warning heard, challenge accepted and hey," I say, shrugging. "It's just a game anyway."

This time he cocks his head a little, like he's confused. "Is that what this is?"

"Oh, come on." I laugh. "I mean, yeah. So let's just—"

"Wait," he says, one hand in the air like he's about to stop time. "Are you fucking with me right now? Why are you doing this?"

"Doing what?"

"Why did you invite me in? Why did you allow me to take off your clothes? Why did you suck my cock?"

"Look, I'm not much of a talker, OK? Let's just fuck to ease the tension a little and then you can take me wherever it is you're gonna take me. I mean, it's getting late. Can we just get this show on the road?"

He laughs. "What the fuck—"

"Exactly," I interrupt. "What the fuck? Are we gonna do this or not?"

"Do what?"

I sigh. It's a loud, thoroughly annoyed sigh. "Are. We. Going. To. Fuck?"

He stares at me for one more second, then grabs my shoulders, spins me around, and pushes me face-first against the wall as he leans into my neck and whispers, "Just remember you were warned."

I whisper back, "There's no point to pleasure without a little panic, right?"

One hand is between my legs before I even stop talking, his fingers probing my pussy, searching for the sweet spot. And when he finds it, I close my eyes and relax.

I'm gonna enjoy this. I do not give a fuck who he is. In fact, I doubt he's even an FBI agent. He's an actor, right? This whole game is nothing but an act. And I need this fuck. Like right now. So I can forget about the dry spell I've been in. So I can come, get it over with, and then be at my best when he finally takes me to the club to fulfill my sexual fantasy.

That thought alone is enough to make me moan. But when you add in the fact that his fingers are now pushing up inside me—

"Yes," I say. "Yes."

THE PLEASURE OF PANIC

He keeps quiet, which is perfect. Because I've had enough conversation for the night. All I want now is action.

He presses his hard cock into my back. "You're small," he says, noting—like I do—that there's no way he's gonna be able to fuck me from behind standing up. I'm too short. This has always been a problem for me. Kinda sucks too. I mean, even on my tiptoes, his cock will still be inches too high to enter me like this.

He lifts up one of my legs, improvising, because he gains entrance to my pussy and puts me off balance so I have to rely on leaning into his arm, which is pressed firmly against the wall on the side of my head. But then he goes one step further. Lifts me up, off my feet completely, pushing my face into the wall to keep me in position, and his cock slides inside me without resistance.

Clever, clever Finn Murphy.

I'm gonna kiss Chella tomorrow. I mean, yeah, I put up a fight over this stupid game of Jordan's, but hell, it's like… it's like having someone take care of your most intimate needs. It's kinda perfect.

Finn nips the tender skin behind my ear, his mouth soft, his breath hot. He says, "You like that?" just as he presses his hips into me, pushing his cock fully inside.

"God, yes," I say back. "More. Fuck me harder. Faster. I need it."

He chuckles as he takes his kisses to my shoulder and then he lifts up both legs, making me steady myself with palms flat against the wall, and starts the pounding.

I have never been fucked like this in my life.

His balls are slapping against my pussy with each determined thrust. His big, fat cock is buried deep inside me one moment, but with each backwards motion, he withdraws almost completely. Making me feel empty. Making me crave him for those few seconds when he's not stretching me open. Making me long for the friction that will bring me to climax.

"Brace yourself," he says, changing position slightly so his hips are almost underneath me, so my top half is crushed against the wall and my bottom half is practically sitting on his cock. He buries himself even deeper inside me—so deep, I let out a gasp from the pain. "Shhh," he says. "It's not time to panic yet."

I agree. That wasn't a cry of panic. It was a cry of pleasure.

He's thrusting upwards now, my ass directly above his thighs as he fucks me hard. Harder than I've ever been fucked before. His breath is quick, and loud, and he's grunting in a low, throaty way that makes me close my eyes and just… disappear into the ecstasy of the moment.

"Yes," I say again.

"Your stockings are so fucking sexy."

"No talking," I say, reaching around to grab a fistful of his hair.

He doesn't respond. At least with words. But he does stop fucking me.

I peek over my shoulder. "Don't even think about it," I say.

"What?" he asks. And I catch a glimpse of a charming, boyish smile appearing on his face.

"If you stop—"

"If I stop… what? What will you do, Issy Grey?" He leans in to bite the outer edge of my ear, which drives me wild. Like sends a shiver through my entire body. "Will you kick me out?"

"No," I say, nearly breathless. "I guess I'd have to just... submit and do what you want."

"Why?" he asks. "Because I've given you a taste of my magic cock and now you realize you can't live without it?"

It's a joke. And normally I'd banter back with him. Have a few laughs. But I'm not in the mood for laughing. I just want to come! So I say, "Yes," instead. "Yes. I need your cock, Special Agent Murphy. I need all of it, I need—"

He pounds me. He fucks me so hard my cheek crashes into the wall with each forward thrust. My legs are trembling, the muscles tired of the exertion of keeping myself balanced on top of him. My arms are shaking too, exhausted from the effort of stabilizing my body as I am fucked from behind, completely lifted off my feet.

His large hands are gripping my thighs and I feel his fingers digging into my flesh—tearing at my expensive stockings. Ripping them so he can slide his fingers under the silky nylon and feel my skin.

And then he lets go of one leg, which puts me completely off balance again. I'm about to protest because my body is spent, my muscles taxed to their limit.

But that's when his fingers find my clit. He begins to rub me. Back and forth so quick, I want to die. "Oh, shit," I manage to squeak out, just as the warm liquid spills out of me and I squirt all over his fingers.

That's it.

I come.

I come so hard my whole body begins to convulse. Sounds escape my mouth that defy description. Moans, and squeals, and shouts of, "Fuck yes! Don't stop!" and, "More, more, more!"

He slows his thrusts until there's nothing left of me. Until I disappear. Until I cease to exist in any world other than the one of post-coital afterglow.

And then he drops my other leg, pulls out, presses his large hand between my shoulder blades, and pushes me to the floor.

I bend low, my head pressed into the hardwood floor of my foyer, my ass high up in the air, as my fingers find my clit and begin to rub.

He spills his come all over my back, the heat of it making me climax again. His moans match mine. Low growls of satisfaction.

Then he bends down, uses my blouse to wipe off his come, and gathers me up in his arms.

He carries me across the room. I don't even open my eyes to see where. Can't open my eyes to see where. But then he sinks onto my couch, me in his lap, and relaxes back into the cushions.

"That was fun," he says, nearly gasping for breath. "But we've got somewhere to be, so…" He slaps my thigh. Hard. Hard enough to make me cry out from the surprise and pain. "So let's clean up and get on the road."

"I don't wanna," I say, turning into his chest, burying my face in the crook of his neck.

"You're not in charge anymore, Ms. Grey. I am."

"How long?" I ask.

"How long what?" he says. His voice is low, but not throaty like it was a few minutes ago. It's soft, and calm, and completely devoid of panic.

"How long will you stay with me? Just tonight?" It might come off a tiny bit desperate, but fuck it. If you can't be needy in the wake of this kind of sex, when can you?

"What do you mean?" he asks.

"The game," I say. "I'm so fucking sleepy right now. Can we just enjoy this and finish the game tomorrow night instead?"

"What?"

I open my eyes, sit up a little so I can look at his face. "Are you gonna make me spell it out?"

"Spell what out?"

"The *game*," I say, getting very irritated. "You know, the one we're fucking playing right now!"

He cocks his head at me. "What. The fuck. Are you talking about?"

"Oh, I get it." I laugh. "You're not gonna break character. OK, whatever. So you got a place in mind for tonight? I mean, if this is my one chance, I gotta take it, right? So I really hope you've got this all figured out and I don't have to make decisions because that was kinda the whole point in playing."

He pushes me away from him, leans back in the cushions even further, and stares at me. Hard. "You mean... the safe house? How the fuck—"

"What? Safe house? What the fuck are *you* talking about?"

"The safe house. I'm supposed to take you to the safe house in Silver Springs."

"Why the fuck would I need to go to a safe house?"

"Uh..." He laughs. "Because you were involved in a drug bust tonight that resulted in you being questioned down at the Federal Building. Not to mention the terrorist connection that came in afterward."

"This is..." I'm so confused. "This is part of the game?"

"What fucking game? I have no clue what you're talking about."

"The game!" I yell. "The fucking game! The one I asked to play—well, I didn't ask to play. Chella made the arrangements. Jordan's Game."

"Jordan, your lawyer?"

"Yes!"

"Why are you playing a game with your lawyer?"

"I'm not! He's..." But I realize I signed a confidentiality agreement. With a lawyer. Who probably takes shit like that very seriously.

"He's what?" Finn asks. And he sounds kinda pissed.

"I can't say any more."

"Why not?" he bellows.

"Because I told you, I signed an NDA earlier tonight so we could talk about it."

"*Who* could talk about *what?*" His tone is angry now, like I'm really starting to piss him off.

"Is this part of the game or not?" I say, suddenly feeling lied to.

"I don't know what fucking game you're talking about, Issy. None of what you're saying right now makes a bit of sense. Are you trying to tell me you just fucked me based on... a misunderstanding?"

"Is that what you're telling me?" I yell.

He inhales. Deeply. Exhales. Loudly. "OK, we're talking in circles."

"All I need to know is if you're playing or not. And I get it, you have to like... maintain the illusion, right? To make it feel real, or whatever. But seriously, dude. I need to know what the fuck is happening. Because I just let you *fuck me!*"

"Let me?" He laughs. "You practically *begged* me!"

I get up out of his lap, walk over to my front closet, pull out a trench coat, slip it on, and tie the belt securely around my waist. "Get out." I point to the door when I say it.

He sits on my couch—zipper open, half-hard cock still spilling out of it—looks me in the eye and says, "No fuckin' way. I'm not leaving until you tell me what the fuck is going on."

"I just did. And if you want to play, fine. But I'm quitting this game right now unless you let me know why you're here. All I need is a wink, OK? You can keep in character or whatever, just give me a signal. And if you can't do that, then you need to get the fuck out of my house or I'll throw you out myself."

He opens his mouth to respond and I can just tell whatever it is he's going to respond with won't be something I want to hear. So I cut him off and say, "And if you have any doubts that I'm capable of throwing you out, Special Agent Finn Murphy—if that's even your real name—then consider this a warning. I'm ranked as a seventh-degree black belt in jujitsu. I can take down men twice your size in four moves."

He huffs some air. Like... as if. But I don't mind. I like being underestimated.

So I finish with, "Just try me, asshole."

CHAPTER SIX

FINN*

OK. This is weird. And all the ways it's weird are ticking off in my head one by one.

She thinks we're playing a game? And from what I can tell, it has something to do with her *lawyer*?

"Get out," she repeats.

"Just…" I hold up one finger. "Give me a second, OK? I need to think things through."

"What's to think through? I asked a very simple question that can be answered with one word. Yes. Or. No."

Right… but she said something about me staying in character. She thinks this was set up? Does she think the entire night was a setup? Like the search warrant, and the FBI interrogation, and the demand to take her to a safe house? And if so… do I play along to get her in my protective custody? Or do I give it to her straight and risk the whole terrorist thing crashing down on top of her?

Well, that's a no-brainer.

So I wink at her.

She recoils a little, tilting her head.

I take it one step further. "I have no idea what you're talking about." Wink.

She opens her mouth to say something, then decides not to.

"But I do have a place in mind for us tonight." Wink.

She squints her eyes at me, like maybe she didn't catch the wink. I decide it might be too dark in here to actually see it properly, so I get up, tuck my dick away, zip my pants but leave them unbuttoned, and walk over to her, hands in the air like I surrender.

"I need to take care of you tonight, Issy. It's my job." Wink. "So just grab a few things, stuff them into a bag, and let's go." Wink.

"Where are we going?"

"It's a secret," I say, smiling. "You'll know when you get there."

"Is it... safe?"

"Safe?" I almost laugh. Because it's a safe house, right? But whatever it is she thinks we're doing tonight, it's got nothing to do with a safe house. What *does* she think we're doing tonight? "Of course it's safe. I just told you, I'm here to take care of you. It was practically an order. So come on, it's getting late. We need to get a move on."

"I need to be back by five AM. I have a seminar tomorrow at noon and I want to get there early."

She's not going anywhere in the morning. But I just nod and say, "Then let's get this show on the road," echoing her words earlier.

She stares at me for a few more seconds. And if I'm reading her correctly, I think it's because she's scared. Not about the terrorist cell who decided to use her company as a front, like she should be, but... of me.

And I don't like that. I mean, I can be a scary guy, but not to innocent women. And after all that just happened since we got to her house, if there's one thing I'm certain of, it's that Issy Grey has nothing to do with whatever threat Declan was talking about earlier. She's just collateral damage.

So I say, "Issy," and offer her my outstretched hand. "Trust me. I promise, I'm not going to hurt you."

Which makes her snort. And then laugh. "You can't hurt me."

I can think up a million ways to hurt a woman, even a capable woman like Issy, and none of it involves violence. You can't jujitsu your way out of emotional damage. "It doesn't even matter if I can or can't, Issy. I'm not going to. So go pack a bag and let's go."

She holds her position for five more seconds. I know, I count them. And then she gives me a slight nod and walks upstairs to what is most likely her bedroom.

"Quickly," I call after her. "We're wasting time."

I put myself back together while I wait. Tuck in my shirt, button my pants, and then I walk around her house and look at stuff in the moonlight. I don't want to turn on a light just in case anyone is outside watching. I didn't see a tail when we drove over here—and I was checking—but you can't be too careful.

I find three things of note.

One—an award. It's a little gold-colored statue of a microphone. The plaque on the base says Empowerment Speakers Award and has her name in fancy calligraphy underneath.

Two—an old family photo. A very small Issy with an older man who might be her grandfather. They're holding hands, eating ice cream cones, sitting on a front stoop, looking pretty happy.

Three—a framed front cover from the *Pan-American Jujitsu Magazine* with Issy Grey's face front and center. The headline across the picture is blacked out with marker.

Which makes me wish this wasn't just the cover, but the entire article so I could read more about her.

I take that off the wall and study it. She looks young. Like... *young*. I don't know a lot about martial arts, it was never my thing. But I do know that there are age requirements for black belts. She's holding a gold medal, smiling since she obviously won some very important competition.

"What are you doing?"

I turn to find Issy standing at the top of the stairs, wearing a fresh blouse, holding a bag. "This was a big deal, huh?" I hold the frame out in her direction.

"Yes," she says, slowly descending the stairs, eyes trained on mine. "And that's very meaningful to me, so please put it back where you found it."

"Sure," I say, feeling chastised. I hang the frame back on the wall and turn to face her.

Neither of us speak.

"I'm ready," she finally says, breaking the awkward silence.

"Right," I say. "Let's go."

I wave her forward towards the door but she shakes her head and juts her chin out. "You first," she says.

Which is weird. But then again, this whole fucking night has been weird. "Sure," I say, walking to the door and opening it up. But when I look over my shoulder, she still hasn't moved. "Issy? You coming?"

She stares at me again. The seconds tick off. I start to feel uncomfortable, like she's onto me. She knows I'm not a player in whatever game this is she's playing. But just when I'm about to open my mouth and try to explain, she steps forward, and I relax.

"Where are we going?" she asks.

"Silver Springs," I say.

"What? That's like two hours away!"

Shit. Is it? I have no idea where Silver Springs is. Fuckin' Declan was supposed to text me the address, so I check my phone, find the missed message, then press the maps app to get directions.

"How will I ever be back in time for masterclass prep tomorrow?"

What does she think is happening tonight? It's fuckin' killing me. But I can't ask so I lie. "What we're doing in Silver Springs won't take long, don't worry. You can sleep on the way there and the way back. I'll keep you safe."

"You keep saying that," Issy says. "But I don't need your protection, Finn. I need—"

But she stops. She was just about to tell me what she needs and… goddammit. I really hate this game we're playing. "You need what?" I prompt her, hopeful.

"I need what was promised," she says.

"Why?" I ask, because asking *what* was promised feels like the wrong move.

"You don't need to know why," she says, walking over to the framed magazine cover to straighten it out on the wall. She turns to me. "You just need to deliver."

Deliver. *O-kaaay.* "Shall we?" I ask, standing just outside the door.

"Sure," she says, and joins me on the front stoop, stopping to lock her door from the outside.

I take her bag—which is pretty light, and that impresses me. I appreciate a light packer—and stick it in the trunk, then open the passenger side door and wave her in.

"Rules say no civilians in the front," she says.

"I'm gonna bend the rules tonight for you, Issy. I don't like the idea of you riding in the back."

"Why?"

"Why are you so suspicious of me all of a sudden? I mean, we just had a good time. What's up?"

"You're just acting weird." But she gets in the front seat. So I close her door, walk around the car, and get in my side.

"It *is* kinda weird, right?" I start the car, check the directions on my phone, and then pull away from the curb as she thinks about that. "I mean... don't you think this is weird?"

"Which part?" she says. "What I asked for? Or that I let you fuck me?"

"Let me?" I laugh, again. "*Begged me*, Issy."

"Whatever," she says, waving her hand in the air. "I never beg. I just take what I want." But I catch a small smile out of the corner of my eye.

"So no, not too weird," I lie.

"Just a little weird?" she asks, still smiling. "It's not a strange request. I looked it up."

"You did?" I ask. Fuck, I'm dying to know what she thinks we're doing tonight.

"Yes. I found a study online that cited almost eight percent of the female population fantasizes about it."

I almost stop the car. Like my foot taps the brake, and we both jerk forward before I realize what I'm doing and correct.

"What the fuck was that?" Issy asks.

"I... uh... there was a cat running across the road. I didn't want to hit it."

Did she imply what I think she implied? Are we playing a sex game?

"Is this a big place?" she asks in my ensuing silence.

"Nope," I lie again. Well, is it really a lie if there's no *place*? I mean, we are going somewhere, but the safe house in Silver Springs is obviously not what she's fantasizing about.

"How many people?" she asks. And when I look over at her, she's biting her lip like she's nervous.

Fuck. I have nothing for that. "You'll see," I say, getting onto the I-70 freeway that will take us up into the mountains.

"Are you curious?" she asks.

"Very." I laugh.

"About which part?"

"Uh..."

"I mean, I know we're not supposed to talk about this or it'll ruin the illusion, but I'm sorta nervous and I can't help it."

Jesus Christ. Pull yourself together, Finn Murphy! You're a goddamned FBI agent. You're a motherfucking force to be reckoned with. This woman has you totally off your game! Step the fuck up and play!

I heed the internal monologue and collect myself. "I'm curious about the whole thing, honestly."

"Because it's weird?"

"I thought we already decided it was normal?"

"It is normal. Well, it's normal to fantasize about it. I'm not sure how many women actually go through with it, so that's... a little bit unusual. But you know what they say?"

"What do they say?" I'm dying. Fucking dying to know what they say!

"'You must make a choice to take a chance or your life will never change.'"

"Who said that?" I ask.

"Zig Ziglar," she replies. "One of my motivational heroes."

"Ah." OK, I like this topic far better than the fantasy sex game we're not playing. So I take the opportunity to switch the subject. "Is he the guy who got you interested in motivational speaking?"

"Yup. His book saved my life."

"You mean like… literally? You were what, on the edge of suicide and then you stumbled onto his words and you decided to give it all another go?"

"No, dumbass. I mean I was at rock bottom, not ready to off myself. That's all."

"Define rock bottom."

"No, again," she growls. "It's none of your business."

"Do you tell your students about your rock bottom?"

"Why?"

"I'm just curious. I find you kinda fascinating."

"Because I'm in this game and I don't look like the kind of woman who'd want to play?"

"Well, yeah."

"I tell some stuff," she admits. "Not all of it, of course."

"Why 'of course?' I mean, 'of course' implies that missing stuff is too private to talk about, or too weird to talk about, or too painful to talk about. So which one is it?"

"You have to pay to hear that answer. That's my livelihood."

I smile, picturing myself at one of her women's empowerment seminars. "Can I come tomorrow?"

"No."

"Why not? Because I'm a man?"

"That's not why. It's just full. I have a waiting list six months long."

"You're pretty popular," I say.

"Very popular. How much research did you do on me before today?"

"None," I admit. Because it would be stupid to lie about that. I really don't know anything about her.

"He had to have been planning this for a while. Couple weeks at least to come up with such an elaborate setup. Fuckin' Chella. She must've given him a heads up a while back and they put this all together." But then she laughs. "I do admit, it was a pretty good scam."

"Which part?"

"The whole FBI thing. The raid or whatever. Like... he must have a lot of connections to pull something like this off, right? Do you know him well?"

"Who?" I ask.

She shakes her head, turns towards the window to hide her smile. "Fine. I get it. Gotta keep up the illusion. I mean, obviously Chella is paying for this, so I'd feel bad if she didn't get her money's worth."

Holy. Fucking. Shit. This is a *business*! I have a pretty good idea who she's talking about. I don't know who this Chella person is, but the *who* in all this—the mastermind, if you will—must be her lawyer, Jordan Wells.

I make a mental note to look that asshole up as soon as we're at the safe house. Could be the break I've been looking for. I mean, Issy just said it herself. He must have some kind of power to set all this up.

Except... it wasn't a setup. The raid was real. The handcuffs were real. The interrogation, the safe house— all real. I wonder if Declan knows anything about this Wells guy? I make another mental note to ask him.

"Hello? Finn?"

"What?" I say, snapping back to the present.

"I said, do you mind if I just close my eyes and sleep a little? I want to be rested for what's coming."

What's coming?

"No, go ahead," I say. "We've still got a ways to go before we get there. I want you rested too." And then I wink. One more time to cement her illusion. To keep her in the fantasy. I need this time to come up with a plan because Issy Grey is gonna be one sexually frustrated deviant when we get to the Silver Springs safe house.

And there's no telling how she might react to the truth.

CHAPTER SEVEN

*ISSY

"Issy." I wake up to a man's attractive hazel eyes staring down at me, and for a second I can't figure out who he is, where I'm at, or what the fuck is going on. "We're here."

But the panic fades as his face comes into focus. Special Agent Finn Murphy. Jordan Wells. The game. My night.

I rub the sleep out of my eyes before I remember I'm wearing makeup and stop. "Where?" I mumble out, still waking up.

"Silver Springs, remember?"

I squint my eyes and stare out the window, but it's total darkness. I can't see shit. "Is this the club?" I ask.

"Uh… yup. Come on, we should get inside."

He opens his door, gets out, and walks around the front of the car to open mine. Suddenly my heart is beating faster, my body is flushed with heat, and I'm nervous.

Finn offers me his hand. "Come on, it's cold out here. Let's get inside."

I get out, more from habit than anything, and he closes the door behind me and waves me forward towards…

"A house?" I say. "Where are all the other cars?"

"What cars?"

"The cars!" I say. "You know, that all the people come in? Hasn't it started yet?" I check my watch. It's after midnight now.

"They'll be here soon. You're supposed to come in first."

"Oh," I say, taking a deep breath to try to get my rapid breathing under control.

"Don't trip," Finn says, grabbing hold of my arm and leading me forward.

I do trip. Like immediately. Because the stone pathway leading up the dark house is uneven, just like the one at my house back in Denver. So I don't pull away.

We stop at the front door, which is apparently locked with an electronic keypad, because Finn punches in a sequence of numbers and the door beeps. He swings the door open to reveal more darkness.

"Go on," he says, encouraging me. "We gotta hurry before people start arriving. You want to be ready, don't you?"

"Yes," I whisper. But this whole thing is creepy as fuck. I really hope Chella knows what she's doing and Jordan is trustworthy. I mean, the guy's a lawyer, so you'd assume. But then again, there's a million lowlife lawyer jokes for a reason, right? You *can't* trust them. What the hell was I thinking?

He closes the door, eliminating the hazy moonlight leaking in from outside, and the entire place is pitch-black darkness.

I hold my breath, convinced this whole thing was a setup and he's really here to—

Stop it, Issy!

I take seven quick breaths, then three long ones—the same technique I've been using to calm myself down for the better part of a decade—and say, "What's going on?"

"What do you mean?" he says, flicking a switch to illuminate the room.

Which is… a living room. And not a well-decorated one, either.

"What the hell?" I ask, spinning around to see his face. "This cannot be the place."

He shrugs as he punches in a sequence of numbers on the door again.

This time locking me in.

I don't ask any more questions. I just react.

CHAPTER EIGHT

FINN✳

Her foot catches me in the mouth, then a fist chops me in the throat. I'm down on the ground gasping for breath in the span of three seconds. One second later the lights go off, and the darkness envelops us.

"What the—" I gasp out, just as I hear something crash across the room.

And I don't get to finish, because she's got something pressed against my throat. A stick, or a bat, or—

"You better start talking right now, Finn Murphy or whoever the fuck you are. Or I'm gonna break your windpipe with this fire poker."

My body instinctively twists, unbalancing her, and the next moment, I've got her on her back and I throw the poker. It crashes against a wall.

There's like half a second when I think I've got her pinned and now I'm on top, but she gets a hand free and jabs me in the eye. I can't help it, I let go of her other hand and she clocks me—hard—right in the jaw. She delivers a second punch to my nose, and the hot sensation of blood dripping pulls me out of my momentary stupor. She's on her feet, standing over me now, when I reach out, grab her ankle, and drop her to the floor. She kicks me in the chest, sending me reeling backwards, and then scrambles away— hidden in the darkness of the room.

"Issy—" I cough. Fucking Declan was right. This chick is goddamned dangerous!

"Who are you?"

I look off to the left where the words come from, but I can't see shit. "Special Agent Finn Murphy!" I yell. "And I'm gonna arrest you now for assaulting an officer!"

"Fuck you!" she yells. And now the voice is somewhere else. Damn, this little bitch is fast. "This is not part of the game, and I'm two seconds away from taking you down for good if you don't unlock that door and—"

I'm on my feet, heading in the direction of where I think the door is—but I don't unlock it.

I flick the light back on.

She's perched on top of a bookcase, crouched down on hands and feet, like a goddamned monkey ready to—

Just as the thought forms in my head, she leaps. Fuckin' knocks me down and chops my throat again.

This time I don't recover so fast. I can do nothing but roll over and wheeze as I try to draw in air.

"Stay down, Agent," she hisses, searching my pockets, then backing away.

I don't answer. Can't answer. I don't know how long I stay there, on hands and knees, my forehead pressed into the dirty wood floor as I try to remember what it's like to breathe, but it's a while.

During the time I'd like to say I got my act together. That I didn't just allow a woman who barely comes up to my shoulders to take me down in the span of three minutes… but I'd be lying.

Because by the time I *can* breathe, she's got my hands zip-tied behind my back and she's sitting on top of me, pushing my face into the floor as she leans down into my ear to hiss, "You've got ten seconds to start talking, asshole. Or I will knock you out, break a window, climb through it, steal your car, and leave you here to stew in your own stupidity until your friends come save you."

CHAPTER NINE

*ISSY

"I'm supposed to protect you, Issy! I'm your goddamn bodyguard!" he yells. Well, it's not a yell because he can barely manage to get the words out.

"Bodyguard." I laugh, but get up off him and start pacing the room. "You're obviously not my bodyguard, because I neither asked for, nor do I require, a bodyguard."

"I swear," he gasps. "That raid was real. That terror threat was real."

"Bullshit! I have nothing to do with that!"

"Right, Einstein." He chokes out a laugh. "You were set up. We explained this to you earlier."

"You told me you were part of the game!" I yell.

"No," he says, finally starting to breathe normal again. "*You* said I was part of this stupid sex game you're playing. I just went along."

"Fucking liar! Caleb sent you, didn't he?"

"Who?"

I kick him in the ribs. Hard. "Don't play stupid!"

"I swear," he says, rolling over a little so he can look up at me. "My badge is in my front pocket." He nods his head towards his jacket, which I didn't search when I found the zip ties.

"Make one move and—"

"I'm fucking zip-tied, Issy! Don't be an asshole. Just get my badge. I'm telling the truth!"

I do a quick pat down on his coat pocket and—fuck. I can feel what's probably a wallet. I pull it out and yup—one of those leather fold-over things that hold badges. Flipping it open reveals an ID, which does in fact, confirm he's FBI.

"Shit," I say.

"Shit is right. You're gonna be charged for this."

"Shut up," I say, pacing. "I need to think."

"You're going down for assault with the intent to kill. They're gonna get you for evading arrest, kidnapping—"

"Kidnapping!" I laugh. "That's a good one."

"You're holding me against my will."

"I'm holding—You're holding *me* against my will!" I yell back.

I stop pacing. He stops struggling and we both just—take a breath. He stares up at me, craning his neck to try to make eye contact.

I wait.

Finally he says, "Listen. I'm FBI. Whoever this Caleb person is, I'm not a part of that. Whatever this game is, I'm not a part of that either."

I don't know what to think, so I keep quiet.

"Someone called into… somewhere earlier today…."

"Somewhere?" I ask, forcing a laugh as I try to calm down. "What do you mean somewhere?"

"I mean, the call was real, it came in—but beyond that I don't know much. I wasn't really…" He sighs. "I wasn't really paying attention earlier today. I had shit on my mind, OK? So I'm not clear on the details, but however it happened that you got on our radar, that was real, Issy. There was chatter."

"What chatter?" I'm really not doing well right now. My heart is skipping beats inside my chest. My breathing is picking up and starting to become erratic.

"Look," he says. "I'm not the best FBI agent, OK? The reason I'm in Denver was because I was demoted. I lost my father a few months back, I've been drinking too much, sleeping too little, and... and... yeah." He lets out a breath that says all the things he couldn't.

I think about that for a few seconds, but my mind is racing, and my heart is pounding, and my hands are shaking and... I hate this. I fucking hate this. I hate that I'm rattled, I hate that every fiber of my being is screaming RUN!

I don't run. I don't run, I don't run, I don't run...

"Untie me, Issy."

"No," I say, swallowing down the fear. "No, I'm leaving you here. I'll make an anonymous call telling people where you are and—"

"No," he yells. "You can't leave."

"I can leave." I laugh. "I'm going to leave. So you better just come to terms with that, buddy."

He rests his head on the floor, craning his neck to look at me. Then he laughs.

"What's so funny?"

"I mean that literally."

"Meant what?" I snap. I'm busy running probabilities in my head. Probabilities of getting out of this alive. What are my chances of survival right now?

"You cannot leave here."

"Watch me." I laugh.

"Go ahead and try."

"What?"

"The door is made of steel. It's on a digital lock and you don't have the code to open it."

"I can go through a window, genius."

"Like I said. Go ahead and try."

What the fuck—? I walk over to the window, tear open the curtains and see—

"Reinforced security shutters, Issy. On every single window. Also on a coded lock. This is a goddamned safe house, OK? No one can get in without blowing a hole in the wall. Which means no one can get out, either. And if you've got some harebrained scheme for giving that a try, I'd like to take this opportunity to caution you against it. They will make you pay for damaging government property. So I hope you've got money stashed away for that. Because fucking up a priority one safe house is gonna cost you dearly."

A sharp pain fills my chest, making me double over. My breathing is far, far beyond erratic now. I start to hyperventilate. My whole body begins to tremble. My knees buckle, and reality flickers, and before I know what's happening—

CHAPTER TEN

FINN✳

She falls to the floor. Like collapses into a heap. Her head misses the coffee table by mere inches. "Issy!" "I yell. "Issy?"

I struggle in the zip ties, but my hands are secured behind my back and I'm not in the right position to break out of them. So I don't bother. I'm a little more worried about her right now than myself. I wriggle across the floor until I am close enough to get a good look at her face. "Issy?" I whisper, trying to see if she's breathing. "Issy?"

She moans.

Thank fuck. "Issy," I say again. "Can you hear me?"

"Whaaaaaa…"

"I think you fainted, Issy. Open your eyes. You're OK, do you hear me? You're OK, you just fainted. You're fine. Just open your eyes."

She shifts her body, turning over on her side. I can't see her face because it's covered by her long, dark hair.

"You're OK," I repeat. "You're fine, all right? You just fainted. It's gonna pass. Just… try to breathe and open your eyes."

She does more than that because suddenly she's up on her hands and knees, her whole body swaying.

"Don't get up!" I say. "Just be still, breathe, and open your eyes and look at me, Issy. Do you hear me? Look. At. Me."

She collapses again. Her breathing is heavy, almost a pant. Like she's having a panic attack or something.

"What… what happened?" she mumbles.

"You fainted, that's all. No big deal. Happens to everyone. It's gonna pass really quick, OK? You're fine."

"My heart," she moans.

"No," I say. "It's a trick. I promise. Your heart is fine, just breathe through your nose for a few minutes. It's a trick. You got overwhelmed and—"

"Shut up!"

Her yell catches me off guard. So much so that I do. I shut up.

"I don't need your help. I don't need your words. I don't need you to tell me when things are and are not OK. So shut the hell up!"

"There she is." I chuckle, relaxing my head on the floor again.

She starts making mad grabs at her hair, pushing it away from her eyes. We're only inches apart—face to face—when her gaze finds mine. Her beautiful blue eyes look like shining sapphires right now. "I don't need your help."

"Obviously," I say. But I feel better. Relieved. I mean, yeah, if she was really hurt and didn't wake up, I'd be stuck here trying to get myself free. And then, with my luck, Declan would show up before I managed that and… yeah.

The last thing I need is a rescue.

But that's not why I'm relieved.

She's OK. She just fainted. She got overwhelmed and scared and who can blame her? It's been a pretty messed-up night for her.

"You can untie me now," I say.

"No." She gets back on her hands and knees, her head hanging, her long hair brushing against the floor as she sways a little. And then she's on her feet. One hand covering her eyes, the other holding onto the back of the couch so she doesn't fall over again.

"I'm not gonna hurt you."

Her hand flies away from her face and she spits, "You *can't* hurt me."

"I know," I say, pulling every FBI trick out of my hat to keep her calm and see reason. "I mean, I know that now. You're pretty tough, chick. Anyone ever tell you that before?"

She huffs air, stumbles across the room, hand outstretched, reaching for the small dinette table, and feels her way around it until she's leaning on the formica kitchen counter in front of the sink. She turns on the tap, sticks her mouth into the flowing water, and drinks.

"Hey," I call. "I could use a drink too."

She pulls back, wipes her hand across her mouth— little droplets of water spilling down her chin—and laughs. "Do you keep whiskey here?"

My neck is tired, the muscles in my shoulders strained from lifting my head off the floor. "Untie me and I'll look."

She ignores that. Just starts going through cupboards, slapping them closed after looking through each one.

"Nothing," she says.

Well, duh, I want to say. "It's a safe house. Not a bar. But we can go get a drink if you want. Talk this over, relax a little, and come up with a plan."

"I already have a plan," she says.

"Ya do?" I laugh. "What is it?"

She grabs at her hair, trying to straighten it out. Doesn't help, it's tragically disheveled. Beautifully unkempt. "You're going to let me out of here, I'm going to take your car, and then we're never going to see each other again."

"Nope," I say. "Not gonna happen that way."

"I'll hurt you," she says.

"No, you won't."

This makes her laugh. But then she cuts it short and seethes, "Underestimate me, Agent Murphy. I dare you."

"Look," I say. "I can see that you're not happy with the arrangements we've made for you—"

"Understatement."

"—so let's just renegotiate, OK? You want to make it to that seminar tomorrow, right?"

She says nothing. Just stares at me.

"We can do that. You untie me, we leave here, go back to your place, you grab a little sleep, and then I go with you to the seminar. I'll just pretend to be a student and that way I can keep you safe and—"

She cuts me off. "How many times do I need to tell you? I do not need your protection."

"I get that," I say, trying to remain calm and reasonable. But the truth is, my fucking neck is killing me, I'm pretty sure there's no circulation in my hands because the zip ties are too tight, my nose might be broken, there's blood all over my face, and she might've fucked up my jaw when she clocked me. So I'm really fucking sick of this shit.

But I deal. Because that's what I've been trained to do.

"I get that *now*," I amend. "But it never hurts to have someone on your side, right?"

"You're not on my side," she sneers. "You lied to me! You lied to get me up here! And you fucked me!"

"You fucked me back. And you kinda beat the shit out of me, so suck it up, buttercup. We're in this together whether you like it or not. Because this night, Issy, this night isn't a game, OK? It's fuckin' real. I'm not after you but people *are* after you. So put your big-girl panties on and *un-fucking-tie me*."

I kinda lose it at the end. Because 'un-fucking-tie me' comes out as a threat.

But it works. At least it might be working. Because she takes a deep breath, looks down at her shaking hands, and exhales out a sigh of resignation.

CHAPTER ELEVEN

*ISSY

I try to keep calm. Run my options through my head. They fly by, like one of those old-time ticker tapes from the early twentieth century that telegraphed important news to people before the internet made information ubiquitous.

What the fuck is going on? There's no way they came looking for me. I've been too careful. I've been too clever. And yeah, I have a decent business going with the whole Go F*ck Yourself thing, but I'm not high-profile. I'm a big fish in a very small pond. I mean, I don't even advertise. My books sold a lot of copies, but I was never on talk shows and shit. So if that FBI raid wasn't part of the game, then who called that tip in?

"Issy," Finn growls. "I'm not going to ask you—"

"You will ask me again if I feel like making you, OK? So just be quiet and let me get a handle on things."

"You can do that after you untie me. Because I'm telling you right now, if I have to break out of these myself, you're gonna regret it."

"You probably don't even know how to break out. You told me yourself. You're not the best FBI agent, right, Murphy?"

"I meant," he seethes, "that I'm not on track for promotion, Issy. Not that I was incapable of something as simple as getting myself out of zip ties. I have seen seven-year-olds get out of zip ties using their shoelaces, so let's not pretend."

I think about this for a moment. He's kinda right about the zip ties thing. I mean, you gotta have time, and be in the right position, but they're pretty simple to get out of if you have those two things.

"Let me out or I'll... I'll..."

I almost laugh. Because he doesn't even have a threat ready.

"I won't fulfill your fantasy," he finishes.

My guffaw is loud enough to startle him. "As if!" I yell. "I'd never let you that close to me again."

"You will, Ms. Grey." He kinda snarls that part. "Because whatever is happening to you right now has nothing to do with some stupid sex game you're playing with your lawyer."

"I'm not playing with him. He's just the—" Grrrrrr.

"He's just the what? Facilitator?"

"I can't talk to you about it, I already explained that."

"Untie me and I'll make sure you can talk about it. You do realize that an NDA is invalid if it involves a crime, right?"

"That's not even true. Lots of people sign NDAs for like... settlements. And it usually involves a crime."

"Those are usually civil actions. Not criminal. Look, you're fucked if you don't get someone on your side real quick, because this shit is happening. Someone called you in tonight. Someone set you up. Someone is out to get you. And if you want to add me to your enemies list, then great. Do that. But when you're sitting in jail wondering where it all went wrong, I'll come visit and remind you."

I let out another long breath of air—

"Untie me."

—and decide that he's right. "Fine," I say, walking into the kitchen to grab a knife from the silverware drawer, and then walk back over to him and bend down. "But if you make any sudden moves—"

"Yeah, yeah, yeah, fuckin' yeah. You'll take me out. Got it."

Asshole.

"Jesus Christ. Are you trying to saw my fuckin' wrists off or what?"

"It's a dull knife, OK? Just hold still."

"Ow."

"I never knew the FBI hired such wussies."

But then the plastic snaps and I back away, because I'm pretty sure he's lying about not trying anything.

They all lie. That's the nature of people.

He's quick too, up on his feet, reeling around to glare at me in seconds. But I'm all the way across the room.

He smiles. It's one of those you-fucking-bitch smiles. I recognize it. Seen it plenty of times in the past.

But then he takes a deep breath, looks down at his wrists, holds them up as exhibit A, and says, "Just FYI, next time you zip-tie someone, don't cut off their circulation."

I sneer at him.

"Now," he says, still glaring, but walking towards the door, "let's go."

"Go where? I'm not leaving until you explain just why the hell you decided to play along with my game when you knew you weren't part of it!"

But he's already punched in the key code and has the door open. "We're going back to your place so I can regroup with my boss and you can get some sleep. You want to make that seminar tomorrow? Then let's go."

Is he serious? Does he really think I'll buy that?

"OK," he says. "Bye."

And then he walks out the door and slams it closed behind him.

It's only then that I realize it locks automatically. Because it beeps. Just the way it did when we came in.

And now I'm trapped.

"You motherfucker," I yell.

FINN*

I'd be lying if I said I wasn't enjoying myself. Issy is pounding on the door screaming every obscenity she can think of. Every threat too. But I just lean back on the hood of the car and smile.

Teach her to zip-tie me. Teach her to kick my ass.

Not that she kicked my ass. She didn't. She just caught me off guard, that's all. I look at my watch and start timing her. "Stop screaming and calm down," I yell.

"The hell I will!"

"Stop screaming for five minutes and I'll let you out. But I'm not letting you out until you calm down. And it's a scientific fact that it takes five minutes to calm down."

She says something back to that, but I don't catch it. And then she stops.

I wait, clocking her.

We're at a little over four minutes and I'm feeling pretty proud of myself when the fire alarm goes off inside.

"I bet that's coded to the fire department, isn't it?" she yells on the other side of the door.

I close my eyes, pinching the bridge of my nose, then walk over to the door, punch in the code and cancel the alarm. But that unlocks the door, and she's got it open before I realize what just happened.

We stand there, not eye to eye because she's tiny and I'm tall, but close enough. Glaring at each other. Daring each other. Planning seven different ways to kill each other.

After almost a minute of silent, mutual hate, she sucks air in through her teeth and says, "Now you may take me home."

"I should leave your ass here on principle."

"I should zip-tie you back up." She waves a fistful of zip ties at me.

"Go ahead and try. You only get the element of surprise once."

"I love to be underestimated."

More mutual hatred.

And then I say, "Fuck it. Get in the car."

I turn my back on her and decide I'm done. If she gets in, I'll drop her ass off at her house and go find Declan. If she wants to stay out here in the goddamned forest, fine by me.

We get in at the same time. Slam our doors at the same time. I start the car and she pushes herself up against her door, like she doesn't want to turn her back on me, not even a little bit.

I back up, spinning the tires in the dirt, and head back out the way we came.

"Well, that was fucking stupid."

"Which part? The part where you turn into a batshit crazy person?"

"No, the part where I waste my night with a stupid FBI agent."

"Well," I say, reaching the end of the driveway and turning onto the highway. "I did fuck you pretty good."

"Shut up."

"Admit it, it was the best part of your night."

"Shut. Up."

114

"I mean, you came hard, right?"

"What the fuck is wrong with you? Didn't your mother teach you manners?"

I laugh. "Is there a protocol for this I'm missing?"

"Yes, it's called shut the fuck up."

"Oh, I get it. I'm supposed to pretend it never happened."

"You don't need to pretend," she says. "It was... what do they call it? Oh, I know, entrapment."

I roll my eyes. "Jesus. For a smart person, you sure don't know very much about the legalities of things. Like your dumb NDA. If he really did set all this up and used the FBI to play this stupid sex game with you—"

"I'm not playing with him, I told you that."

"—then you have every right to report him. He can't touch you. Really. I'm not lying. This is my *job*."

She turns her head away and stares out into the passing night.

"And if you weren't playing with him, then who?"

"I thought it was you, dumbass."

"How do you not know who is supposed to be fucking you, Issy? How does that even make sense?"

"It just does. You'll have to trust me."

"Well, I don't trust you. Not after you went insane back there."

She breathes out through her nose.

Silence.

"Just fuckin' tell me what's going on. I can help you. *Will* help you. And he won't touch you. I promise."

"It's not him I'm worried about, OK? He's a stand-up guy. He's not gonna—"

But my laugh is so loud, she stops mid sentence. "Stand-up guy? Are you kidding me?"

"He runs… he runs a sex fantasy fulfillment business, OK? It's all legal."

"Oh, I'm sure it is."

"It is. He's a lawyer, for fuck's sake. A very fucking successful one. He wouldn't cross any lines."

"Nope," I say. "He didn't cross any lines at all tonight."

"You don't know it's him, OK?"

"You seem to think it's him."

"That's because none of it made sense."

"You thought you were gonna be taken to a sex club to be fucked in front of—"

"Just never mind that part, OK? My friend set this up for me as a Valentine's Day gift. To make me do something outside of work. So I went over to the tea shop to talk about it, Jordan was there, and I told him what I wanted, and then he closed my file and said…" She sighs. Loudly.

"Said what?"

Silence.

"Goddammit, Issy. What did he say?"

"He said… he said no, OK? He said no, I wasn't right for his game, and he closed my file and walked out. There, are you happy now?"

I want to laugh, but it doesn't seem appropriate. So I hold it in and try to be professional. "So if he said no, then why did you think you were supposed to let me fuck you tonight?"

"Jesus, could you be any more vulgar?"

"Answer the question. God, I'm gonna get it out of you eventually, why do you insist on making this so difficult?"

"I thought it was part of the game, OK? Like… he's supposed to be this master sex game planner. So I figured none of this FBI stuff made much sense, so it must be the game. That's all it was. A stupid misunderstanding. I assumed something, I was wrong, now let's drop it."

"Master sex game planner. I really need to meet this guy."

"Why?" She laughs. "You gonna buy a game from him?"

"Me? No. I don't need a game to get fucked."

"I'm sure you don't, playboy."

I think through her comments for a while. She stays silent. Just leaning her head up against the window, looking outside like she's wishing she could be anywhere but here.

I want to tell her things. Things like, *Well, I had fun. Hope you did too.* Or *Maybe we can do it again tomorrow? And this time I can zip-tie you up, wink wink, if you know what I mean.*

But I don't.

Because she said none of the FBI stuff made much sense.

"Not any sense," I say.

"What?" she says, dragging her gaze from the window.

"You said none of this FBI stuff made *much* sense. Not *any* sense. Which means it made a little sense."

"You're really reaching now."

"Am I?"

"You are."

I'm not, but I drop it. Because I knew she was hiding something back at the office. I knew. Felt it in my bones.

And now I'm gonna make it my mission to figure out what it is.

CHAPTER THIRTEEN

*ISSY

The problem with this night is... some of it was fun. I mean, I'm pretty disappointed that this isn't a game. Unless he's lying, but I really don't think he's lying. He can't be that good an actor. And we really were down at the Federal Building and I really was locked in an interrogation room, and he and his partner really did question me.

So what the fuck is going on?

And, more importantly, why the fuck is this happening to me? I mean, I was just minding my own business, doing my thing, and then wham. Bullshit everywhere I turn. It's bad enough that Chella talked Jordan into a game for me. I mean, that's a little bit humiliating all by itself. But then to be turned down?

"I didn't ask for any of this," I say, looking out the window as the world whips by. We're on I-70 now, heading back towards Denver, and I can just see the glow of city lights peeking over the top of the mountains. There's no traffic, so we should be back in downtown in like twenty minutes.

"OK," he says. But it's one of those OK's that really means, *You're full of shit.*

"I didn't."

"Fine. I'm agreeing with you."

"But your agreement is really just placating me."

"If you say so, Issy."

I huff out a breath of air and decide to drop it.

"But you don't make sense. And you know that. Your background is… well, spotty."

Yup. It is. But there's no way he could find out about my past. Like, literally, no way. That girl doesn't exist anymore. So I don't agree or disagree with his initial assessment.

"Which means it's either completely made up or you've somehow erased parts of it. So which is it?"

I ignore him.

"I'm gonna figure it out."

"Why?" I say, turning my body to face him. I'm angry now. "Why do you need to figure it out? Why can't you just drop the whole fucking thing?"

"Because you're somehow involved in a terror threat."

"Says you," I spit. "That's probably bullshit. You guys probably made that up to make me vulnerable. To make me cooperate. And it's not gonna work."

"We didn't make it up." He laughs. "This is the fucking FBI, Issy. We've got better things to do than play sex games with you."

"Could you just shut up?"

"Fine," he says, pressing a button on the navigation panel. Music starts to play, something beat-y, and hypnotic, and dark, which does nothing for my already dark mood. But he stays silent all the way into downtown. All the way to my house.

I open the door as soon as the car stops, just trying to get away from him as quickly as possible, but then he shuts the car off.

"No," I say, shaking my head, one leg already out the door. "No, you're not coming in."

"Fine," he says, shrugging. "But I'm not leaving either."

I get out, slam the door, walk up to my house, keys already in hand, open the door, slam it closed behind me, and flick on the light.

And then I do most of that backwards. I open the door back up, slam it behind me, skip down the porch stairs, run down the walkway, and open the car door back up.

"Forget something?" he asks, while texting on his phone.

"Someone was in my house."

He stops texting. "What?"

"It's ransacked, Finn!" I grab my hair with frustration. "Someone went through my house!"

His door is open, he's out of the car, he's got a gun out as he stalks up my front walk, and then he looks at me, nods his head, and I open the door for him.

He goes in like… well, an FBI guy. Pointing his gun this way and that way as he steps over the mountains of debris, searching for people in the house.

When he goes upstairs, I look around nervously.

Someone was in my house. Strangers did this to me.

I suddenly feel very violated.

"No one," Finn says, coming down the stairs, holstering his gun. "Whoever it was did this hours ago. Probably right after we left."

"How do you know that?" I ask, still expecting people to jump out at me.

"It's my job," he says simply. Which doesn't appease me. He's poking at his phone, puts it to his ear. He says, "Declan, call me back. Something is wrong."

"What's that mean? Who's Declan?"

"Let's go," he says, pointing at the door. "I'm taking you to my house until I can figure this shit out."

"Wait," I say, putting my hands up.

"Yes, Ms. Grey?" he says, not even looking at me because his eyes are still taking in the scene.

"You want me to go to your house with you?"

"Yeah, to keep you safe."

"And that's it?"

He just stares at me. Dumbly.

"Not to fuck me again? Not to play one more round before this night is over?"

Now it's his turn to laugh. "Issy," he says, pulling out his professional voice. "This isn't a game. I'm not your hired help for the night. I fucked you earlier because I think you're sexy, that's it. But if pretending to play this stupid game makes you go along with my duty to keep you safe, I'll keep playing along."

We stare at each other.

"Yes, Issy. This is all part of my secret plan to spread your legs open and lick your pussy. Better?"

I turn away so he can't see me smile, then gather up my self-respect, turn back, and say, with a straight face, "Fine. It's not a game. I'm just a job to you."

He tips a pretend hat at me, then waves a hand at the door. "After you."

It only takes a few minutes to get to his place over in Lower Downtown, but the seconds drag on like years in the silence. He says nothing, just compulsively checks his phone, like maybe he thinks his ringer isn't working and that's why this Declan guy hasn't called him back yet. Then he sends another text, trying to get an answer.

"What did you just text?" I ask.

"Business," he says back.

Whatever.

He lives in a trendy new condo building right next to a bar called Bronco Brews. That's the place with the fake water tower on the roof, like this is New York or something.

"OK," he says, flicking the light on after he opens his apartment door. "Come in and let's just try to grab a couple hours of sleep before dawn."

It's already after four AM, and I'm not sure I could sleep, even if I had the time. My seminar is at noon, but I need to get my shit together before I walk in and try to change the mindset of three hundred women. I can't go up there and talk to them all freaked out about shit like this.

"Hey," I say, walking into his living room and dropping my bag on the floor.

"What's up?" he asks, taking his holster off and locking his gun in a safe hidden in the wall.

"Just answer me this, OK?"

"Sure, what is it, Issy?" Now he's walking into his bedroom, taking off his suit coat as he disappears.

"If that raid last night was real—"

He pops into the doorway again and my eyes immediately track to his fingers, which are unbuttoning his button-down shirt. "If?" he says. "If it was real?"

"Fine," I huff. "It was real. Wouldn't they have like… crime scene tape and shit all over my place? Am I even allowed to go back in there?"

"It's not a murder scene." He disappears into his bedroom again.

I wonder what he's taking off next. But then I hear the jingle of his belt and know.

"Right, but don't they have to send in a forensics team or something?"

He appears in the open doorway again, this time bare-chested and wearing cut-off sweat shorts. I stare a second too long, and when my eyes meet his, he's smiling. "Someone's been watching too many police procedurals on TV." And then he winks. "Just change out of those clothes and try to get some sleep, OK? I'm fuckin' tired, I gotta be up in like two hours, and I need to just forget about this day."

I look down at my bag, thinking about what I have inside it.

"Now what?" he asks, leaving the bedroom and walking towards me. He goes into the kitchen, grabs a glass from a cupboard, and fills it with water from the fridge door.

"I'm just gonna sleep in my clothes," I say, trying to look at anything but his naked torso. He's very fit. Like *very* fit. I'm talking six-pack. I'm talking that v-line of muscle that disappears under the waist line of his sweat shorts. I'm talking—

"Why?"

"I didn't bring… anything appropriate."

His eyes dart to my pack, then meet mine again.

He smiles.

We both go for the bag at the same time. I'm closer, so I get to it first, but his arms are long and he snatches it away. I jump, trying to get it back, but he holds it over his head.

Have I mentioned he's a foot taller than me?

"Give it back," I say.

"What'd you pack?"

"None of your business. Now give it back."

He turns his back to me and starts unzipping the bag while I desperately try to reach around his broad shoulders to no avail. "What is…"

"Give it back," I say, pulling on the strap, and this time I succeed. Or he lets it go. Or whatever. It doesn't matter. Because he's holding up what I did pack.

"Dayum, woman. You were gonna wear this for me tonight?"

I close my eyes, rub my fingertips into my temples, and say, "This isn't happening."

"Are you into…"

"Shut up and give it back."

"Issy." He laughs. "You're a kinky little bitch, you know that?"

I snatch the nightie—it really doesn't qualify as a nightie. People don't wear open-tit lingerie to bed. People wear open-tit lingerie to sex clubs. Which is where I thought I was going tonight.

"You gonna put it on?" Finn asks.

I open my eyes, snatch the… costume… out of his hands, throw it over my shoulder, and say, "Not in your dreams, playboy."

But he's already reaching into the bag again. "Je-*sus*," he says, his voice low, almost a whisper. Like he's found buried treasure. "Holy shit. You're really into this, aren't you?"

He's looking at my boots now. Black. Thigh-high. Grommets and laces all the way up the back. Made of latex.

125

He drops them to the floor. "What's this?"

I take a deep, deep breath.

"OK," he says, waving the riding crop in the air. "Hold on, sister. We gotta get this out of the way before we go any further."

My blood pressure is rising so rapidly, my head begins to pound.

"Do you like to dish it out?" He whips the crop back and forth in the air so it makes that whoosh sound. "Or do you like to be the one being dished on?"

I grab the crop, pull it out of his hand, and hide it behind my back. "Are you done?"

"I don't think so." He laughs as he reaches back into the bag and removes nipple clamps. "My *God*," he says, looking at them in the palm of his hand, then at my tits, then at them again.

"OK, all very funny," I say, trying to be nonchalant. "We're done here. I'm gonna sleep on the couch in my clothes, you're going to your room. Good night."

"Oh." He grins. "Oh, no, no, no. I mean... come on, Issy."

"Come on what?"

He walks towards me.

I back away.

But his long arms—damn his long arms—reach around behind my back and take the crop.

I give up and don't fight him. Fuck it, right? Just let him have his fun. He'll tire himself out like a child and then he'll let it go.

But he whacks me on the ass so hard with the crop, I jump. "What the fuck?"

"Did it make you wet?"

"You're insane."

"I'm insane? Woman, you're the one who went out on a date with me tonight and packed kink!"

"It wasn't a date. It was a *game*."

"Oh, excuse me," he says, closing his eyes and placing a mea culpa hand over his heart. "You're the one who let me take you out with the intention of putting all this on."

He opens his eyes.

We stare at each other.

"So," he says, reaching for my wrists and pulling me towards him. His chest is hot. And bare. And muscular. He smells faintly of aftershave. And sweat. And the city. He smells like sex, I realize. Because I already let him fuck me. We've already done this. "This is your fantasy, huh?"

I look up at him. I have to crane my neck back to see his face because he's so tall. "So what?"

"Then let's do it."

"You mean, let's play the game you were sent to play?"

He shrugs. "Yeah, if that's what you need to go forward. Let's play the game, Issy."

Is it a game? Or isn't it?

I can't tell anymore.

He takes off my coat, just like he did earlier. Takes off my jacket, just like he did earlier. Then unbuttons my blouse, opens it up, except he doesn't pull off all the buttons this time. His hand grabs my breasts through my bra, squeezing.

And it's all very familiar. Should be, because we've already been here and back.

The crop smacks my ass again, only this time I don't jump.

I moan.

"I'm winning at the moment," he whispers into my neck, biting my ear. "But if you put all this on, you'll steal the game right out from under me. Because I'll forfeit and you'll win the prize."

CHAPTER FOURTEEN

FINN✳

So we are playing a game?" she asks.

"Come on," I say, still leaning into her neck. "Just forget about that stupid game. We've got some chemistry here, right? I mean, you did let me fuck you earlier." She huffs some air, but I cut her off. "You liked it. You came. Couple times. And even though you're putting up this fight and holding out hope that this is a game so you don't have to take responsibility for that, it's not, Issy. It's just two strangers who click. That's all. And when that happens you don't just throw it away. You let it lead you. You give it a chance. You make a decision to go down a new road. Because clicking with people is a special thing that doesn't happen every day."

"You didn't answer the question."

"Jesus. No," I say. "At least not _that_ game. I have nothing to do with this Jordan Wells shit. At all. I bumped into you the same way you bumped into me. And yeah, I misled you a little to get you to stay with me tonight, and yeah, that was part of my job. But no one told me to fuck you, Issy. Or like you. That was just... me."

She thinks about this for a second. "I still have a lot of questions."

"Like what?" I ask. "Ask me. I'll tell you anything you want to know."

"Why did the FBI show up at my office?"

"I don't really know for sure, but I'm assuming you're just caught in someone's web."

"Bad luck," she answers.

I shrug. "Bad luck."

"I don't buy it."

"Me either." I laugh. "But no one's after you now and we can't get any answers until morning, so why dwell on it?"

I squeeze her breasts again so she won't forget we have other options. Better ways to pass the time than focusing on what's probably nothing more than some bizarre random circumstance.

I lean back a little so I can see her face. Her eyes are darting back and forth, like she's thinking pretty hard about something. She sighs, meets my gaze, and says, "You just want to see me in the costume."

"True." I smile. "And you want to put it on. Just admit it."

She tries not to smile, but fails, so she turns her head to hide it.

"So let me put it on you."

"What?"

"You heard me," I say, reaching around her back to unclasp her bra. I drag it, and her open blouse, down her arms and let them both fall to the floor. She takes yet another deep breath, like she wants to give in to an urge to fold her arms across her chest and cover herself.

But she doesn't give in. She looks up at me and holds her position, arms down at her side.

I unbutton her pants, slide my hands under the fabric of her slacks, and let my fingers slip between her legs.

"You're excited," I say, leaning down once again, this time to smell her. Her scent is not perfume, but something else. Something softer. Sweeter. Shampoo, or hand lotion, or hell, maybe she's just sweet on the inside and it leaks through her pores to balance out the tough-girl exterior.

"Mmmm," she moans.

"So what do ya say? You up for a wardrobe change?"

Her back stiffens at the question, but my fingers are ready. I push one inside her and it glides easily through her wetness. "Say yes," I whisper. "Just say yes, Issy. Accept the challenge and we'll turn this whole night around. Make it something new. Something special."

"Special." She chuckles. "I don't even know you. I know nothing about you at all."

"Well, how about this?" I say back, one hand sliding her pants over her hips until they fall down her legs, the other still inside her pussy, busy taking away the last of her inhibitions. "I'll dress you up and for as long as it takes me to do that, you can ask me questions. I'll answer every single one with the truth. You bare yourself to me, I'll lay myself open to you. Deal?"

She bites her lip, but nods her head at the same time. "You're just gonna lie, so why bother."

I hold my hand up, palm towards her like I'm taking an oath, and say, "Promise. The truth, and nothing but the truth."

She hesitates. And when she says nothing at all, I take that as a yes. "Excellent," I say, walking around her to reach for the discarded costume. "Excellent."

Her eyes track me, her body turning as I pick up her outfit. Damn, this might be the funnest mistake of my life.

"OK," she finally says, biting her lip. "First question. Why did you lie to me earlier?"

I hold up the lingerie and shake my head a little. This, all of this—that magic bag she's carrying around—is definitely a sex fantasy come to life.

"Wait," I say, looking down at her.

"What? You said you'd answer anything. Don't back out on me now, Agent Murphy."

"No, I mean, wait a second. You're accusing me of playing a game with you, but..."

"But what?" She's still resisting the urge to cover herself. But she doesn't bring her arms up. She steps out of her pants and kicks them aside instead.

"But... what if you're playing a game with me?" I ask.

"What? What's that even mean?"

"What if... someone bought *me* a game with Jordan Wells and you're the player and I'm the unsuspecting victim?"

"Oh, for fuck's sake. Nice try. I'm not even gonna answer that."

"Why?" I ask, walking over to her again, unable to resist the feeling of the soft silky fabric of her costume between my fingers.

"Because it's ridiculous. I'm the one who has no clue what's happening. I'm the one who met with Jordan. I'm the one who got turned down. You said you didn't even know him. And that's enough questions from you. Unless you'd like me to play dress-up with *you* while you ask *me* questions." She grabs the lingerie from my hand and holds it up. "Choose."

My laugh bellows all the way up to the ceiling. "I don't think so." I snatch the costume back, bend down, and reach for her ankle.

She gasps, pulling away.

"Cooperate, Issy. It's better that way."

"I'm ticklish," she says, once again pulling her foot away from my reaching hand. "I'll handle the foot department."

"No way," I say, serious. "I'm definitely handling the boots."

She stifles a grin, bites her lip, and shakes her head all in the same moment. "You have a foot fetish?"

"No… uh, well, I don't think so. I just like the thought of slipping your feet into those sexy-as-fuck boots. And," I say, taking hold of her ankle—she hisses in a breath through her teeth, like this is painful—"I'll take these ones off, as well."

I slip her shoe off before she can think too hard about that. Clearly, her feet need the attention if it makes her that uncomfortable.

When I look up at her, I'm grinning. So big.

She counters with, "Why were you demoted? When you left the FBI in DC?"

Shit. Why'd I have to go admit that to her? "It's a long story."

"Those boots will take a long time to put on. We've got time. Now talk."

I eye the boots and decide she's right. There's no zipper, it's just laces and grommets for as far as the eye can see.

Which absolutely delights me. So fuck it.

"OK," I say, cupping her foot. It's tiny, just like her. And soft.

She grits her teeth, holds onto my shoulder for balance, and mumbles something like, "Oh, my God. Oh, my God."

"I'm Irish."

"Yes," she hisses, like she's trying to distract herself. "Your name doesn't hide that fact."

"Right. It's like a goddamned stigma. But what can you do?"

"You could change it, I guess." She's calmer now, because I've let go of her foot and she's not balancing on one leg. But she winces and grabs my shoulders again when I reach for the other one and slip that shoe off too.

"I could, I guess. But doesn't change who I am."

"Who are you?"

"Finnegan Murphy."

"Finnegan." She laughs. "It's silly and sexy at the same time."

"So I've been told before. Back east the Irish have a certain… reputation."

"Oh," she says.

"Is that an, *Oh, that's interesting*, kind of oh? Or an, *Oh, that's too bad*, kind of oh?"

"Bad, dummy."

I swipe a finger up the underside of her foot until she tries to hop backwards. I have her by the ankle with the other hand, so she gets… maybe two inches of space.

"Stop it!" she squeals.

"Then be fair. You want to know things about me? I'm telling you them. But you can't judge me until I'm done."

"That wasn't part of the deal."

"Well, it is now. Because that's playing fair. And we're playing fair."

"Then don't tickle me."

"Deal."

I smile up at her, but she's scowling. "Go on."

"OK, so I'm from a big extended Irish family. And my father was FBI, and his father was FBI, and his father before that was FBI too."

"Got it. You've got no ambition of your own."

"Fuck. You." But I follow that up immediately with, "I'm sorry. Forget I said that. It's not fair."

"Jesus. Fuckin' men. You're all the same."

"I'm gonna do you a favor now, and forget you said that. Because it's not fair either. You don't know me. I don't know you, and hopefully, once we tell our stories, we'll see eye to eye. Maybe you'll change your mind about me."

"I'm not telling my story, you're telling yours because we made a deal. So one more time, Agent Murphy. Why did you get demoted?" This time it comes out with a little more venom. But she's also eyeing the boot I'm holding with apprehension.

I place my hand on the back of her upper thigh and say, "Relax. It's not torture. It's fun."

She forces a smile, but shakes her head.

I start unlacing the back of the boot. I swear, there's like forty-seven eyelets to deal with. But I'm not complaining. That's forty-seven chances to drive her wild as I lace them back up.

"OK, back to the fuckin' question. The demotion in DC. What was that about? You disappoint your dad or something?"

"You're a goddamned mind-reader, Ms. Grey."

"So you did."

I nod.

"What did you do?"

"I did… a whole lot of nothing for a very long time. And then one day… I had enough, you know?" I look up at her as I lace her boot.

"He was a good witch? Or a bad witch?"

I think about this and want to say good, because there's good in everybody. And it's easy to see the good over the bad when it comes to family. But I can't lie. I promised her the truth. So I don't bother trying and answer with, "Bad witch."

"Oh."

"He's dead now, so… whatever."

She pouts her lips a little. "Well, sorry about that. That he's dead. It's hard to lose people."

"Thanks," I say. "And appreciated."

"Were you close at least? Even if you disappointed him?"

"Yeah. I guess you could say we're close." Then I wince. Because I said that like he's still alive. It's so hard for me to believe he's dead and… "I mean… I went into the FBI because he wanted me to, and I thought it'd make him proud of me."

"Is he?" Then she winces, and not because I've got the laces all undone and I'm reaching for her foot to slip it inside the boot, either. It's because she's talking about him in the present tense too. "Was he? Before he died?"

"It depends when you asked him, I guess."

"OK," she says, thinking about that for a moment. "Go on. We seem to be taking a while to get to the point here so…"

"Yeah," I say. "Right. DC. So I went into the FBI Academy in Virginia. Graduated pretty high up in my class. Not top, but near the top. And I guess that's expected because of who I was and all."

"Come on. You're taking way too long to answer one stupid question."

That's because I don't really want to tell her the next part. I deflect and wrap both hands around her calf, sliding them up to her thighs. I'm watching her face as I do this. She closes her eyes and sighs.

Which makes me smile.

"So on graduation day I'm standing there, all dressed up, feeling pretty fucking good about myself. And my dad comes over with a little box. A gift, ya know?"

"Was it a watch or something?"

My hands stop what they're doing as I gaze off into space, thinking back on that moment. "No, it wasn't a watch. It was a phone."

"Huh," she says. "Like a cool new iPhone? Kind of a weird gift, but OK."

"No, it wasn't a cool new iPhone. It was a cheap-ass thing you buy in the checkout lane at Walmart."

Now she's squinting her eyes. Trying to fit the pieces together. I'm just about to give the big reveal when she says, "Oh. Shit."

"What?" I ask.

"It was a burner phone, wasn't it?"

"How the fuck did you guess that?"

"Was it? Was it a burner?"

I nod.

"Fuckin' A. He was dirty, wasn't he."

"How the fuck did you jump to that conclusion?" I ask.

"Sorry. OK, well, good." She draws in a deep breath and lets it out.

"No," I say. "He was the bad witch, remember. He was dirty as fuck, Issy. And that phone was... it was his way of saying, 'Welcome to the family, Finn. Now you're a bad witch too.'"

"Shit. You had no idea?"

I shake my head. "Not a fuckin' clue."

"What did you do?"

"I took it." I look up at her as I say this, my eyes looking right into hers. "I answered it when it rang. I got a new one sent to me every few weeks or so. And I answered those too."

"So you fell in line."

"Yeah. That's exactly what I did."

"So what happened? That you got sent to Denver?"

I start lacing up her boot, winding the laces back and forth across the back of her calf, all the way up to that little dent behind her knee. And each time I poke the lace head into the eye, she makes the cutest little whimper sound. Like I'm driving her crazy. "So mostly I'm just doing my job. Sometimes it would be a month in between calls. But when it rang, that fucker rang, ya know?"

"What did they make you do?"

"Whatever."

"Kill people?"

"Yeah, some. But they were all thugs, right? Enemies. Different gangs, different cities."

"Gangs?"

"Remember when I told you I was Irish?"

"Oh, fuck."

"Oh, fuck is right." I inhale. Exhale loudly. I finish lacing the boot, tie it off at the back side of her knee, and reach for the other one.

"You still haven't answered my question."

"Why did I get sent here?"

"Why?"

"Because one day…" The whole fucking thing flashes through my head in this one moment. Everything that went down that night. "One day I looked him in the eye and said, 'Nah. I'm not gonna do it. I'm done.'"

Issy is quiet now. So I just go on.

"And he pulled out a gun and put it to my head. And he said, 'The only way you're done is if you're dead, Finnegan.'"

"Jesus."

"And… well—" I consider lying again. But what's the point? "I shot him first. Because even though I really didn't want to believe he'd shoot me… I knew he was gonna do it."

Issy's mouth is hanging open. Her eyes wide.

"Because he had this look of surprise on his face when he realized I had my gun out. And then he laughed, and I could almost feel the muscles in his arm, like he was about to pull that fuckin' trigger. And I just happened to pull mine first."

"You're here because you killed your FBI dad?"

I shrug. "Ya know, Issy, I'm not really sure why I'm here." I continue lacing her boot, and feeling proud of how it all looks. I'm practically an expert. This one goes much quicker. Not that I'm trying to be quick. It actually feels good getting some of this shit I've been carrying around for the past few months off my back. "I'm just taking it one day at a time. I'm not doing a very good job at that, but I'm trying."

"Do you regret it?"

"No," I say. But that's all I have for that. And I'm tying the bow at the back of her knee anyway, so her time is up. I sit back on my heels, admiring my work. She twists around to try to get a glimpse. "You're goddamned sexy, you know that?"

She shrugs when I look up at her. "It's the boots."

But I shake my head as I stand back up. "Nah, It's not the boots. It's just... you." And then I place my hands on her cheeks, lean in, and kiss her. Like really kiss her.

When I pull back her eyes are open. Watching me. "So," I say.

"So," she says.

"Am I a good witch or a bad witch?"

CHAPTER FIFTEEN

*ISSY

"I'm not sure yet," I say, answering his question. "You definitely come off as good witch. On the outside, I mean. I can't explain it, but bad guys don't admit shit like that to people they hardly know."

"But you're not sure about what's on the inside."

I stare at him. This man I didn't know yesterday morning. This man I met under the strangest of circumstances. This man who has proclaimed himself my protector.

This man killed his own father.

If my silence makes him nervous, he doesn't show it. He bends down, picks up the costume, and says, "Take all the time you need to come to a conclusion. But while you're doing that… may I?"

He shakes the lingerie in his hand, shoots me a wicked grin that has bad witch written all over it, and then he winks.

His wink is a thing, I decide. To put people at ease. To make them forget bad witches even exist and there's nothing to see here but goodness.

And it works. For me, at least. Because I feel pretty OK about his confession.

Why is the question. Why do I feel OK about it?

Is this a game with Jordan? Or is this all real? Would a guy admit to being a dirty FBI agent, and killing his dirty FBI agent father, and being demoted and sent to—

"Hey," I say. "So what happened after? I mean, you didn't really answer my question. How the fuck did you get to Denver?"

"Well… the FBI is a gang too. We cover for each other. And I'm pretty sure my father wasn't the only dirty guy in the DC bureau."

"So they covered for you?"

I nod. "Gave me some paid leave, then swept the whole thing under the rug and sent me out here."

"Like a new start?"

"Brand-new city, brand-new partner, brand-new start."

Do I believe him? I guess I don't have much choice. I either believe him and stay here, or take my chances and leave.

"So… should I go on?" he asks. And he's not talking about his story. The story is over. He's asking about the costume.

I should get the fuck out of here. I should put my clothes back on, walk out that door, and never look back. Just leave.

But I nod yes, anyway. I give him permission to dress me up and keep the game going. Because this is a game. None of this can be coincidence. But if I'm gonna buy in, I need to go all in.

He chuckles under his breath as he hold the negligee up to study how it works, and mumbles, "OK, don't make a fool of yourself, Murphy."

In his defense, it does look a little weird, since, you know, there's no cups. It's just round open holes where tits go.

"Need help?" I say, trying to forget everything he just told me.

"Nope. Figuring this out is like the highlight of my life so far."

"You must have a very boring life."

He stops his lingerie analysis to look at me. "Hey, there ain't nothing wrong with boring, babe. Not a damn thing wrong with boring."

"So you don't miss DC?"

He places the nightie over my head, pulls it down, totally messing up my hair, and then picks up one arm and fits it into the straps.

I almost die. This is fuckin' hilarious.

"No," he says, taking his attention to the other arm now. "It doesn't matter where you are. People are the same."

"So they're corrupt here too? That's what you're saying?"

He pulls the nightie down, but it gets caught on my breasts, so he reaches underneath it, lifts my tits, fits them into the little cut-out holes until they spill out, and then straightens out the front so the lace ruffle on the edge is neat.

I absolutely die this time and there's no way in hell I don't laugh.

"What?" he says. "Did I do it wrong?"

I shake my head, still smiling. "No, it's right."

"Then why are you laughing at me?"

"It's… it's pretty adorable, actually."

"That I dressed you up as a kinky slut?" He waggles his eyebrows at me, just to make it clear he's joking.

"That you took it so seriously. I mean, your boot lacing is top-notch. Not too loose, not too tight—which is pretty hard to accomplish when you're dealing with forty-seven eyes."

He sucks in a huge breath of air, leans back on his heels, and raises his chin, proud as punch. "Thank you. And the answer to your last question—and I do mean that literally, since we're gonna be too busy to talk in like, oh, ten seconds—is yes. Denver is as corrupt as hell. Everyone knows it, nobody cares to fix it, and I'm no better or worse than the rest of them, I guess. So I choose... indifferent witch. Because after wrestling with this shit for almost a decade, I've decided if you choose a side and stand for something, those people will disappoint you eventually and you'll have to renounce them and choose another. So why bother?"

"Hmm," I say.

"You don't agree."

"No, that's the funny part. I absolutely agree. I've been indifferent witch for a pretty long time now."

"But... your job?"

I shrug. "My job is to give people hope. To help them realize their mistakes, make the right changes, and then move on. So that's what I do."

"It's all bullshit?" he asks, raising an eyebrow. And just a smidge, just a teeny-tiny dash of disappointment leaks out of him.

"No, it's not bullshit. I believe in self-defense, so I show them how to take a man down who's twice their size. And I believe in self-preservation, so I tell them to think of themselves first because you can't take care of anyone else unless you're taking care of you. And I tell them they're worthy of that, because the world has taught them they're not. But I don't teach them anything more than self-reliance and confidence. I don't sugarcoat anything. I ask them to be true to themselves—whatever that may look like—and that's it."

The eyebrow drops back into place. The dash of disappointment morphs into more than a little bit of respect. And the Q&A time is over, because he reaches into his pocket, where he must've stuffed them earlier, and holds the nipple clamps in the palm of his hand. "How sure are you of these?"

I inhale. Exhale. And say, "I don't even know how to put them on."

We both laugh at that. Like... silly, this-is-great-fun kind of laughing.

"I've never done this before either," he says. "Let me make that disclaimer before we start."

"Should we Google it?" I ask, still giggling.

"Nah," he says, pinching one open and bringing it towards my nipple. "How hard could it be. Just—"

I jump back, grabbing at my nipple. "Holy shit! Ow, ow, ow, ow!"

He winces. "OK, let's Google it."

Twenty minutes later we're sitting on his couch, engrossed in a sexpert's video series on YouTube. In fact, we're watching Butt Plugs 101 right now because the autoplay is on and this chick has like, every topic imaginable.

Finn looks over at me, hesitant to take his eyes off the demo on his laptop screen. "Did you—"

"No," I say quickly. "I didn't bring a butt plug."

"Just checking," he says. "Trying to make your fantasy night everything you thought it would be."

"Honestly, I've never even thought about butt sex."

"No?" He laughs. Loud. "Surely you've—"

"Nope."

"Never?"

"Never."

"Jesus."

"Is that weird?"

"I dunno." He shrugs.

"So you... have? Done that? With other people?" He pretends not to hear my question. "Finn?"

"Come on," he says. "Don't make me answer that."

"Why, you're embarrassed?"

"No, I'm not embarrassed. I just want to concentrate on you, that's all."

"Awww... you're trying be a good witch."

He laughs, slaps the laptop closed, and says, "I'm ready. You ready?"

I nod. "Just remember, she said—"

"I heard her. I was sitting right here." He reaches for the clamps, stands up, pulls me to my feet, and comes at me again.

I put my hand up to stop him. "Whoa, there, buddy. Didn't you pay attention? You gotta get my girls ready for this. She said you gotta talk dirty to them first."

"To you, dingbat. Not them." He laughs.

"OK, so talk."

He shrugs. "What kinda dirty talk do you like?"

"You know," I say, unable to look him in the eye. "The usual."

"Oh, my God. You've never done that either? Jesus Christ, Issy! You're practically a virgin."

"I have," I say. "Just... it didn't go very well."

146

His eyebrows slide up his forehead in… what? Surprise? Curiosity? "Explain."

Curiosity, I guess.

"I mean… it was all kinda weird."

"Like he wanted you to call him daddy kind of weird?"

"Daddy? What? No! Is that a thing? Gross!"

"Nope," Finn says, shaking his head. "No one does that. What'd he say?"

"Oh, man. Don't make me repeat it."

"Come on, I gotta know where your boundaries are. You heard the sexpert. Gotta be safe and shit."

"OK," I say, taking a deep breath. "He wanted me to like… tell him what to do." Finn blinks. "Like, explicitly." Finn blinks again. "Or he wouldn't do anything." Three more blinks. "What?"

"That's it?"

"He wanted me to say things like, 'Put it in my pussy.' But then he'd be like, 'You didn't say, 'Put your cock in my pussy.'"

"OK."

"What? That's weird, right?"

He crosses his arms, places a hand over his mouth like he doesn't want me to see him smile, and then says, "Totally weird."

I slap his arm. "That's normal?"

He shakes his head no, but it turns into a nod pretty quick. "Totally vanilla ice cream, babe. Sorry. Pretty much standard dirty talk right there."

"OK, so what do guys say?"

He opens his mouth. Closes it. Tries again. Fails. Says, "Maybe we should skip the dirty talk."

"No, I wanna hear it. Tell me."

"Are you sure?"

"Mmmhmm. Yup. Hit me with it."

He thinks about this for a few seconds, then says, "OK, but I'm only doing this because you're making me."

I laugh. "Got it. Go for it."

"You can't call me a pervert when you do the whole sex fantasy debrief with your friend, Bella."

"Chella. And I won't, I promise."

"OK, but just remember—"

"I won't tell her anything, promise."

He closes his eyes, steps towards me, threads his hand into my hair as he leans into my ear and whispers, "I'm gonna put my fingers inside you now, Issy. Right up in your pussy. And you're gonna be wet for me, understand?"

I turn my head to look at him, but he holds me in place by gripping my hair.

"Just agree," he coos.

"Yes," I say.

"Yes, you'll what?"

"I'll…" I swallow hard. "I'll be wet for you."

I can feel his smile as he kisses my neck. "Good. Then I'm gonna finger you and play with your clit, just to get you ready for my nipple clamps, got it?"

I'm too busy picturing that in my head to respond, but he nips the tender skin under my ear and says, "Got it?"

"Yes," I say. "Got it."

"Shit like that," he says, pulling back and releasing my hair.

"That's it?" I ask.

"It's not good enough?"

"No, it's pretty good. But… do you have more?"

He tilts his head like a confused puppy. "Are you fucking with me?"

148

"What do you mean?"

He tilts his head some more. "You've done this before."

I press my bare breasts against his chest, lean up on my tippy toes so I can kiss his chin, and whisper, "Mr. Murphy," as I take those kisses to his neck. Then I slide my lips down his bare chest, dragging my fingernails down his abs as I lower myself to my knees, and look up at him as I take his hard cock out of his sweats and begin pumping him in my hand. "This is my first time," I coo. "Don't be mad if I can't please you."

And then I place the tip of his cock against my lips and kiss it as I look up at him with innocent, wide eyes, and say, "Be gentle with me. My pussy is tiny and your cock is so, *so* big."

He's transfixed. And I almost laugh. Almost.

And then he grins. "You're a dirty, bad, little slut. And I'm gonna spank you hard for lying."

He pulls me to my feet as I continue laughing. Then one at a time, the clamps go on. And not the gentle way we just learned about on YouTube, either. The hard, tight way that pinches and makes me gasp. Then he's got the riding crop in his hand and he's bending me over the arm of his couch.

"Count," he says, as he holds me there with a hand planted firmly in the center of my back. "And don't fuck it up or you'll get extra."

He whacks me hard, but not too hard. And I count each one, but I do mess it up.

Because this... *this* is what I signed up for.

This is the game I wanted to play.

CHAPTER SIXTEEN

FINN✳

"You're very, very bad," I say, swatting her ass.

"Nine," she cries out.

But I roll my eyes because that's the third time she got the count wrong and I had to start over. So I stop. I wait.

She lifts her head, looks over her shoulder at me, and says, "What?"

"You're faking it."

"What?"

"You heard me. You're faking it!"

"I didn't even come yet, how do you—"

"I mean the spankings, Issy. You lured me into this and now you're—"

She gets up off my knee. "Lured you? Ha! You were the one who was all excited about dressing me!"

"You pretended that you've never had butt sex!"

"I haven't!" she says, putting her hands on her hips and tapping the toe of her boot on the floor.

Which I admit makes her tits bounce a little and distracts me for a moment. But I rally. "And then you're all, *Daddy-talk isn't a thing, is it?*" I use a fake girl voice for that part.

She shrugs, smiles, then shrugs again. "It's still gross."

Which I agree with so I got nothing for that. But I'm definitely not done. "What the fuck are you doing tonight?"

"I'm trying to have my sex fantasy, which, by the way, isn't going very well."

"I'm not in the game!"

"Well, you were playing along."

"Because you were practically throwing yourself at me."

"Oh!" she exclaims.

"And I'm a fucking guy!"

"No," she says, crossing her arms over her breasts. "Nope. You're not getting out of this that easy. I mean, it's like you're not even trying."

"Trying what? I just wanted to fuck you!"

"And yet here we are, arguing!"

"Yeah, because you're faking it."

"Well, you didn't even remember the crotchless panties!"

"What?" I'm confused, confounded and—"What crotchless panties?"—curious.

"In the bag," she says, pointing to it. "You didn't even see them. And I wasn't gonna point it out because we'd finally come to some kind of game-play consensus and—"

"Issy," I say, taking her arm and pulling her close to me. I stare into her eyes. Dead. Serious. "I'm not playing the game with you. I'm not a part of this. I'm not your fantasy guy!"

"Then how the fuck do you explain this night? Huh? There's no way this is all just a coincidence. So I'm not falling for it."

More toe-tapping from her.

I grab my hair and try to figure out just how I got mixed up with this girl.

I woke up this afternoon, drank a little bit—which I'm not proud of, but whatever—ended up at the diner. Declan came in, we got the call about Go F*ck Yourself,

we went over there, everything seemed normal until…
then Issy turned into a Tasmanian Devil, we took her back
to headquarters, the terror threat came in, I was assigned
to take her to the safe house…

"I think you're playing."

"Well, I—" I don't know what to think. I mean, it
sorta makes sense when I run it through my head like that,
but this right now—her missing crotchless panties, her
titless negligee, her fuck-me-hard lace-up boots, and the
fact that I was spanking her with a riding crop twenty
seconds ago…

That is decidedly not normal.

"I think you're right."

"Of course I'm right."

I look at her. "Someone set me up."

"Of course they did."

"We need to talk to Jordan."

"Yes." She nods. "I agree. He's target number one on
the agenda tomorrow."

Which makes me glance up at the clock over the
fireplace. "You mean today."

"Jesus, how the fuck did it get to be five AM?"

"Well, honestly, I'm surprised it's not later. We packed
a lot of shit into the last eight hours."

Which is exactly how long I've known her.

And *that* is ridiculous.

"What time do you have to go into the office?" she
asks.

"I don't. I'm on Issy Grey bodyguard duty, remember?
I'm assuming Declan will get in touch. Until then, I'm sure
he assumes we're up at the house in Silver Springs. Why?"

"Well, I have to be down in the Tech Center by noon.
I've got the seminar, remember?"

"I thought you had those at your office?"

"No. Well, I do. But this is like… the call for students. The free seminar, right? To get them signed up. So I got that at noon."

"Should I take you home?" I ask her.

She bites her lip, and for a second I think she's gonna ask me to fuck her first. Which makes me roll my eyes internally and say, *Jesus Christ, Finn, get a grip.*

She doesn't. Ask me to fuck her, that is. She says, "Do you think it's safe there?"

"Well, do you really think this is a game?"

She shrugs.

"Then no, I'd have to say no. It's not safe and you should stay here, and I'll take the couch, and—"

"Don't be dumb," she says, waving a hand at me. "We've already had sex. And I'm not kicking you out of your own bed."

"Do you want like… a t-shirt and shorts to wear?"

She looks down at her outfit and sighs. "Sure." Like she's disappointed she has to take it off. Or that this fantasy of hers is all fucked up.

"Can I ask you something?"

"I guess," she says, propping a foot up on the coffee table so she can start unlacing the back of her boots.

I swat her hand away and take that duty on myself. You know, because I'm a gentleman and shit. "What was the fantasy? I mean, specifically?"

She smiles, then giggles, then shakes her head. "Never mind. It's just something I saw in a movie once and it kinda made me hot, so I figured it might be nice to try it in real life. Like… expose myself in a new way. Feel something different. I don't know if you've noticed, but I'm a bit of a control freak."

"Nah," I say, laughing to myself as I concentrate on pulling the laces apart.

"For real, I am," she says. "And sometimes it exhausts me. To, like, be in charge of everything."

"So you wanted to be dominated?"

"No." She laughs. "No, that wasn't it."

"But the boots? The crop?"

"I just wanted to *lose* control, not *be* controlled. I wanted to feel out of my element. Like... I might have a problem."

"Nah, I think that's normal. Everyone wants an adventure, right?" I finish unlacing the first boot and grab her foot to slide the boot off. It makes a sexy whooshing sound as her leg comes free from the latex. "And actually, this fantasy game makes a lot of sense. This Jordan guy, he takes away your control and assumes it himself. So you know it's all planned, you feel safe, and yet it's still enough to get your heart racing, right?"

"Yeah," she says, as I take my attention back to the boots. I'm oddly familiar with them for only having met them a couple hours ago. "I guess so. But this is a disaster. And if you're really not playing—"

"I'm not, I swear to God, I'm not."

"Then that's even worse. You probably think I'm a freak."

"Because of these boots?" I ask. "I love these fucking boots."

"Yeah," she says, looking down at me from over her shoulder. "They are pretty hot. I've had them for years. First time I've put them on though."

I finish unlacing boot number two and pull it off, then look up at her. See her. Not her tits, popping out of the lingerie. Or her pussy, which is visible, since I'm sitting

155

down and she's standing in front of me and I forgot her crotchless panties. But her.

"Was it everything you thought it'd be?"

She smiles, then nods her head. "Yeah. Maybe better."

My hand finds the back of her soft upper thigh. I can't help myself. "Why better?" I ask, caressing her leg as we stare at each other. I like her face, I realize. She's not one of those runway-model beauties. She's... very cute. Soft, almost round cheeks. Full lips, but small mouth. Wide eyes and perky nose.

She places her hands on my bare shoulders, kneeling on the couch, her knees sinking into the cushions on either side of mine. "Because if this is real—if it's not a game— then I think I just found someone cool."

I smile. I can't help myself. "Who the fuck are you? And why would you trust me, after what I just told you?"

"You... we... people"—she finally finds the words she needs—"people do things. Sometimes they're not proud of those things, but they refuse to be stuck on the same track, doing the same shit, repeating the same mistakes over and over and over again. So if you are telling the truth, then I *get* your story."

"Why?" I ask. "Why... what... how?"

"I just do. I mean, I have a ton of other questions for you, Agent Murphy. I do. And I'll need answers to them eventually. But right now..." She sighs deeply, looks away from me, but then her eyes dart back. "I've had enough. That's why. I've just had enough. If it's all just fantasy, fine. Because I kinda need one."

"The missing spaces in your past," I say.

She bites her lip. But unlike all the other seductive stuff she's done tonight, I'm convinced she's not even trying to be sexy right now. She's just... her. Then she shrugs. "That, Agent Murphy, is a very long story. And we're too tired to bare our souls to each other right now. But"—she leans her face into my neck, inhaling deeply, like she's trying to capture my scent—"we can still end this properly."

End it?

I dunno if I want to end it. But her soft breathing, her body positioned over mine—her pussy, I realize—her bare breasts right in front of me, just begging to be touched—that's a very, very good way to keep the night alive.

My hands find her small waist, gripping it, urging her to sit down on my lap. Which she does. And then she starts moving back and forth across my cock. I'm still semi-hard from when she almost took me into her mouth, but that doesn't last long. It only takes seconds for me to grow long and thick for her.

She bows her head, pressing her forehead into mine. I gaze up at her, my hands on her ass now. "Like you said, there's pleasure in panic or something like that."

Did I say that? I don't remember and I don't care either. I want to be inside her. Right now.

She lifts her hips up, reading my mind, and then her hand is between her legs. I look down in time to see her bring my cock out from my sweats and place it near her opening.

She flicks it back and forth, the wetness of her desire coating the tip of my head. And then she sits down, I slide inside her like we're meant to fit together this way, and we both moan.

It's different than the last time we fucked. Completely. It's slow, and easy, and there's nothing fast and hard about it at all.

Her breathing keeps pace with mine. It's labored, and heavy, and intoxicating.

I let my fingers find her asshole, which makes her panic for a moment, but only a moment. She relaxes because I'm gentle. My probing is safe. And my intent isn't to penetrate her, but pleasure her.

Maybe that's what I meant. The pleasure of panic.

She's still gripping my shoulders, but now she lets her back arch as her head falls back, her hips leaning into mine so I'm deep inside her belly. And then she begins to grind in earnest. Her eyes open. My eyes open. Meeting in the middle as she fucks me, and I finger her, and then my free hand drops to her clit and I begin to massage it. Every time she thrusts forward, I pinch it, which makes her wince, but not in pain.

The thought of spankings, and riding crops, and fuck-me boots are far behind us now. As far away as yesterday morning is.

I study her like she's a precious piece of art. I watch her face as her expressions change. I see every emotion she's feeling. I see lust, I see longing, I see the sensual satisfaction I'm bestowing on her.

She takes it. All of it, and all of me, and then I've got my arms wrapped around her back, and she's got her arms wrapped around my neck. And our thrusting—our fucking—becomes stillness. The moment freezes, my cock buried so deep inside her, I feel nothing but her wet pussy gripping me. Welcoming me. Begging me to—

It's one of those silent orgasms. There's no yelling, there's no grunting, there's no sweat. It's just stillness until I explode, and she explodes, and we mix together, creating something new. Something perfect.

Breathing hard, she sinks into my chest. I hug her so tight, I start to worry about cutting off her breathing. But when I loosen my grip, she says, "No."

And I obey her command. Because it's the right thing to do .

We stay like that for several minutes. Silent. I feel my cock relax and then slip out of her. My come spills out with it, coating my legs, which makes her sigh.

Her mind must be in the same place as mine, because she whispers, "I'm on the pill,"

Which is great, because I lost all fucking control and didn't even think about it.

Then she says, "This was way better."

And even though she doesn't explain, I know. I get it. I understand her.

"So much better, " I say. And then I stand up, bringing her with me. She wraps her legs around my waist as I carry her to the bathroom and set her down on the counter. Which makes her gasp, because it's granite and cold.

I find that adorable, so I smile the whole time I'm turning on the shower and slipping my sweats down my legs. And then I lift the negligee over her head, throw it into the corner of the bathroom, lift her up, and carry her into the shower, pressing her back up against the tile wall.

We say nothing as we fuck again. This time I pin her in place the way she captured me out there on the couch. She goes limp as I fuck her hard, one hand under each of her knees, holding her up. Her arms are wrapped tightly around my neck like she'll never let go as she grinds her clit against the top of my shaft until she can't take it anymore.

She bites my shoulder as she comes.

And this time, I don't come inside her pussy.

159

I drop her legs. She plants her feet on the floor and descends to her knees without even being told. She looks at me as I come inside her mouth, taking me deep, but not all the way into her throat. My fat cock fills her up, her lips wrapped tightly around it, with water running down her face. Her cheeks pink from the steam and the sex.

After, I wash her hair as she washes mine. It's weird. She's a stranger, yet she feels like she's always been in my life. Like this is just what we do. We fuck on the couch, then we fuck in the shower, and then we wash each other's hair. Like this is how it's always been and always will be.

When we're done, I dry her off, she dries me off, and we say… nothing.

I lead her into my bedroom, hand her a t-shirt and a pair of boxers. She puts them on, like she's done this a million times before.

I put on a new pair of cut-off sweats and pull the covers aside, watching her ass wiggle inside my boxers as she crawls over to the other side.

Her side.

Then I flick off the lights and join her.

My arm stretches out and she automatically makes my shoulder her pillow as I wrap her up against me.

It's insane.

Fucking insane.

Because even though we just met ten hours ago, she has *always* been here. That side of the bed, which has been empty since I moved into this apartment, has always belonged to her.

"Tomorrow," she says, the word thick with sleep. "You'll still be here, right?"

I can't stop the smile. Even if I wanted to, I wouldn't be able to. "I'm not going anywhere, babe. At least not without you."

I don't see it, but I feel it. Her lips curving upward against my chest.

She falls asleep immediately but I... I'm afraid to fall asleep. I'm afraid this is just a game. She's just a dream and if I close my eyes she's gonna disappear.

But I lose that battle.

Slowly. Surely. It finds me. It controls me. It reminds me why I'm here, what I'm doing, and that Issy Grey has nothing to do with any of it.

And then I fade into the darkness that I've been accustomed to.

CHAPTER SEVENTEEN

✳ISSY

I wake to the sound of the TV in another room and for a few confusing seconds, I have no idea where I'm at. But then I smell him—the shampoo we used last night in his shower—and the whole thing comes back to me.

Not like a nightmare though. Which I have to ponder for a moment before I let my thoughts wander down the inevitable path.

Like a dream. And even though most of it has the potential to be—well, let's be honest here since I'm only talking to myself—scary as fuck, I'm decidedly pleased with last night.

The sex. Was. Fantastic.

And I'm not even talking about the wall sex at my house, or the kink-play we did when we got here to his place. I'm talking about the stuff we did after that. The slow stuff. The seductive stuff.

"Oh, you're awake?" Finn is standing in the doorway, leaning up against the wall. His head is cocked to one side, like he's not sure what kind of mood I'm gonna be in, and his expression is something between fear and excitement.

The pleasure of panic, I realize.

It's sexy as fuck. And he's looking hotter now—wearing nothing but those same cut-off sweat shorts—than he did last night in his black Fed suit.

"I'm awake. What time is it?"

"Nine am. I should probably take you home."

"Oh." Well, that deflates me.

"So you can change, ya know. And get ready for your seminar."

"Oh. So… what are you doing today?" I'm trying to feel him out, which is what he's doing to me.

"What do you think I'm doing?" He grins. Wide. "I'm your bodyguard, Ms. Grey. I'm following you around, playing chauffeur, and generally being your muscle."

I smile. Pretty wide.

"Not that you need muscle," he continues, walking slowly towards the bed.

I can't take my eyes off him. The planes of his stomach are perfect. His unshaven jaw just makes me want to picture him between my legs. And his shoulders. Damn. They are so wide. Wide enough to be the perfect pillow for my head last night.

I cuddled with him.

The thought is startling. Mostly because I'm not really a cuddly person, but also because I might want to turn into a cuddly person. With him.

"What are you thinking about?" he asks, sitting on the bed near me. He sinks into the mattress and I let my body roll towards him a little, until my face is right next to his thigh.

I lift my head, scoot closer, and rest it right on his leg.

Yup. He makes me want to cuddle.

"Do you want some breakfast before we go?"

"What are you making?" I ask, looking up at his hazel eyes.

"Cereal," he whispers.

"Sounds great," I whisper back.

"OK," he says, throwing the covers off me and slapping my thigh. "Get up. And come as you are."

He leaves without looking back so I get up and follow. Just like I am.

Boxers and t-shirt. Both his.

Maybe I'm his too?

I don't know why I'm thinking this shit. This really isn't me. I'm not usually this girl. Not with men, at least. Yeah, I put on a good front for the business. And yeah, I've been through some major shit. I've done things. Things I'd call courageous.

But this is something else. It's... vulnerability.

I hate being vulnerable. It's why I crave control. It's why I'm always the one in charge. It's why... it's why I needed this game.

It's not a game, Issy Grey. This shit is real and that should scare you so bad. Because what he told you last night is information you didn't need to know.

"Dayum," he says, when I appear in the main room. He's got one of those open-concept places where the kitchen, dining, and living rooms all run into each other. "Your bedhead is pretty fucking sexy."

I sigh. Because he's saying all the right things. And man, I really hope this isn't a game, because I like him. He's done so much right since we were forced together last night. And men who still say all the right things the next morning have potential, right?

Even if they did kill their—

"Here," he says, handing me a bowl of cereal. It's got multicolored mini-marshmallows in it, which only makes me like him more.

I take it and climb up into a bar stool at the island. He pours some milk into his bowl, then starts eating it with a giant spoon.

I look down at my bowl. I've got a giant spoon too. Which makes me chuckle. Because I'm not even sure it'll fit in my mouth.

"It'll fit," Finn says, winking at me. "I got that demonstration last night about the volume capacity of your mouth, so I know things." He taps his head with his spoon to illustrate his point.

"You're dirty," I say, scooping up some cereal and shoving it in my mouth.

He watches me. And I'm thinking, who makes eating cereal sexy?

"Dayum," he says again.

"What's that mean, anyway?" I ask, chewing slowly. I haven't had sugar cereal in like a decade. It's delicious. Why don't I eat this crap daily?

"Just…" He shakes his head. "I was thinking about you all morning."

"How long have you been up?"

"Hours," he says. "Many, agonizing hours."

"Why didn't you wake me?"

"I wanted to enjoy the fact that you were sleeping in my bed for a little longer." He grins around his spoon and I have to look away because I think… I think I blush.

"Anyway," he says. "I was thinking about you all morning. Wondering if you'd be mad at me when you woke up. Wondering if you'd try to ditch me. Wondering if it was just gonna be a one-night thing, or…"

"Or?" I ask, when he doesn't finish.

He shrugs. "I don't wanna be that guy."

"What guy?"

"The one who falls for the girl and she's just… being casual, ya know? So she gets spooked and ghosts on him. I don't want that. So I'm just gonna put it out there. I know what's happening is kinda weird, but I like you. And I hope you don't ghost on me."

I don't know what to say to that, so I take another bite of sugar and chew slowly to think about it.

I was gonna say, *I'm not a ghoster.* But it's a lie. And I don't want to lie to him. I am a ghoster. I'm the fuckin' queen of ghosting on people. I've done it so many times, in so many places, I just can't deny it with a straight face. And I don't really want to start this conversation unless I can finish it.

I'm not ready for that. At all.

Finn takes the hint and reaches for the TV remote, turning up the volume.

I swivel around in my chair to stare at it, for lack of anything better to do, and that's the moment that makes my heart skip.

Makes my hand freeze halfway to my mouth.

Makes me gasp with surprise.

Makes me question every thought, every action, every choice I've made over the past eight years.

Because that's when my past catches up with me.

The room goes dark everywhere except the TV. It's like I'm in a tunnel and there's a spotlight on the screen.

Two faces.

"Holy shit," Finn says. "That's Declan."

But that's not the face I see. It's the face of the man standing beside Declan.

It's Caleb.

"And he's with…" Finn continues. "What the fuck?"

And isn't it ironic that I was just thinking about how well I ghost and there he is? The man I walked out on eight years ago. The man I ran from.

The only man who knows who, and what, I really am.

CHAPTER EIGHTEEN

FINN❋

"Issy?" I ask. Because while I was talking about Declan being on TV with Caleb, she zoned out or something. "Issy?" I say again. But it's like she doesn't even hear me. She gets up, walks over to the big screen mounted above the fireplace, and just stares at the interview going on in front of the Capitol building.

"Issy?" I ask, walking over to her. "Are you OK?"

"What is this?" she asks, turning to look up at me.

"This?" I ask, looking at the TV. "I dunno," I shrug. "An interview." I read the ticker at the bottom of the screen out loud. "FBI joins forces with the Inmate Exoneration Project. Celebrating the release of Caleb Kelly after being incarcerated for—"

"Eight years," she whispers. "Eight years." She looks up at me, eyes wild. "They let him out?"

"Do you know him? Oh, man. That was the Caleb you mentioned last night, wasn't it?"

Fuck.

"Holy shit," she says, spinning around, grabbing her hair in confusion. "Holy shit, holy shit, holy shit!"

"What?" I ask. "What the fuck is happening? Do you know him?" Which is a stupid question, because obviously she does. "Did he hurt you?"

She doesn't need to answer. I see it all over her face.

"What did he do? Issy? What did he do to you? Is he the reason your background profile is so incomplete?"

She just looks at me. Then she says, "They said he was going away forever! They promised me!"

"Tell me what's going on! How do you know him?"

But she just shakes her head. She turns away, walks to the bedroom, closes the door, and locks it behind her.

I turn back to the TV and try to figure out what the fuck is happening. Then I have my phone and I'm calling Declan. It goes right to voicemail, and for a second I think of course it does, he's on TV. But it's not live. There's a little banner with the time stamp, and it's from earlier this morning.

What the fuck?

The bedroom door opens, Issy appears—fully dressed in yesterday's clothes—and says, "We need to find Jordan. Right. Now."

"Why? Does he have something to do with this?"

"I don't know," she says. "But I need answers. I need to know what the fuck is going on. And I swear, Agent Murphy—"

Agent Murphy? I thought we were past that.

"—if you're involved in this, if you were sent to distract me so I didn't find out until it was too late—"

"Issy, you're not being rational!"

"No?" she asks, pretty much hysterical. "No? Well, isn't it interesting that you show up in my life the night before that asshole gets out of prison? Isn't it weird that I was tied up all night fucking around with you while this was happening?"

"I've got nothing to do with any of that!"

"Really? Then why is your partner at the FBI standing next to him saying he's a supporter? Huh? Answer me that."

But I can't. Because I don't know. And it looks pretty fuckin' bad because yeah. This has *Finn is involved* written all over it.

She walks to the door, but I grab her by the arm. Her hand is in throat-chop mode immediately, but I know that move now, so I duck. "You're not going anywhere without me."

"The hell I'm not! I'm gonna hunt down Jordan Wells and get to the fuckin' bottom of this!"

"You've got that seminar in like…" I check the clock on the wall. "Two and half hours. And it's all the way down in the Tech Center, which is a thirty-minute drive. So how the fuck do you plan on finding Jordan Wells before that, huh?"

It's lame. I know it's lame as I'm saying it, but it's all I got. And I don't expect it to work, or stop her for more than a brief pause to tell me to go fuck myself, sans asterisk—

But she stops. Blinks. Says, "Shit."

Which gives me another second. "I'll get dressed, you stay here, and then I'll drive you down to your seminar or whatever, and then when that's over, we'll go hunt down Jordan together. Deal?"

She's shaking her head the whole time I'm talking.

"Issy," I say, grabbing her hand. Not her arm, but her hand. Which she looks at like she might be thinking about breaking my fingers, so I let it go and just make that little surrender gesture, the both-hands-in-the-air one, and say, "I swear to fucking God, I'm on your side here. I swear. I just tried calling Declan to see what's up and he didn't answer."

"Of course not, because then you'd have to provide me with answers! He's your partner! You have to be in on this!"

"In on what? I'm new in town, remember? He's dirty, I'm here to…"

"Be dirty with him, right?"

"That's not…" I want to say it's not true, but it kinda is true.

"I knew it!"

"Wait," I say, getting in front of her so she can't leave. "Wait, wait, wait. OK, I am here because of him." I shake my head, unable to articulate well under this kind of stress. "But I'm on your side, OK? Not his. Yours! And if you give me five minutes to get dressed, I'll prove it."

"How?" She's tapping her toe, arms crossed over her chest.

"I'll use everything in my power, every FBI resource at my disposal to hunt down Jordan Wells and make him talk."

She stares at me, more angry than scared. But still, I can just tell—this is fear talking. She's afraid of Caleb. And I don't want to bring that up because… because then I'll have to go down that road with her.

I'm not ready to do that yet.

"I'm on your side, Issy," I say, voice low and even now. "I'll prove it. I will. I'm still your protector. So whatever Caleb did to you, he'll never do it again. I'll make sure of it."

She swallows hard. Like her brave exterior is wilting right before my eyes. So I take another step closer, approaching her like a wild animal, and slowly, so very slowly, take her in my arms.

"He won't get you," I murmur. "He won't get you. I promise. I won't let him. We're gonna figure this shit out together and it's gonna be OK."

She just shakes her head no and begins to cry.

And that's the part that scares *me*.

Because Issy Grey is a pillar of strength. And if she feels vulnerable enough to cry and break her tough exterior in front of a man she barely knows… well, she must have a very good reason.

I take her back to her house to change clothes. Whoever was there is gone now, but I go in first to make sure. Gun ready, trigger finger ready. Clearing each room.

She walks right past me up the stairs.

"Goddammit! What the hell, Issy?"

"No one's here," she says. "And if they're still hanging around, they're outside. Point your gun outside."

Shit. I go back to the door, which she left open, and press myself up against the foyer wall as I look out, gun in low ready, and scan the street.

The apartment buildings on either side of her little plot of land act like a wall. Which is good, I guess. People can't really sneak up on her. They have to approach from the front.

Unless they come in from the back, dumbass.

Shit. I'm off my game right now. I'm preoccupied with what she's hiding in her past. I'm not being careful enough. I kick the door closed, then go towards the back of the house.

She has a yard, but it's very small and like the front, it's flanked on either side by the windowless apartment buildings. The patio space is about twenty feet wide, equally as long, and backs up to an old brick garage. Pretty easy to secure, I realize. This place is set up like a tiny fortress in the middle of the city.

I can hear the shower going upstairs when I go back inside. So I look around at the mess. Couch cushions are thrown about, table upended and...

Oh, I want to kill someone now. Because the frame that was on the wall—the one with her young smiling face and a gold medal win—is on the ground, the glass smashed to bits.

Which means this was personal. Whoever came here was looking for her. Not money, not jewelry, not hidden information.

Her.

Fuck.

The shower upstairs stops, then I hear the old floorboards creaking as she walks around. A few minutes later the hairdryer is blowing, then a few more and she's walking again.

What could she be hiding?

It could be anything, but somehow I know it's not just anything. It's something big. Something dirty. Something like what I'm hiding, maybe.

My stomach seizes and I feel sick all of a sudden. Because I'm getting a very bad feeling about this whole fucked-up situation.

Caleb Kelly. And Declan was at his side. So I know exactly what this is about.

The fucking Mob.

Issy Grey.

It's a weird name. Almost... fake.

Which has me thinking about her missing background. Was she...

No. Not her.

But she was young. Young people do stupid things. I know that better than most. I did stupid things. My father did stupid things. And now he's dead and I killed him and now I'm here. Doing more stupid things.

Yeah.

The stairs creak, making me look over at Issy as she descends. She's transformed. Neat feminine suit, cream-colored wide-leg pants, which look amazing on her small frame, and a fitted matching jacket with a silky ruffled edge over a pale pink cami. She's wearing make-up and jewelry and flat pink shoes.

"God," I say. "I want to back you up against a wall right now."

She doesn't smile, she sighs. "I'm ready. We better just... go." Then she looks around, spies the broken framed picture on the floor, and shakes her head. "I can't think about this now. I have a job to do. I have three hundred women coming to that seminar to find something. Some kind of hope to keep going. I might be their last chance to turn their lives around and I *can't* let them down."

"We'll figure it out, Issy. I promise."

"You better not be involved in this, Finn. Or I will..."

I wait her out as her threat trails off, wondering what she might do to me. Not that I'm worried about it, I'm not involved in any of this. But I want to know. It'll tell me something about her. Tell me how deep this runs.

"I'll just... break down. I don't think I can take another betrayal. I really don't."

And that's all I need to know. This is life-changing bad. This is more than some stupid game. This might be her, hanging by a thread. She is those women coming to hear her speak today. She's been them, changed her future, somehow, some way, and this, what's happening to her right now, might snap that thin thread she's been hanging on by. "I'm not involved, Issy. I swear, I'm not."

"We'll see," she says. But it's a very weak truce. Because I haven't told her all my secrets. Some of them can't ever spill out. Some of them should never see the light of day.

I make myself smile. I force it to look real. Because she's so lost right now. So sad. So… vulnerable.

"Come on. I can't wait for your seminar. I think this day might change my life."

She smiles. It might even be a real smile and I make a promise to myself today to fix this. Whatever is happening, whatever she's afraid of, I will stand in front of her. I will protect her. I will make it right.

We're just driving past the Capitol building when Issy says, "Pull over." She looks over her shoulder, halfway out of her seat, and says it again. "Pull over. Find a parking garage."

"What?" I say, stopping at a red light. "Why?"

"That's Jordan's building back there. We have some time. Let's just go in there and see if we can find out where he is. I need to talk to him. And if that doesn't work, let's stop by Chella's Tea Room. She'll know where he is."

I turn right, pull in to the first parking garage I see, and drive up the ramp to park.

She's got her seat belt off before I even cut the engine, and she's out of the car one second later.

I catch up to her, wanting to say all the right things, but failing. Because no words come to me. Something is happening to her world right now. Something terrible. So I just walk next to her as we make our way down to street level and approach the forty-story building that houses her lawyer.

The lobby is sleek and sophisticated. There's a doorman and a reception desk, so Issy heads over that way, me trailing behind her.

"Excuse me," she says to one of the receptionists. "I'm trying to find out if there's an emergency contact for Wells, Wells, and Stratford. They're on mid-winter break, I guess, and it's very important I get in contact with them."

The receptionist just stares at her. "Mid-winter what?"

"I dunno," Issy says. "They're like, all on vacation I guess."

More confusion from the receptionist. Then she looks at her co-worker and says, "Mellie, is Wells, Wells, and Stratford on some kind of break today?"

"No," Mellie says. "I saw Wells Senior go up just a few minutes ago."

Issy looks at me. I stare back at her. And we both shake our heads.

That motherfucker.

That arrogant motherfucker is lying.

CHAPTER NINETEEN

J✱RDAN

"So what do ya got?" I say, not bothering to look up as Darrel is about to knock his knuckles on the frame of my door.

"Jesus, man. You've got like a sixth sense about people or something."

I smile, taking a moment to look up from the case file I'm studying. "Gotta be one step ahead at all times. You should know that better than anyone. Come in. Tell me what's good."

"Well," Darrel says, easing himself down onto the chair in front of my desk. "We've got sixteen active cases right now and they're all pretty much on track."

I glance up at him again. "Jesus. When did we get so busy?"

"Word travels, I guess. Anyway—"

But he's cut off by Eileen, my assistant, who does manage to knock her knuckles on my door frame before I can stop her. She's sneaky like that. Maybe she should be the house private investigator? "Mr. Wells," she says.

"What's up, Eileen?"

"Someone's here to see you. He's very insistent."

Darrel and I exchange a look that says, *Yup, we know who this is.*

"You want me to leave?" he asks.

"Nah," I say. "It'll be short, I'm sure."

"Right this way," Eileen says outside in the hallway.

"I know where his office is," comes the voice trailing behind her.

"Shit," Darrel and I say at the same time. That wasn't who we were expecting.

Ixion appears in my door, doesn't bother to knock, and walks right in like he owns the place. We've been friends… well, we haven't exactly been friends for a very long time. But we've known each other since we were little boys. And back in our college days we might've thought about being more than friends.

He's still kinda pissed about that game I played with him and his new girlfriend last month, so while I shouldn't be surprised he's here—I am.

He should be thanking me for that shit. No one ever thanks me. I mean, he got a new lease on life, he's not living out in that shack up in Ten Miles from Nowhere, Wyoming, and he's back in Denver. Where he belongs, I might add. With a pretty hot chick I introduced him to. You'd think a guy would get a thank you for that, right?

I laugh. "Well, this is a surprise. Come on in, Ix. Oh, you already have. In that case, have a seat. Can I get you a drink? Darrel, get the man a drink."

He doesn't sit and one look over at Darrel says he's not here for the drink. He just lifts up his sunglasses so they're resting on his forehead, places both hands flat on the top of my desk, glares down at me, and says, "What the fuck are you doing?"

I exhale. That exhale says *I'm annoyed, I'm busy, and you don't have an appointment.* But I pride myself on being professional, so I say, "What the ever-loving fuck are you talking about now? I mean, Jesus Christ, Ixion. I get it. You don't like me. You think I'm a bad guy. You think I fuck with people's lives. So why do you insist on"—I make air quotes with my fingers—"bumping into me every chance you get?"

I see this fucker everywhere. The goddamned symphony—though that was partly my fault. At Chella's little tea room, which I love and frequent often since she makes the most delicious pastries in town. He's even working out at my fucking gym now. And it's like... it's like he just inserted himself into my world or something. And believe me, if I had known getting him down here for that last job I hired him to do was gonna subject me to his unending angst and anger, I'd have left his ass in jail.

"I heard you had a game going."

"Darrel," I say, not taking my eyes off Ix. "Do we have a game going?"

"We've got sixteen games going," Darrel replies.

"Sixteen games," I say, still looking at Ixion. "So which one are you interested in?"

"You know what game," he says.

"No, Ixion. I really don't. So either get real specific or just get the fuck out."

He points his finger at me. Glares at me. Leans forward a little, letting me know just who I'm talking to, and says—

Could he kick my ass? I'm not sure. He's big, but I'm smart. I think smart beats big every day of the week.

"—I'm not gonna play with you." Eyes narrowed, jaw clenching, teeth bared. And not in a smiling way either. He's always been dramatic like that.

I open my mouth to say something witty, and childish, and *mean*... but I can hear Eileen outside in the hallway, talking loudly.

"What the fuck?" I say, looking at Darrel. He shrugs, and then a man appears in my door, flanked by...

"Oh, this is fucking great," I say.

"Who the fuck are you?" Ixion asks. As if he's got any right to know anything.

But the guy pulls out one of those flip-open badge-holder wallet things and flashes it at me. "FBI, motherfucker. That's who I am."

I look at Ix. He looks at Darrel. Darrel looks at me. I look back at Ix.

Ixion says, "I'll be back," then flips his sunglasses down on his face like he's the goddamned Terminator, and walks out.

OK. Annoying ex-friend—lover? Not quite—taken care of. Now back to Angry Guy Number Two. "How can I help you, Agent"—I read his badge because he's still flashing it at me—"Murphy?" I squint to see it because it's still kinda far away.

"Do you know who this is?" He jacks his thumb at Issy Grey.

"Nice to see you again, Issy. No hard feelings about last night, right?"

"I knew it!" she yells, jumping and kinda spinning in place like an over-excited puppy. "You did this! I knew it!"

"I'm gonna need to ask you some questions, Mr. Wells," Agent Murphy says.

"I'm outta here," Darrel says, getting up from his chair. "I'll catch up with you later." He walks towards the door without a second glance back at me.

"Thanks, Darrel. Remind me not to make you a *real* partner in crime, because you'd probably bail on me the first time things got heavy."

He waves a hand over his shoulder as he turns the corner and disappears, ignoring my deteriorating mood. Which is why I keep him around. He kinda gets me.

"OK," I say, clapping my hands and rubbing them together. "Issy, do you mind closing the door? Whatever this is, Wells Senior doesn't need to hear about it. He's got a bad heart."

Agent Murphy kicks out and the door slams shut with a bang.

I smile. I'm not gonna let this day go to shit. I've got too many things in play to let one ex—lover? Friend? Whatever Ixion is—a jilted game player, and an FBI agent take away my Zen. "I think you two had better sit down and take a deep breath." Issy Grey opens her mouth to snarl at me, but I hold up a finger and say, more forcefully this time, "Sit. The fuck. Down."

She sits, he doesn't. But that's typical, right? Men.

"Did you approach," Murphy says, "Miss Grey last night about a sexual fantasy fulfillment game?"

"Nope."

"Liar!" Issy says, kinda yelling. Which makes her boyfriend here shoot her a look, which I think says, *Let me handle this.*

I look at Issy Grey, because I have a file on her, and I know she doesn't let anyone handle something she can handle herself. So I expect her to put up a fight.

But she doesn't.

Which piques my curiosity.

CHAPTER TWENTY

FINN✳

"OK," I say, "Let's just all calm down."

"I'm calm," Jordan Wells says. "It's you two who might need a Xanax."

"You have some nerve, you know that?" Issy is sitting in one of the chairs in front of Jordan's desk. Her legs don't even reach the ground. I mean, her toes do, but she's kinda swinging her feet because she's nervous. Which is adorable. And kinda makes me happy.

Jesus. What's wrong with me?

"Did you or did you not have a conversation with Miss Grey last night about playing a sexual fantasy game?"

"No comment," Wells says.

I just look at him, then remember he's some kind of high-powered lawyer here in Denver and adjust. "OK. But I'm gonna take you down to headquarters for questioning if you don't cooperate."

Jordan shakes his head. "No, you're not. Unless I'm under arrest and you're prepared to handcuff me, I'm not going anywhere and you're not doing anything."

Issy sighs.

"Just make this easy, Wells. Just cooperate. Her fucking house was ransacked last night, OK? Someone broke in and went through her shit. Broke her things. Personal things. Things that meant something to her. And we think it's got something to do with your game."

"Number one," Wells says, holding up a finger. "I don't have to answer your questions. It's called the right

185

to remain silent. Number two, I have no business dealings with Ms. Grey whatsoever, isn't that right, Issy?"

We both look at her. She shrugs. "I think you do and you're just not telling me."

"Number three," he continues, "the very short conversation we had last night at dinner…" He looks at Issy again. "It wasn't dinner. What would you call it? Drinks?" He shrugs. Issy looks like she might stand up and throat-chop him—and right about now, I'm silently rooting for her to do that. "Regardless, that conversation happened after we signed an iron-clad non-disclosure agreement."

I force myself not to look at Issy. "So you're hiding behind that." Piece of shit.

"Look," he says. "I'm not obligated to say anything to you, Murphy. But in the interest of making you get the fuck out of my office without causing a scene, I'll tell you something useful."

I wait for it, but he does one of those dramatic pauses. So I say, "Well, what is it?"

"I turned her down," he whispers, then looks over at Issy. "You told him that, right?"

She sighs. Looks kinda scared and small. And I suddenly have a lot of hate for this lawyer.

"She told me that," I say.

Which makes Jordan raise his eyebrows and look over at Issy again. "You better be careful. That NDA is no joke."

"You and I both know that NDA means nothing if a crime has been committed."

"What crime?" Jordan practically snorts. "If there'd been a crime you really would be arresting me. But instead, you're here making idle threats trying to scare me into falling for your stupid federal interrogation techniques. I'm the most powerful defense lawyer in the Rocky Mountain region, Agent Murphy. And while that might not mean much to a guy who comes from DC"—it's my turn to raise my eyebrows, because this means he's been digging up dirt on me—"it means a lot *here*. Because I know every judge, every state congressperson, every local police chief, and even the fucking governor. So you'd better get your shit straight if you want to play bad cop with me. Got it?"

"If you're not playing a game with me," Issy says, "then why did you lie last night?"

"What did I lie about?" Wells actually has the gall to look confused.

"We called your office last night," I say. "And we were told your entire office was shut down for a mid-winter holiday. So why lie? Why not just take the call?"

CHAPTER TWENTY-ONE

J✳RDAN

"Who called?" I ask.

"The fucking FBI called, that's who," Murphy says.

"No, who *specifically*?" I ask again. People, man. You gotta lead them down a path by the goddamned hand or they just don't get it. Luckily, that's my specialty. I am the best at swaying a jury. It's like my God-given gift.

"I don't know who. Someone from the fuckin' office."

"Don't you think you should find that out?"

He just stares at me. So I scratch my neck, wait him out a few seconds, but he's either unable to find the right connection or refusing to do so. I whisper, "Agent Murphy, if someone from your office said they called me last night, and they told you I was unavailable… well, you might have a problem in your organization."

Which makes him blink.

I look over at Issy. "Whatever it is you think I'm doing to your life right now…" I shake my head. "That's not me, Issy. I swear. Not me."

"Then who?" she asks.

"Well," I say, tapping some keys on my keyboard and pulling up her file. I point to the screen, which she can't see since she's facing the back of the monitor, and say, "Probably one of the very questionable people from your past. Eh? Maybe? Possibly? Could be?"

"Stop it," Murphy says. "You don't have to be a dick."

"No, I don't. And I'm not, believe me. If I were being a dick, you'd know it. I'm being immature and smug at the moment. But not a dick."

"That right there?" Murphy says, pointing. "Is dickish."

"Whatever you say. My point is, Issy Grey has quite the checkered past." She looks at me, wide-eyed. "I'm the best, I think I just made that clear a few seconds ago. And if you were going to be one of my players, it was my job to make sure I knew the risks. And even though you're pretty high up there in the risk department, Ms. Grey, I sat down with you as a favor to our mutual friend. And once I heard the specifics of your... *needs*... I decided to walk away. And that's exactly what I did."

"So you're blaming her." That's Murphy.

But I can see in his eyes that he already knows everything I just told him. Issy just stares at me, blank-faced, unable or unwilling to comment further. So I continue.

"I know why you're here, Agent Murphy." Now I've got his attention.

"What?"

"It's just my job, don't take it personally."

"You've been digging in my past?"

"Let's just say... yes." And I can't help it, I smile.

"Is everything a game to you?" Issy is back now, pissed off. About me knowing her better than she thought, or knowing her new boyfriend, I'm not quite sure.

"Um. Pretty much, yeah," I say. "Why not, right? Why not play life like a game? It's as good a strategy as any."

"You're fucking with the FBI," Murphy says, dead serious.

"Are you sure about that?" I say, leading him by the hand again. He just stares at me, so I continue. "Are you really sure about that, Agent Murphy? Because someone at the FBI, an organization to which you belong, fed you a lie last night about me being unavailable. Let me guess," I say, looking back at Issy. "Something happened last night after our little chat?" She squints her eyes at me. "And they wanted to question you about it. You're a very smart woman, Issy. I knew this intuitively, even before I started looking into your background. So you, rightly, said 'Lawyer!' And they countered with, 'He's unavailable.' Am I right?"

She swallows, licks her lips, then says, "Close."

"OK," I say, folding my hands on my desk and glancing up at Murphy again. "So I was here last night. Pretty late, in fact. I didn't get any calls. No calls came into reception, either. So…" I open my hands up. *Obvious answer, people.*

"You're telling me my department is dirty," Murphy says.

"Is that what I'm telling you?" I ask back. "Or is that something you already knew, Finnegan Murphy?"

"Good for you, you've got a file on me."

Ah, he's starting to get it now.

"This isn't looking good for you, Wells. You're playing a game you can't win."

But I just say, "Whoever makes the rules wins, Murphy. You know that just as well as I do."

CHAPTER TWENTY-TWO

*ISSY

Whoever makes the rules wins.

Well, I can't argue with that.

We left Jordan's office after that little remark. He encouraged us, actually. Got up, pointed to the door, and said, "If you don't mind, please close the door on your way out."

"He's hiding shit from his father," Finn says. "Did you catch that little remark?"

I did, but so what?

"We could take this to him. I'm sure Wells Senior would be very interested in knowing what his son—and full partner in his very high-profile law firm—is doing."

"We could," I say, looking out the window as we travel down I-25 towards the Tech Center. "But we'd be following the wrong leads."

Finn is quiet after that. Quiet the whole rest of the way. We're already off the freeway, turning into the hotel, when he finally says, "We're gonna figure this out."

"Yup," I say. "We are. For sure." And then I look at him. Wait for him to look at me as we pull up to the valet. "But it's not going to be good. It might be better to just walk away."

"What?"

"Just pack up my shit, leave the country—"

"What the fuck are you talking about?"

"Finn," I say, turning in my seat. "That guy on TV this morning. Caleb Kelly? He's fuckin' Mob, OK? And your boss, partner, whatever the fuck he is, was standing next to him. The FBI is dirtier than you ever imagined and we, the two of us, are right in the middle of it."

"We're not running," he says.

"No? Then what are we doing?"

"We're gonna tell them to go fuck themselves."

Which makes me laugh. Just a little.

"That is your creed, right?" he asks.

"It is," I say.

"Then live by it, Issy."

This hits me hard. "I do live by it." And I seethe out the words. "Don't think one night of sex and danger makes you an expert on my life, OK? You don't know shit."

"Then tell me."

"Why should I tell you? We're not even on the same team."

"What team is that?"

"Hell if I know what team *you're* on. But my team is called Issy Grey. That's who I play for."

Then, before he can comment further, the valet is at the car, opening up our doors. I get out, hike my purse over my shoulder, and look around until I see Suzanne standing in front of the revolving doors holding a stack of files in her arms.

"There you are!" she says, walking quickly over to me. "Oh, who's this?" she asks, looking up at Finn.

"Finn Murphy, meet Suzanne Levy. Suzanne, Finn. Now let's get to work. I've got women to inspire."

Once inside we take the elevator up to the banquet floor and come out into a room overflowing with women. The registration tables are busy, the vendor tables are packed, and I let Suzanne lead me into a small room where we've got command central set up.

I've done a lot of these seminars over the past several years, but this is only the second one I've done here in Denver. I like this place. I like Chella, I like my little downtown office. I like the women I've met so far. I like the mountains. I even went skiing for the first time last month and liked that too.

But I can like a lot of places. I'm not partial to places. I'm partial to survival. And seeing Caleb's face on TV... well, that's enough to kick me into survival mode.

I shouldn't even do this seminar because I've already made up my mind to run again and that just gives Caleb time to come find me. But I can't let all these women down. Today's seminar is free. That's how this works. I give a free seminar, inspire them, and the ones with the money get the hope.

But that's not how it's gonna work today. I'll be gone by the time they come looking for me. I have an online class ready to go just for this kind of emergency. They can take that. It's free too. So I'm actually looking out for them. I'm thinking of them as I take care of myself, so I'm not gonna feel bad about this. I can interact with them online. I won't leave them stranded. I'll figure out a way.

I look over at Finn, who's got one arm across his chest and one hand up to his mouth, like he's thinking pretty hard about something. And since he's staring straight at me, I can only assume it's me he's thinking about.

"OK," Suzanne says. "It's go time. I'll go start the introductions."

I nod at her. She knows something's up, but she won't ask. Not right before a seminar. Suzanne has been with me since my very first book. She was the first point of contact at the agency I submitted the proposal to. She saved it from the slush pile, pushed it hard, and when her boss said no, she called me herself.

Which was probably unethical on her part. But in her defense, she quit that job immediately and started working for me. We've been a team ever since.

Until now. Because this is all over. It was a good run. A pretty wild ride. I mean, looking back on all I've accomplished in the last eight years, it's a miracle, really. Suzanne will go her way, I'll go my way, and everything will be done virtually from now on.

"Hey," Suzanne says, squeezing my arm. "You're gonna be great."

Which isn't some meaningless affirmation to calm my stage fright. It's not even about the seminar today. It's about tomorrow. It's written all over my face. It's in my expression, playing out through body language. She sees it coming. She must just… feel it. And we've had a contingency plan in place since the very first webinar. She knows there's more to my life than I tell the clients. Much more.

"Yeah, everything's gonna be great," I reply.

She smiles at me, then opens the door—letting in the dull roar of three hundred people out in the ballroom—and then closes it behind her, stifling it again.

I look at Finn. He says, "I don't know what's going through that head of yours, but whatever it is, don't."

I smile. It's kinda real. I like him. He's not too uptight, but not too easy-going either. Kind of a middle-of-the-road guy. Which I can appreciate. I spent most of my life living the highs and lows, riding them like a surfer rides a wave. I had no clue how much energy it took to live like that until I started doing yoga, and tai chi, and meditation.

Life just got… simple when I let things go. And I've always had the kickboxing and the jujitsu, which kinda took all that stagnant energy and gave it a home.

Being Issy Grey has been bliss. But I wasn't always Issy Grey. I found bliss once. I can find it again.

"Look," I say, turning my back on him. "I appreciate your help and everything, but—"

"No buts, Issy. And let's just not talk about it now, OK? There's time later."

"Sure," I agree. Because I can hear Suzanne talking into the microphone in the ballroom. She's talking me up. Telling them how we met, about the book, and the first seminar. Then finally, how many people have taken the coaching classes and graduated. Giving these newcomers hope by letting them envision themselves at the end of the journey.

And then she gets to the last part. The part where she finally has them welcome me to the stage.

So I look at Finn and say, "See you on the other side."

And his expression changes and he knows what that means, but it's too late. I walk through the door and out into a standing ovation.

CHAPTER TWENTY-THREE

FINN✳

I am Team Issy.

That's all I know. That's all I think about as I stand off to the side of the stage and watch her as she takes a room full of sad and desperate women and turns that into hope.

She starts with her story. And even though I wish I was hearing it in private, and even though I know this is probably only a fraction of what's happened to her because no one shares everything in public, it satisfies me. It cements my feet firmly in front of her. It makes me want to fight her battles, keep her safe, and love her hard.

"I was lost once," is how she starts the story. "Unrecognizable when I looked in the mirror. I was eighteen, and who isn't lost at eighteen, right?"

I watch the crowd of women, many of whom nod their heads, thinking back on their own misspent youth.

"And I got involved with a man. A very bad one, at that."

Which I can only assume is Caleb Kelly. Newly released prisoner. Everything that's happening points to the mob.

But I know. I already know. Not the specifics. I don't need the specifics. When a woman runs from a man, it's usually for one of two reasons. She runs for her life or the lives of her children.

Issy doesn't have children, so it's the former.

Whatever he did to scare her so bad, well... it doesn't need to be said.

She doesn't say it now, but we all know.

As I glance around the filled-up room I see some of them are crying. Some of them look angry. Some of them look lost.

All of them look at Issy.

She looks very small up on that stage. But then again, she looks very big too. Her voice is loud, and strong, and confident. Even though something very bad is happening to her today.

She puts on the brave face. The face of a warrior. The face of a winner. The face of a woman. And she takes their pain and remolds it into hope.

I've seen other self-help speakers. Not a lot, but there was a time in my life a few years back where I was all gung-ho about remaking myself. Becoming a better man and shit like that. So I read books, and I went to seminars—much like this one, but then again, nothing like this one at all. And I took a few classes and yeah. It helped.

But I never, *ever* experienced *this*.

Issy Grey is a phenomenon.

She is world-class.

And soon, woman are shouting out to her as she talks. Things like, "Yes." Things like, "Holy shit." Things like, "You're my hero."

Because her story goes from bad, to worse, to evil. And she goes from pitied, to sympathetic, to admired.

And she tells them almost no details. No names. No specifics. Nothing like that. It's just… this time, and this guy, and this gun.

Gun.

Gun.

It echoes in my head. And I need to know more. I need to know all of it. Not so I can understand her. I already understand her. But so I can join her. So I can walk by her side. So I can take up her banner and proclaim myself loyal.

Eventually I find myself sitting in a chair near the front row. The woman next to me is crying and I have a sudden urge to take her in my arms and tell her it's all gonna be OK. That she is strong. That she is valued. That she's capable.

But I don't need to, because the woman sitting next to her does it first. I don't think they're together, either. I think… I think two hours ago they were total strangers and now they're hugging like sisters.

Issy has a plan. She doesn't talk about what it will cost them, at least not in dollars. She talks about the parts of themselves they need to leave behind to move forward. She talks about guilt, because failure and guilt go together. She talks about forgiveness. Not for the people who hurt them—although that's encouraged too because, to quote Issy herself, "Forgiveness is freedom"—but for themselves. Because everyone makes mistakes and mistakes don't define you unless you let them. Mistakes are just tools to make better decisions in the future.

And by the time the seminar is over, we're a family. Just me, Issy Grey, her assistant, Suzanne, and three hundred sad, but hopeful, women.

She says thank you, directs them to her website where a free online course is waiting for them, and then exits the stage.

I can hear them all whisper. "Free? Did she say free?"

Yes, that's what she said. Which means there will not be another masterclass.

The woman in front of me already has the website pulled up on her phone. Her excitement about the course is hard to contain, so in a matter of thirty seconds, all the women around me are gathered in front of her phone. Filled with hope. Filled with relief. Filled with thoughts of salvation.

I stand up, because I know I should make my way back to that little staging room. I know I have to stop whatever escape plan Issy's about to enact. I know all this, but I find myself transfixed. Stilled. By this woman. By her performance? No, by her honesty. Her sense of responsibility to these three hundred strangers.

So I take just another minute, just sixty more seconds. And I see them. Like really see them.

And I realize...

We are *all* Team Issy.

CHAPTER TWENTY-FOUR

*ISSY

There's always a bunch of commotion after a seminar. People want to talk to me, get my opinions, tell me their story. And I want to listen. I usually do listen. But today... today I need to get out of here. I spy Finn in the open door of the staging room. He towers over most of the women. His eyes are searching for me, because I get lost in a crowd. And then his gaze finds mine and he smiles.

I smile back, even though I don't feel much like smiling. Talking to people about their lives, the things that hold them back, and how to find hope for the future is an exhausting thing. And this time afterward is typically how I recharge the sadness I see on their faces as I talk.

But today it's Finn's smile that recharges me. I sign books, because that's my job. And I listen to them, and smile, because I owe them that. We're in this together, all of us, so I owe them that. And I'm grateful. Even though this life is over for me, it's just starting for them.

The free online course will help them. I'll try to answer emails for a while, but I'm leaving town today. I'm disappearing, turning into someone new tomorrow.

I look at Suzanne and she sighs, looking straight at me. She knows what's coming, but she doesn't know why. She has no details.

"What's wrong?" she mouths from across the room.

"I need to get out of here," I mouth back. Slowly, so she can read my lips.

She nods, then starts talking loudly, trying to get everyone's attention.

I take one last look at Finn, who is caught in the crowd, trying to make his way towards me, and turn away.

There's a door in the back of the room that leads to a more-or-less private hallway. And there's a stairwell there. I know that much. So that's where I end up.

"Issy!" Finn calls from behind me. "Wait!"

I want to run. Right now. Because I kinda like him. Even though I've known this man less than a day, it was kind of a fun day. The pleasure of panic. I guess it's true. Danger, even just the perception of danger, brings people closer. It creates bonds that don't evolve in any other situation.

But it wasn't just the *perception* of danger, was it?

"Issy," he says again when I disappear into the stairwell and let the door close behind me.

But he follows, and a few seconds later he's jumping down the flight of stairs I've descended and blocking my way. "Where are you going?"

I sigh, shaking my head.

"You're not giving up?" He says this like, *You, of all people, giving up?*

"I gotta leave, Finn. I'm sorry. I like you, and if things were different, we'd probably hit it off. Probably date. Maybe even last a while. But I'm not going to put myself in danger for the possibility of a relationship. You're some kind of distraction, I think."

"Issy," he says, holding his hand up, palm towards me. "I swear—"

"I don't think you're in on it, Finn. But someone is fucking with me. And maybe you too." I shrug. "Your partner, Declan. He's dangerous. He's got a position, and power, and a badge. And he was standing next to Caleb Kelly on TV this morning. A man... a very bad man, who should be in prison, but isn't." And I don't want to say the rest, but it comes out anyway. Because it must be said. "He should be in prison, and isn't. Just. Like. You."

That hits him pretty hard. He deflates a little. But he's not done trying. "Just..." he starts, but stops. And I get it. It's hard to know what to say when you're unsure of what's happening. "Just hold that thought," he says, taking my hand, leading me down the stairs. "Just hold that thought because we need to stop time for a little bit and just clear our heads."

I let him lead me, because that's where I was heading anyway. And when we burst through the doors on the ground floor, he looks both ways, like he's undecided. Like he has no plan. And I just want to pull away. Leave this hotel, leave this town, get on the road and leave it all behind.

I can start again. I've done it before.

But then he goes right. He heads down the hallway. We enter the edge of the lobby, and he looks down at me and smiles a smile that says, *Don't underestimate me.*

We get in line at the front desk. "What... what are you doing?" I ask.

But before he can answer, one of the reception people calls him forward to the counter.

"We'd like your best room, please," Finn says. "We don't have a reservation."

"Let me check for you," the man at the desk says, his fingers clicking over a keyboard. He lifts one eyebrow, looks up at Finn, then over at me. "The best?" he asks. "Are you sure?"

"I'm sure," Finn says.

"What are you doing?" I whisper.

"Stopping time," he whispers back. He hands over his credit card and ID, and a few minutes later he's leading me towards the elevators.

I exhale on the way up to the top floor, torn between leaving and staying. I'm totally on board with a timeout. But we can only run from reality for so long before—

"Stop," Finn says. "Stop thinking about the future. We're in the here and now, Issy. Be present."

Normally that might rub me the wrong way. I'm always present.

Except for today. Today my world got upended and it's been a very long time since I needed to concentrate on my own advice. The stuff I say on stage at seminars. The stuff I write in books. The stuff I tell *other* women to do.

So I need the reminder.

He flashes the key card at the door, it blinks green, and he opens it to reveal an entire wall of floor-to-ceiling windows with a view of both downtown Denver and the snow-capped mountains off in the distance.

The door closes with a heavy thunk, and then he's leading me over towards the windows. He spins me around, drags my jacket over my shoulders, down my arms, and tosses it aside. His strong hands are immediately on my arms, caressing them as he leans in to kiss me. I melt as he pushes me up against the cool window, a chill tingling up my spine as my back connects to the glass.

"Take me," I whisper. "Just take me."

I know what he's doing. Trying to take my mind off what's happening. Using sex as a distraction. But it doesn't matter. He smells like conviction and stability. And when my hands find his biceps, he feels like a rock. Like a wall. Like he was made to stand in front of me.

And even though I don't want to admit it, I need a protector right now. Him. I need him right now. Because everything I've built is about to crash down on top of me. Pin me to the ground and leave me to suffocate under a pile of rocks and debris called Lies.

Lies I've told. Lies I've lived. Lies that are about to come yank me back into the life I left behind.

I didn't run far enough. Not nearly far enough. Because my past has caught up and now it's time to pay my debts. So if he wants to help me forget for a day, I'm not gonna stop him.

"Please," I whisper. "Just take all of me. Right now."

"No," he says. "I'm not going to take you. I already did that yesterday at your house. Now I just want to worship you."

He lowers himself, his hands on my breasts. Just briefly, just for a moment he squeezes them. And then his hands descend with him, pausing to unbutton my slacks. Drag my zipper down. Slip them, and my panties, over my hips until they fall to the floor at my feet. His eyes never leaving mine.

He smiles.

I smile back. I can't help it.

And something leaves me in that smile. The fear. The tension. The frustration.

His hands are on my thighs now, his thumbs pressing into the long muscles, easing their way between my legs until he makes me want to open them for him.

No words are exchanged. They're not necessary. Just a few gentle touches that say more than words ever could.

I close my eyes because his breath is tickling the soft skin as he breathes in my scent.

What do I smell like?

Fear. And loneliness. And anxiety.

Panic. I smell like panic.

His tongue is there, flicking against my clit just as these words form in my head.

And there it is. The pleasure of panic incarnate.

I grab his hair, then loosen my fingers, wanting to be gentle with him for some reason. I open my legs wider as he forces his chin between them, his unshaven jaw scratchy and perfect as he moves his mouth against my opening.

Worship me, he said.

Yeah… that's how it feels.

My knees buckle, but he holds me up. My legs begin to tremble, but he keeps me steady. Licking me, sucking me, his hands reaching up now to squeeze my breasts. I want to melt. I want to succumb to the feeling of floating that's threatening to overtake all my practical sensibilities. I want to give in and give up at the same time.

And just as that thought manifests, I slide my back down the cool, cool glass of the window, unable—or unwilling— to keep standing up.

He chuckles a little, readjusting his body for my new position, resting himself on the floor, face between my now wide-open legs, hands on my still-trembling thighs.

My breath is ragged and uneven, but it matches the irregular hard thumping of my heart inside my chest. And when he places his whole mouth over my pussy, his tongue flicking incessantly against my clit, I can't hold it in anymore.

I can't keep it together.

And he says, "Just let go," his words vibrating into me, like he's reading my mind.

So I do.

Because I have no choice. I can't stop it, and I wouldn't want to anyway.

He licks at the wetness spilling out of me, my body writhing from the climax, my spine stiff, then soft, then stiff again as the waves of pleasure wash through me.

And then he stands, leans down, picks me up, and carries me to the bed where he lays me down. Gently, like I am something precious. And begins to undress himself.

I watch. I watch every single moment of it. I memorize the way his fingers unbutton his shirt. I burn the image of his chest muscles, his abs, that cut line that disappears into his pants, into my memory. So I can think about it—dream about it—later.

He takes off his jacket, then his shirt, and he's bare from the chest up. I'm still wearing my cami top, so I sit up a little and bring it over my head, then reach around to unfasten my bra as he unbuckles his belt, removes his pants, and stands in front of me. Hard. Long. Thick. His cock almost pulsing with anticipation. I look at it, crave it, then look up at him and find his attention on my mouth.

I know what he wants.

We want the very same thing.

Him inside me.

So I lick my lips, position myself on my knees, and reach out for his cock.

His hands are immediately on my head, urging me to take him. I don't hesitate. I open my mouth and push forward until the tip of his swollen head hits the back of my throat and I have to stop and regain some control.

I breathe through my nose as I look up at his face. He's lost now. Lost in the feeling of being inside me. Lost in the idea of what's coming next.

And when my mouth is filled up with saliva, I flatten my tongue against his shaft and withdraw, until the tip of his cock is between my lips.

"Fuuuuck," he moans softly.

And I like that moan. So I rub the head of his cock between my lips, kissing it, worshipping him the way he worshipped me.

"Do you want to come in my mouth?" I ask him.

He smiles. "I appreciate the offer. But no. No," he says again, shaking his head. "I do want to come inside you, but not there."

I lean back, my heels touching my bare butt. And then I scoot over, pat the bed, and say, "Come here, then. Because I want to ride you."

God, just saying that out loud is enough to get my pussy throbbing. But watching him do it has me nearing the edge of climax again.

I close my eyes as he moves onto the bed and when I open them again, he's lying back, head slightly elevated and resting against the headboard. Making sure he can see me when I make the next move.

If he minds sharing control, he doesn't show it. So I go slow. I twist, bring one leg up and over his hips, positioning my pussy right over his upper thighs. His cock is long, reaching up to his belly button. It jumps when I take it my hand and begin to pump him, my hand immediately wet from my own saliva.

I lift my hips up, place him at my opening, then flick his head around before letting go and sitting down.

We both moan. It's relief. And filled expectations of what's to come.

His arms wrap around my body, completely encircling my back. My hands rest on his shoulders as I rock forward, then push backward, forcing him to fill me up. My nails dig into his skin and he lets out a long, low growl, immediately gripping my ass with the same intensity.

We stare into each other's eyes. But we're really seeing our souls as they consider the possibility of mixing together.

"Come here," he says.

And I don't know how I could possibly get any closer to him.

But I do.

My head bumps against his, our eyes so close our souls touch.

CHAPTER TWENTY-FIVE

FINN✳

Even though this started out with me on my knees, worshiping her pussy with my tongue, I have an overwhelming urge to ravish her.

"I want to flip you over," I say.

"Do it," she says.

"I want to grab a fistful of your hair and pull your head back so far you have to look me in the eye when I slip my cock between your ass cheeks and fill your pussy."

"Do it," she says. Our heads touching. Our eyes meeting. Our souls connected.

I shake my head. I want to be gentle with her. I want to make her feel special. Cherished. Loved...?

How could that word even come up? Even as a passing thought in my head?

I haven't even known her a day.

And it feels like a lifetime...

But I have no idea who she really is, what kind of trouble she's been in, or where she plans on being tomorrow.

With me. She's going to be with me tomorrow.

She grinds her hips down, forcing my cock even deeper inside her.

"Yes," she moans. "Yes."

Her nails are digging into my shoulders, pinpricks of pain that mingle with the pleasure. She notices something—an expression on my face, or the growl that comes from my mouth—and takes these things as some kind of signal to do it again.

Which she does. Only this time her nails drag down the curve of my shoulder. When I look down, there's a bright red welt rising up off my skin.

"You want it rough?" I say, grabbing her hair and pulling until her head jerks.

"I love it rough. I love it. Give it to me rough, Finn. Make me remember this night forever."

But I only hear the begging. Not the warning of what's coming tomorrow. Tomorrow is far away. Hours upon hours away. And hours to Issy and I are like years to other people. I have years to think about that last sentence.

I hug her tightly. Her legs grip my thighs like she knows what's coming and she'll do anything to keep my cock from slipping out of her pussy.

But it can't be helped.

I rock forward, get my knees underneath me, then bounce her back onto the mattress.

She laughs like a girl. Like a woman who is about to get the fuck of her life. Her legs wrap around my middle, scissoring me in her grip, like she's gonna use some secret jujitsu sex position on me.

God, I hope she does that.

"You like it this way?"

She nods, still laughing. "More," she says, teasing me. "More."

I reach behind my back, grab her ankles, and slowly push her legs open. She bites her lip, chews on it for a second, then closes her eyes and sucks in a breath of air when she's spreadeagle, my hands pushing her knees into the mattress. I lean forward and kiss her belly.

She writhes, bucking and squirming, pressing her breasts up towards my face until her nipples seem to be begging for my lips.

I can't deny them. Even if I wanted to, it's beyond my control. My tongue flicks against her peaked nipple, making her moan, and then I nip it with my teeth. Not too hard, but hard enough to make her squeal, "More, more!" again.

"I've got more for you, don't worry," I say, backing away. Giving myself enough space so I can flip her over on her stomach. Her knees bend, feet swinging up until they hit my chest. I grab them both, bring them to my mouth, and kiss her toes.

This… I have to stop and laugh. Because this *undoes* her. She screams, "No! Oh, my God! No, no, no!"

But I just say, "Be still."

"I'm ticklish! I told you that!" She laughs.

"I'm not gonna tickle you, Issy. Be still."

"Just your touch—"

But she stops. Because I'm kissing the sole of her left foot, my lips barely brushing against her tickle spot.

She holds her breath. I know this, because I'm watching her. I count to ten, then fifteen, still kissing the soft pad of her foot. And then at twenty, it comes out in a rush.

And I say, "See?"

And she sees. She goes still. Her whole body stops fighting. Her mind relaxes as I hold her foot up to my lips.

I reach down and place my other hand flat on her back, right between her shoulder blades, pressing the breath out of her again. Pushing her down, stealing her air and making her exhale.

And when her chest is empty of every molecule of oxygen, I grab her hair, right up next to the scalp, and I pull her head back. Slowly. So slowly. And let her breathe in. I let her take what I'm offering, forcing her head and back to arch as I knee her legs open and position my cock right between her ass cheeks, just the way I imagined it. And when we're eye to eye... soul to soul... only then do I lunge my cock deep into her pussy.

She's propping her upper body up with her hands flat on the mattress. And I'm riding her ass. My groin pounding her, my balls slapping against her skin.

She repositions her knees, so she's up off the bed a little, giving me more room to fuck her. And just as she starts begging, "More. Harder. Harder still!" I slow.

I still.

This time her begging cuts off. Because she only feels what I want her to feel and I want her to feel *me*. I'm not just a man behind her. I'm not just another guy trying to make her fantasy come true.

I'm Finn Murphy and I want her to know... *this* is what I can give her. Me and only me.

"Open your eyes," I growl. Her pussy feels so tight. So wet. So perfect I want to come right now. But I don't. Because I'm not done with her yet. She tries to obey my request, but can't quite do it. I'm easing in and out of her so slowly now, she's whimpering. "Open. Your. Eyes." I say it again.

This time she does it. And in the same moment, I release her hair and wrap my hand around the front of her throat. Not choking her. Not even squeezing. Just holding her in position.

But it's enough.

She whispers, "Please."

And that's as far as she gets, because just as her request escapes her lips, I thrust forward so hard, she exhales again.

Empties herself for me so I can fill her up.

"Come inside me," she says.

I thought she'd never ask.

I lean down so my chest is pressing right up against her back, reach underneath her belly so my fingers can find her clit, and strum her. Back and forth so fast, she begins to wail. Begins to beg. Begins to yell, "Yes! Oh, God, yes!"

She clamps down on my cock, gushing on my dick and coating it with her sweet release. Her whole body goes rigid as she gasps, sucking in air like she's desperate for it, her throat constricting underneath the grip of my hand.

And when she empties herself of breath this one... last... time...

I spill into her.

My mouth is on her ear, kissing it before I lose control and drop my lips to the fleshy part of her shoulder so I can nip her skin and make her whimper.

Sweat breaks out on my stomach, making our bodies slick from the sex. I grab her tight around the waist and roll over, taking her with me.

We suck all the breaths now. Greedily. No longer cherishing the deprivation of life-giving air. Her chest rises with mine as I hug her close and hook my leg around hers, caging her in so she can't even think about that escape plan she's been cooking up all day.

"You're not going anywhere," I growl into her ear.

She smiles. I can't see her smile, but I know she smiles. She wants me to keep her prisoner here with me forever. I know it.

"Because you're my bodyguard."

"Yeah." I laugh. But then I shake my head. "No. Because hours to us are like years for others. And we've spent a lifetime together since we met last night."

She exhales again. "Finn," she whispers.

"No," I say. "No. I'm not gonna let you run. I'm not gonna let you. People love you, Issy. You know things and you share those things with them. Those women need you and an online course is a good start for a lot of them, but they need more than that. They need to see you. Feel you. Hear you. Know you. And I need all that too."

She squirms in my strong embrace. I don't want to give in and let her go. Not even to just change position. But I do. Because she's asking, and right now I want to give her everything she asks for.

When she's done squirming we're face to face, her eyes on me, my eyes on her, mirrored smiles in the fading, hazy light of sunset filtering in through the floor-to-ceiling windows.

"You don't know me," she says.

"Wrong," I say. "I know you."

She shakes her head. "No. I think if you really knew me, you'd... you'd be ashamed of me."

"Issy—"

"Finn," she says, placing her fingertips on my lips. "Just listen. I have a story to tell you. One that starts and ends just like the one I told on stage today. But it's all the parts in the middle that I left out that matter."

"So tell me," I say. "Tell me everything so I know what I'm up against."

"Up against?" she asks.

"Yeah. Tell me who I gotta kill to make it right." I regret that immediately. Because she knows now. She knows a little bit about what I'm capable of. And I don't want to scare her.

She huffs out a breath. "I wish it were that simple."

It is that simple. But I have enough sense to keep it to myself this time.

Because Issy has no idea who I really am either. It's me who carries the shame and guilt in this room, not her. There's no way she can be as dirty as I am.

She is pure in my eyes. Pure and innocent. Sweet and strong. Perfect.

No. It's me who has the shameful story to tell. And if she thinks that what I told her last night is all there is… well, I'm gonna disappoint her.

But not yet. There's time for that later. Now, I just want to know her. "Tell me," I say. "I'll make it all go away. And if you still want to leave this life behind when that's all done, we'll leave together."

She stares at me. We are eye to eye. Soul to soul. Her forehead is sweaty from the sex and her hair is damp. I brush a piece off her cheek so I can see her unspoiled.

"It all started when I was eleven and he was twenty-eight."

I have to repeat those words in my head several times to make sense of them. To force myself to accept what is surely coming next.

Death.

Because I'm going to kill that motherfucker and I'm going to make it hurt.

CHAPTER TWENTY-SIX

*ISSY

I regret the words the moment they leave my mouth. I want to take them back. Eat them up. Swallow them down and keep that shit buried deep, deep inside me.

But I can't. There is no such thing as rewind in real life.

"Caleb?" he asks.

I just enjoy things as I nod. The view. The sunset over the mountains off in the west. The room. His body. What we just did. How I feel about him.

"He... how?"

I hear the anger inside him building. I hear the fear too. And there's a part of me that wants to say, *Just kidding. Nothing happened.* But there's no rewind. And fuck it, right? So I say, "My mom had me when she was fifteen." And then I glance up at him, kind of afraid to see the pain on his face, but used to it. I've told the story before. Probably a dozen times to various people over the years. So it's not like this is something new.

"OK," he says. I can hear his heartbeat in his voice. You know how a person's voice shakes a little when they're angry, or afraid, or frustrated to the point of tears?

He's definitely the first one. Angry.

I take a deep breath and begin on the exhale. "She was fifteen, kinda wild, kinda remarkable. The kind of teenage girl who gets attention. Not because she's bad, or beautiful, or smart. But because she was just born... special. You ever know someone like that?"

He's just staring at me when I glance up again. "Yeah," he says. "You. You are that special someone, Issy. You're strong, and sensible, and courageous. I can't take my eyes off you. Even if I wanted to, I can't. You're the only thing there is to look at. Everything else just fades into the background."

I press my lips together. Afraid. That he's lying. And not even that I'm not special. Just afraid of falling into him. Losing him. Because this... this whole situation isn't going to end with the happily ever after. It's just not.

So I take a deep breath and continue. "I found a photo album of her once. My grandpa had it in the attic. I lived with him in Montreal until I was eight. By then my mother was... what? Twenty-three? Jesus. She was so young."

"Was?" Finn asks.

"We're getting there," I sigh. "So I was up in the attic one day looking for old clothes of my grandma's. For a school presentation. I was doing a report on Viola Desmond and wanted an old-fashioned dress. I don't know why I thought my grandma would have one of those." I laugh. "Because she was young too, when she died. Only thirty-nine. But I was like seven then. So I had no concept of what old was. And I found a photo album. It was all about my mom. This woman I barely knew because she was twenty-two years old and wasn't raising me. I saw her every now and again. Sometimes she'd show up on my birthday. She came by the Christmas before, I remember that. Brought me a book called *How to Be a Lady*." Which makes me pause to laugh. "Ironic, since she wasn't what I'd call a lady. More on that later."

I feel Finn let out a breath. A sigh comes with it.

"My mother was… I dunno the word for a person like her. I'm not really sure what it's called. Maybe charismatic? But that word, for whatever reason, makes me think of a man. So not that. Maybe alluring. It was in her eyes, I think. She had very dark hair, like me. And pale skin, like me. But she had these weird brown, not-brown eyes. Unlike me, because mine are blue. But it wasn't her looks, it was her… personality? Her soul?"

"Charming?" he asks.

"What?"

"She was charming, like you."

I shrug. "Maybe."

"She was… captivating?" he tries again.

"Yes," I say. "Yes. Captivating."

"Like you."

"Maybe."

Which makes Finn smile. And I stop my story, all thoughts of my story, to enjoy his smile. Because he won't be smiling much longer if I keep going.

"Go on," he says, after his smile fades and I stay quiet. Still trying to burn that smile into my memory. One day I might need that smile. One day I might have nothing left *but* that smile. So I like to keep things like that tucked away for future use. "I want to hear the rest."

He really doesn't. What he really means is that he *needs* to hear the rest.

Which I get. So I do. Go on.

"So when my mom was twenty-three and I was eight, she showed up at my grandpa's house with this guy. Her new husband."

"No," Finn says, jumping ahead.

I nod. "That was Caleb Kelly. He was a little older than her, but still very young. Like twenty-five, I guess. And there was a lot of yelling, and a lot of crying, and a lot of threats. From both sides. My grandpa, who already had lawyers in place for this, kept his head. I do remember that much. All the drama came from them. He knew this visit would come eventually and he was well-prepared. But she was married now, her life was in order, and her record was clean. So… what's a judge to do? Right?"

"Fuck," Finn whispers.

"It took three years of legal battles, but she won. Mostly because my grandpa was really sick by that time. He died shortly after I was sent to live with her in Philadelphia. And then my new life began as the daughter of a Mob… well, what was he back then? I dunno. Not a boss yet. But he was making a name for himself."

"Caleb Kelly is…"

"One of you," I finish for him. Because that's just the truth.

The silence that ensues is painful.

I burn that into my brain as well. Because one day there might be a time when I'm happy. When I'm satisfied. When I feel safe. And then I'll take this moment out and turn it around in my hand, looking at it from all angles with detached acceptance. And it'll bring reality crashing back into focus.

"And then… and then he started touching me. Pretty much almost immediately."

There's this low rumble that fills the room. It takes several full seconds to realize that it's Finn. Some deep, animalistic growl emerging from his chest.

I go on, because this story isn't even close to over yet. "I started taking kid karate when I was six. You know those classes, right? Fifty small children in a room wearing white gi and white belts. Screaming and punching and kicking the air like kids do. Well, I took that seriously. I dunno why, I just did. I had passed the kids' black belt test by the time I went to live with my mom, and even though he'd have never encouraged me to continue if he knew what I'd eventually become, Caleb let me continue. Used to parade me around his gang, I guess, if you want to call them that. It might've been more of a cartel by then though. Make me fight them. He used them to scare me, and then he used me to scare them. And I just kept going to the dojo, kept getting better, because it got me out of the house. It was all I had back then. The fight was all I had."

"So that's how you won that world championship?"

"Yup," I say. "That's how I did it."

"Did he rape you?"

"More times than I can count."

Finn's body was stiff before, but now it's rigid. Like death.

"Until I came back from winning that world championship. I was seventeen then. And he came at me, drunk. I was riding high. Feeling powerful, and angry, and... So I took him out. Kicked his fucking ass. Broke all his fingers for touching me. Kicked him in the balls until he was writhing in pain on the floor, unable to even move. And then I called the cops, filed a report and, well, the rest you can figure out. My mother cried, begged me to..."

Finn waits. But this is the hardest part for me to say. I can tell him I was raped, no problem. But what came after... that's the part that hurts. "Begged you to what?"

I shrug. "Stay quiet, what else? She said they'd come after me. After her."

"Did they?"

"Of course they did. They killed her two days after he was found guilty and sent to prison."

"And you? What did they do to you?"

"They tried to do things to me, but…" I smile. Because that's a moment I take out often. That memory of that has gotten me through so many, *many* hard times. "Well, I'm still here."

"So Declan…"

"I dunno, Finn."

"Do you… know me?"

It would be a strange question coming from anyone else. But it's not coming from him. He is Irish Mob. I am too. By default, but still. That connection is there.

"Murphy," I say, thinking about his last name. "No, I don't think so. I was already back in Montreal the day the indictment came down for Kelly in Philadelphia. When my grandpa died he left me a key to a storage unit back near our old house. I went there to gather up the lost pieces of my life, and then I just… disappeared. Because he didn't just leave me money, he left me a new ID. A new name, a new past, a new everything."

"So your sealed juvenile file?"

"It's not me. None of that is real."

"What was your old name?"

"Izett Gery."

"Izett," he says, trying it out. "It fits you."

"I know it's stupid to keep my same first initials. And I was fully aware that my new last name is an anagram of my old one, but it's what I had. It's what my grandpa left me. So I took the gift, left Canada, and started over as Issy."

He thinks about this for a while. "You're not surprised that Caleb found you, are you?"

I shrug again, then decide to just admit it. Why not? Why not embrace the truth? It gives you power over your fears. So I say, "In a way... I think I've been waiting for this day."

"And you still want to run?"

"Well." I huff out something that might be a laugh. "I'm not stupid. I know he's going to win, especially now that he's out of prison and he's found me. So running makes sense. Staying?" I say. "Fighting? That's a death wish."

"Yeah," he agrees, hugging me tighter. "I get it. Revenge isn't worth it sometimes."

"Besides," I say. "I think I already got my revenge."

"By sending him to prison?"

"No. That wasn't me. That was the government. I got my revenge when I became the person I was meant to be. When Izett Gery finally became Issy Grey. When I wrote my book it had a story in there, kinda like this one, but not this one. And people responded to it. They saw strength in me. Which made me believe in myself. Made me take on the role of helper. So I started those courses and began speaking. And that's the best I can do, right? Just be me, the way I was meant to be me. And go on. So I think success is my revenge."

"If you leave tomorrow, I want to go with you."

"Why?" I ask. "I mean, we've known each other one day, Finn. One. Day."

"I don't care," he says. "You make all the sense to me, Issy. It's like... all the questions I have about my life, what I'm doing, where I'm headed, why I'm here... they were like a cloud. A mist. Something intangible, like an obscure haze that had no definition. And then you come into my

227

life and suddenly, all those stray particles coalesced and became something real."

We both think about that for a little bit. I picture him in my head. Standing in something that looks like a cloud slowly moving around at his feet. And then it begins to move quicker, spin faster, until I appear—an apparition made of water molecules or some other life-giving element—and become his reality.

It's a beautiful vision, even I have to admit that. Like a line of poetry.

But there's this little nagging question in the back of my head. This feeling that something is wrong here. Not him. I believe him when he says we have this connection.

But what of the mist that wasn't me? All those particles still left behind?

What of that?

"If you leave with me you'll be on the run too."

"I've been on the run since the moment my father handed me that box on graduation day, I just didn't realize it."

"Will they come looking for you?"

"Who is they?" he asks.

"Them, the Bureau. Them, the Mob. Whoever. Who'll miss you if you run, Finn? I guess that's the question I'm asking."

He thinks about this for a long time. A long time. And then he says, "You know what I hate about stories?"

I'm more than a little confused at the topic change, but that's overridden by my own curiosity at where this might be going. "Stories as in books?"

"Or movies," he says.

"What?" I ask. "What do you hate?"

"The endings." He pulls me tight against his chest and I take him in. His scent, the curve of his biceps as I trace my finger down the length of his arm. His large hands. "I never get the endings."

"What do you mean? You don't like them?"

"No, I like a good ending as much as anyone. But I don't get them. Because there's no end to a story. Just because you run out of pages doesn't make it the end. So I get to the end of a movie or a book and I think… I feel like I was cheated, ya know?"

"OK. I've read some good endings. Seen a few movies that leave me satisfied when they're over. But I get what you're saying. And I guess the author or movie director just wants people to make that part up."

"Right," he says, playing with my hair, twisting the dark strands around in his fingers, looking at me thoughtfully as he does this. "Just make it up. That's my whole point. We're making all this up, Issy. Every second of our lives we're creating our own reality."

"What's that got to do with people missing you if you leave?"

"Those people don't count unless I let them count. So yeah, I guess the Bureau might wonder where the fuck I went. In fact"—he laughs—"I know they will. And I guess the Mob will be more than a little interested, if only because they want to know what my future looks like as it pertains to them. But that story is over now. They're at the end and there's no more pages, there's no more film to see. Because this is my story, not theirs."

"It's deep," I say, after giving his answer some consideration. "But not what I was looking for, exactly. So I'll rephrase the question. What will those people *do* if you disappear with me?"

CHAPTER TWENTY-SEVEN

FINN✳

I know what she's asking.

And she knows I'm evading.

So it comes down to this. Do I give her what she's looking for and scare her away? Or do I let it ride and see how far we get?

I'm still trying to decide when she says, "You know what Jordan told me? Last night when we were discussing the game?"

"I thought you weren't allowed to talk about it?"

"Well, fuck that NDA. I'll take my chances. Because he knows more about this shit than he's saying. I might not know everything, but I know when someone's feeding me bullshit to evade the topic."

"What?" I ask, smiling down at her. Looking into her blue eyes. Soul to soul. Because she knows I'm doing the same thing. "What did he tell you?"

She looks at me, but doesn't smile. "He said… some people like a panic game. That's what my friend signed me up for. A panic game. And that could mean a lot of things. Strangulation was one of them."

"Jesus." I laugh. "Do you like that shit?"

"Um…" She giggles. "I mean, maybe. It was pretty hot when you had your hand around my throat, but that's not the point. It was just one option of the panic game."

"OK, so what were the other options?"

"Submission, because I'm a control freak. So he said some women like me crave submission. But that's not what we settled on when all was said and done. We settled on chaos. The kind of panic that comes with chaos because I'm so rigid, I guess. So controlling. So orderly. I need everything to go a certain way because that's what keeps me sane. It was just a guess, and he happened to guess right. But it was only a guess until I thought about it more. Jordan Wells might think he knows me, but he doesn't. Me, or at least the real me, was never written down in a file somewhere. They're not locked away in some sealed juvenile record, they're not on any social media, and there's no photo album to find in an attic one day by accident. The most important parts of me, the things that make me me, are all in my head. They're memories. So all the things that make you you, they're up here, Finn."

She taps my head with her finger.

"They're not what you did. They're not what you're doing. And they certainly not where you're going, because that hasn't happened yet. They're just... a stack of memories and nothing else."

I nod, getting it.

"So forget about what life looks like if you come with me and tell me what life looks like now."

And here it is, the moment of truth. Because she has now spelled it out for me. And I have a choice. I can tell her or not. But if I don't tell her, then she's not gonna stick around. That's the part I get.

"They're gonna miss me," I admit.

"Why? Because you're an invaluable FBI agent?"

I almost snort.

"Because you know too much about the Mob?"

I shake my head. "No. Neither of those things. I hate being an FBI agent. I mean it was the only thing I wanted to be until my father gave me that phone. But every moment after that one was tainted by corruption. So I'm not some integral part of their team. I'm a fucked-up partner, I have no good insight into their mission, and I have no promising future with them. Even if things go my way out here in Denver, it's over. It's been over since the day it started."

I know she's got lots of questions about that, but she's patient with me and lets it go.

"And no, I'm not part of the Mob, either. I have ties, for sure. But they can't trust me. No one trusts me, Issy. No one until you, and that's probably just me making a lot of assumptions." I'm still looking at her. I search her eyes for some kind of sign of what she's thinking, but find nothing.

"So why would they miss you?"

"Because... I do actually have another reason for coming to Denver."

"And that's because...?"

"That's hidden behind a well-written NDA."

"Ah," she says. "And you're not willing to break it, even if it does involve a crime."

"I can't. Not yet, anyway. But the way things are going, that could change very fast."

"How?" But then she sighs. "Never mind. I understand."

She says she does, and maybe she thinks she does, but she doesn't understand. And she's not giving me a pass. And this isn't over.

She's just being... agreeable.

I don't want her to be agreeable, so I need to tell her something true. Something real. Something more.

"So the endings, right?" I say, continuing my train of thought. "That next blank page in the book. I know we've just met and we don't really know each other at all. But I have this feeling about you, Issy. Like we've known each other for years. Lifetimes, maybe. And I've never felt that way with anyone else. I've never just bumped into someone by accident and... wanted to be with them. Wanted to share things with them. I guess what I'm trying to say is... before you, I've never wanted to keep the story going. I've never wanted to fill up that blank page. And I know that's not enough and makes no sense, but it's what I feel."

"It's the panic," she says, smiling again.

"What?"

"You're thinking, *Why the fuck am I telling this girl this shit? Why am I trying so hard? Why do I care?* And it's the panic. The rush of being on the same team with someone for once."

"And yet here I am, spilling my guts, but at the same time not telling you what you need to know."

"Why?"

I shrug. "None of that shit is who I am, Issy."

"OK. Then who are you?"

"Just a guy doing his best to make the right decisions. And not repeat the mistakes of my father. Not end up buried in concrete on a construction site."

She nods her head at me thoughtfully. "Will you ever tell me why you're here?"

"Here?" I say, touching her chest.

"No," she says, sitting up and pointing to the wall of windows. "Here."

"Yeah, I will. When the time is right."

"You do realize that's the wrong answer." But she's smiling when she says it.

"Yeah," I say, smiling back. "I do realize that. But it's the only one I've got right now."

She eases herself back down, resting her head on my chest. "Where would we go?"

I place my hand on her head, enjoying the fact that she accepted that answer as truth. "Did you have somewhere in mind? Because I don't care about the place. Only the person I go with."

"I was thinking Kansas."

"What the fuck is in Kansas?"

"Nothing," she says, sighing. I look down at her just in time to see her eyes close. "That's the whole point. There's nothing there but farms, and fields, and tractors. I'd buy a big old piece of land and just forget about the rest of the world. Live alone." She lifts her head up to see me now. "Unless you come. I'd make an exception for you."

"Would ya?"

"Mmmhmmm. I would. I'd get a horse and a chicken coop. And maybe start a garden, even though I can't grow shit. I'd try anyway."

"Well, Kansas it is. Maybe we better get the fuck out of this hotel and go pack."

"I'm not taking anything."

"Nothing?"

She shakes her head. "There's nothing there for me. I mean, I love the house, but obviously I can't take that with me."

"The trophy?" I ask. "The framed magazine cover? The family photos?"

"Wow," she breathes out.

"What?"

"You were in my house for like ten minutes and you just picked out the only three possessions that mean anything to me. That's some trick you've got there, Agent."

I shrug. "I guess that's what I do, right? I'm a fucking FBI agent."

"For better or worse."

"Yeah," I say. There's something nagging me. Telling me to pay attention. But I don't want to pay attention. Because I think that nagging feeling is guilt.

Guilt for wasting my twenties being a carbon copy of my father.

Guilt for killing him.

Guilt for accepting the deal they gave me to stay out of prison.

Guilt for being here with her. Because somehow, some way, I'm gonna fuck this up just like I fucked all the rest up.

"OK," she says. Like she's been thinking about my questions. "I guess you're right. I really don't want to leave those things behind. I know the frame is smashed and the picture was just a digital printout, but I'd rather glue and tape it all back together if it means I can keep something that my grandfather held in his own hands when he was alive. And I know I have that family photo on my phone. But that photo was taken the day before my mom showed up with her new husband and upended my world. To me... it was the last day I was ever truly happy."

"And the trophy?" I ask. I just want her to keep talking. I want to listen to her for days. Years. Lifetimes.

"I was presented that award the first year I started public speaking. I was brand-new to the speaking circuit, but my seminars always sold out. People were talking about me. They wanted to interview me. The wanted my opinion. And I remember thinking—who the fuck would want my opinion on anything? And if they only knew who I really was..." She sighs. "Well, when I got that award I decided... that very day, I decided that I didn't think they'd care who I was. I really didn't. These people—these strangers—knew the real me. They heard me talk once, maybe twice, and they knew me. And the people in my past never had any idea."

I just want to look at this woman. I never want to take my eyes off her. "That's how I feel about you," I say. "Like I know you. And I realize I don't, but I feel like I do. And sometimes, you just gotta go with the feeling."

She smiles, pats my arm, then leans up to kiss me. First on the lips, then on the cheek, then on the neck. "You know what the silliest thing about that trophy is?"

I can't imagine anything about that trophy is silly. But I really want to hear her talk some more. So I say, "What?"

"It's so stupid." She laughs. "It's like six inches tall, made of gold-colored plastic, and the base isn't even wood, it's resin." She stops to look up at me and smile. Then she shrugs. "But I don't care. It's solid gold to me. It's worth a fortune to me. Because that day I got that, that's the day I thought to myself, 'Well, that settles it. You really are Issy Grey now. Because that stupid award says so.'"

"Maybe you've always been Issy Grey?"

"Maybe." And then she thinks about this for a few seconds and amends. "Yeah. I have. I've always been her. It just took a while to figure that out."

"Well, I'm envious," I say. "Because I've always just been me. And I wish I was someone else."

She tilts her head up at me and says, "Well, I think you're pretty perfect just the way you are. And yeah, maybe you've made some mistakes."

That's an understatement.

"But were they honest mistakes? That's what I ask the women in my classes. Like... did you set out to fuck people over? Or was it more about circumstance?"

"Does it matter? I mean, if you kill your father, does it matter that it was the only choice at the time?"

"Well, let me ask you this, Agent Murphy. Suppose you were a woman. Now suppose you were young, and naive, and a man came into your life and told you everything you wanted to hear. And he made you feel good. And special. And perfect. Now let's suppose he was lying." She swallows hard. Takes in a deep breath. "Let's suppose he hurt you. Badly. And let's suppose you did something you didn't want to do, but he was holding a gun on you, and you were holding one on him, and you just happened to shoot true first. Do you think it matters now?"

"Legally?" I ask.

"No," she says, poking me in the chest, the tip of her finger right over the center of my heart. "Emotionally."

"No, it doesn't. But she still did it."

Issy shrugs. "I guess my point is, do you live with it and vow to never let yourself get in that kind of situation again? Or do you beat yourself up until you can't take it anymore and give up?"

"I don't know, Issy. I just know what I did was wrong. And I wish I could take it back."

"You don't get a rewind."

"I know that."

"So you just come to terms with it. You make that incident your own personal catharsis and try to be a better person."

I know what she's saying is true. I get that. It all makes perfect logical sense. But my problem is—and this I can't tell her, so she can't help with it—my problem is... I never became that better person.

I'm still the same guy.

"Ready to go again?" she says, winking at me. Trying to lighten the mood.

And I appreciate it too. More than she knows. I just want to enjoy her right now. Just accept that this good thing came into my life and enjoy her before she figures out I don't deserve her.

So I say, "So fucking ready," and dive under the covers, scooting my way down her body, my hands reaching up to squeeze her tits, and the moment she opens her legs, I start eating her out.

I make her come all over my face. I sit on top of her, pinning her to the bed as I fuck her tits with my cock. And then I ease it into her mouth and watch her suck me off until I can't take it anymore and make her stop.

And then I fuck her slow again.

I want her to think of me as a slow, careful lover. Even when I'm not.

We sleep, wake, order room service, fuck, and sleep some more.

And pretty soon the dawn is breaking and she's groaning about sleeping longer, and I'm thinking, *I wish I could keep you in this hotel room forever. I wish I could stop time. So you never learn the lies I'm telling. So you never see me as the man I really am.*

But I want to pretend a little longer. So we do sleep some more. And we order room service for breakfast so we can stay in the fantasy a little longer. Live the dream to its fullest.

The problem with dreams is... you always wake up eventually.

So I'm gonna take her to Kansas. Today. We're gonna buy a fuckin' farm. Some beat-up old house with a falling-down front porch. The roof will leak, the floors will squeak, and the hot water will never really get hot.

But we won't care.

We're gonna raise chickens, and get a horse, and grow a garden.

Hell... maybe we'll even grow a family.

CHAPTER TWENTY-EIGHT

✳ISSY

I'm checking my email on Finn's phone because the battery is dead on mine, and even though there's a million messages about the seminar yesterday, I don't even pretend to read them. I just hold the phone in my hand, stare down at it, and think. I need to make sense of this. Because it makes no sense.

I've known this man a day and a half and I'm rearranging my life for him.

Well, no. That's not really true. I'm accepting his offer to navigate this Caleb bullshit alongside me.

And the only thing I can come up with that makes any sense at all is that... everyone wants to belong. That's my feeling, anyway. That's one of the major takeaways I've gotten out of this whole life-coach thing over the past several years. People are unhappy when they don't feel supported and it's hard to feel supported when you're fighting for your life.

That doesn't have to mean literally. Not everyone has had to fight like I did. The fight could be as simple—and overwhelming—as trying to pay rent, or heat your house, or feed your kids.

And if the sense of belonging isn't there, then hopelessness takes over. There's a big difference between being solitary and being alone.

I look over at Finn as we navigate our way back into downtown Denver and use him as an example. He comes from a family where blood means everything. Where loyalty is counted in the secrets you keep and success is earned by doing what you're told. Even if that involves putting your life on hold.

This has to be the reason he wants to come with me today.

He's given them enough and now he wants to take something for himself.

I see women come into my classes and seminars like this all the time. They got married, had kids, devoted years and years to taking care of other people and now... the husband left. Maybe cheated, maybe not. Maybe she cheated. The kids are older, no longer attached to her every second of the day. Or maybe she had no children. Maybe she had no husband. They are all different in that respect.

But the one thing they have in common is they feel lonely. They feel adrift. They feel lost.

But I don't really care why the women come to me. I just want to help them find peace, whatever that means to them. The way I found peace in helping them. It just feels good to do that and I'm sad that there will be no more masterclasses in my future. The online stuff is nice, for sure. But it won't ever replace the sense of pride I felt walking into that office on the first day, bearing witness to their broken dreams. Or the sense of joy it brings me when I watch them grow, and change, and blossom as the weeks and months go by. And there's no man, no amount of money, no amount of personal success that can replace how I feel about them the day they graduate.

Not all of them have their shit together that day. Not all of them have achieved whatever it was they thought they wanted when they started the class. And not all of them have found their peace. But all of them are on their way.

And I helped them do that. With words.

It amazes me every time I think about it. That something so simple, something free, something we all have access to—put together in the right order and said with conviction—can change lives.

I am not the world's most tragic girl, by any stretch of the imagination. But I've paid my dues. So maybe… maybe today is my graduation day? Maybe I put in the time, did all the homework, and now it's time for me to move on too?

Maybe I've been using *them* to fix *me*, instead of the other way around?

"What are you thinking about?" Finn asks as we sit at a red light on Champa Street.

"Everything," I say, looking over at him to smile. "Do you think this is like, meant to be or something?"

"What is?" he asks. "Us?"

I nod. "Yeah. Because, well… we met the day before yesterday, Finn. That's kinda crazy, right?"

He exhales, but it's kind of a laugh. "Totally," he says, easing the car forward when the light turns green. "But you know what?"

"What?" I ask.

He looks at me for a moment, then takes his eyes back to the road and the morning traffic. "I've been in a cage for so long I barely know what it means to be free. And this, what we're doing today, feels a whole lot like freedom to me."

"What if we hate each other tomorrow?"

"Do you think we will?" he asks. And it's not a joke. It's not mean, either. In fact, it feels like the most honest question I've ever been asked.

So I say, "No. I don't."

"Me either."

"I think… I think I see some frustration in the future. I see some challenges. Like what if you snore like a fuckin' bear?"

He laughs.

"You didn't last night, but that doesn't really count. I wouldn't call anything we did last night typical."

"Maybe it is? Maybe that's our new normal? Fucking, and laughing, and talking, and room service. Maybe that's the rest of our lives? Maybe I never sleep deep enough again for you to find out the answer to the do-you-snore question?"

"What if we get caught?" I ask.

"Who's gonna catch us?"

"The Bureau? Caleb?"

"And then what?"

"I dunno, maybe they kill us?" I say.

"What if we stay and toe the line? What will they do to us then?"

"Same, I suppose. Eventually."

"Do you want to stay and fight?" He looks right at me when he asks that question.

I shake my head. "No, that for sure leads to death."

"Are you having second thoughts? Because if so, I get it. You barely know me and—"

"I'm not," I say quickly. "I'm not."

"Then what's this about?"

"I just… it feels a little like quitting to leave all those women behind. I mean, I know the online course is good. I've been building it for a while now, preparing for this day. I have a shell company to keep it anonymous, I have the website all ready, I have like almost a hundred videos for them to watch. And it's all free, so…"

"Are you worried about money?"

"No," I say, frustrated that when I need the right words, I can't find them. I'm a goddamned award-winning speaker who gets paid to find the right words and now they're failing me. "I actually made a ton of money off the book. So I have that in savings overseas. And that last masterclass got me into a solid six figures for this year already and it's only February. So it's not the money."

"Then…?"

"I just feel kinda like a quitter."

"Well, we can always tell the world what kind of man Caleb Kelly really is. You have a lot of information, Issy. And so do I. We could bring him down. Maybe alone it would've been a tough sell, but together?"

"But you're one of them, Finn. How could the world trust you? Caleb and his people will drag your name through the mud. Turn you into a joke. And the FBI won't help, not when they find out why you really joined."

"I think they'll come around once they find out what we know."

"Will they?" I ask. "Knowledge is a strange thing. You can know something. Something wonderful. Something meaningful. Something true. And even then, oftentimes it changes nothing. You could know the secrets of the universe, but what do you do with that knowledge? And what good is knowledge anyway? What good is truth that isn't accepted? What good is a secret you can do nothing with?"

"Well, that's just it, isn't it? We *can* do something with our secrets."

"I don't think so, Finn. I think the world already knows our secrets. Some place, deep down, they know these things already. Maybe not the specifics, but they know bad people are out there. They know there's corruption. They know all this, and they don't want to think about it. They don't have time to care. Because caring means they have to reevaluate their priorities. Their worldview. Caring means they have to change."

He looks over at me as he turns into the alley behind my work. Pulling up next to my car. The only car in the parking lot since Suzanne won't be back and no one is coming in for a consultation today. We get out of his car, get into mine—he drives. And pull back out into the street to head over to my place.

"Are we talking about them? Or you, Issy?"

Some people might take that as an accusation. Some people might be offended. Some people might even get angry.

But it's an honest question.

Those were the words I was looking for and couldn't find.

"Why am I doing this?"

"Leaving?" he asks.

"No... why did I start this business in the first place?"

"Oh," he says, surprised at the change of subject.

But was it really a change of subject? Haven't I been talking about this the entire time?

"To help people, of course. I mean, you can't be doing it for the money. Otherwise you'd be charging for that online course."

"I'm not doing it for the money," I say.

"I know. So why don't you tell me why you're doing it? Because you're the only one who knows."

"I'm doing it because I care about them," I say. "I want them to feel cared for when they're with me. I want them to feel that because I never did."

He leans across the center console, places a hand on my cheek, kisses me on the lips, and whispers, "Yeah, it's official."

Which makes me laugh. "What are you talking about?"

"I love you."

"Oh, Lord," I say, still laughing. "You've known me *one* day."

"We're working on day two, lady. Don't shortchange me on the morning after."

"You're crazy," I say.

"Maybe. Maybe not. Maybe all the panic we've been through just made us unusually close. Maybe telling secrets gave us a bond you can't get any other way. Or maybe," he says, soft smile creeping up his face, "I'm just the kind of guy who knows a good thing when he finds it."

I feel tears welling in my eyes. Which isn't me at all. I mean, I didn't even cry last night when I told him I was raped repeatedly as a child. By a mobster who is now most certainly after me. Who probably wants to kill me or, worse, rape me again.

Anger, hate, rage, violence—none of that stuff fazes me anymore.

But tenderness?

Yeah, that gets me every time.

I'm just not used to it.

"Hey," Finn says. "Get used to it."

It's like he can read my mind. How could he know me so well? Why do I feel like we're meant to be together?

I'm not one of those girls who waits around for Prince Charming. And he's not even Prince Charming. He's fuckin' King Death or something. He admitted to killing his own father. And I dismissed it. I... I *validated* him for doing that.

247

"I like you," he says. "Maybe love is too strong a word for day two, but I'm in, ya know. Whatever it is you want to do, I'm in. If you want to run, we'll run. If you want to fight, we'll fight. If you want to go public, we'll do that. Hell, we can do all three if you want. I don't care. I feel like with you, I can do anything, Issy. You... empower me. So just tell me and we'll do it together."

I place my hand over his. "I want all three."

"Done."

"It's not done, you weirdo. Doing all three is impossible."

"Says the woman who already did the impossible."

"What are you talking about?"

"You survived, Issy. And from what you've told me, that was an all-of-the-above kind of strategy. So let's do it. Let's leave today, make a plan, get that asshole Caleb—and Declan and anyone else who's dirty as sin—and take it all public. Put it all out there for the world to judge. I've got tricks up my sleeve, don't worry about my reputation. What you see is not what you get."

"I don't know if I believe that."

"Which part? The tricks part? Or the surviving part?"

"They're gonna get you," I say. "And I can't let them."

"If that's code for I'm-gonna-leave-him-so-I-don't-ruin-his-life, then forget it, babe. You're stuck with me."

"But—"

"Just trust me," he says. "I know that's a hard thing for you, but trust me. I got this."

I decide to accept his offer. Because I'm tired. I'm tired of making all these decisions on my own. I'm worn out from being the strong one. I'm fucking exhausted from maintaining control. I just want someone on my side. I just want a partner.

And I want to believe that the pleasure of living comes from the panic you endure when you change your life from one thing into another.

And it hits me then. Just as these words go from being an ethereal mist around my feet to something concrete in front of me... this is exactly what Zig meant when he said, "You must make a choice to take a chance or your life will never change."

And that feels so right all of a sudden. So on track, so inevitable, so certain, and necessary, and fated that I believe it.

But I shake my worldview one more time and take that conclusion one step further.

It's not the words I believe in... it's *us*.

His phone rings in my hand, startling me. But when I look at it, there's no incoming call.

I squint my eyes, tabbing at the screen as it continues to ring, trying to find the call.

I look up at Finn and find a look of panic on his face. "What the—"

But that's when I realize the phone in my hand, *his* phone in my hand, is not the one that's ringing.

And my phone is dead.

"Finn?" I ask. I look at his coat pocket and realize the ringing is coming from there.

I reach for it, but his hand on my wrist stops me before I can get my fingers inside.

"Don't," he says.

"What is that?" I ask. "Is that a..."

He shakes his head. "Just don't, Issy. Not now."

"Is that a burner phone in your pocket?"

JA HUSS

I slap his hand away, reach inside, and pull out one of those cheap-ass phones you can buy in the checkout line at Walmart. The screen says, *Blocked.*

"What the fuck is this?" I say, my voice rising in pitch. "Are you still working for them? Like right now? Even after you got a second chance?"

"Issy—"

"No. Tell me," I yell. "Tell me right fucking now. Are you still with the Mob?"

But I don't need him to tell me. Because it's written all over his face.

Finn Murphy is nothing but another goddamned lying *man.*

"Issy, please."

I throw both phones at him. One hits the window, screen cracking, the little burner bounces off his cheek, leaving a bright red mark on his skin.

"You fucking liar." I shake my head. "You motherfucking liar. And I almost left town with you. Were you gonna turn me in to Caleb? Was this all a game to you? Were you gonna—"

"Stop it," he says. "Just listen to me."

I point my finger right in his face and say, "Fuck you. Get out of my car, leave, and don't ever contact me again."

And then I take a deep breath, feeling a little vindicated that I figured him out before we left town and he ruined my life—but also a little sad that I fell for his charm. And his smile. And his eyes. And his dream.

But I let that breath out, open the door to the car, slam it behind me.

And walk away.

CHAPTER TWENTY-NINE

FINN✳

"Issy!"

Goddammit. I get out of the car, jog to catch up with her, and take her arm. She does some… I don't fuckin' know, some martial arts thing on me, and has my arm twisted behind my back as she says, "Go away. I'm done. You had every chance to tell me you were still as crooked as the tree roots in my front yard, and you didn't."

I shake her off and she lets go, her small face looking up at mine, anger, and fear, and… anger written all over it. "That's not what this is."

"Bullshit! Why do you still have that fucking burner phone then?"

"I can't say, but—"

"You can't say? I just told you the most fucked-up thing that ever happened to me. I just told you my stepfather raped me as a child. And you're standing here telling me you can't say why you've got an extra phone in your pocket?"

I want to tell her, but she's never gonna understand. Ever.

"OK, then," she says. "Get the fuck off my property, Agent Murphy." She turns, walks away, and just when I think she's never going to talk to me again, she stops. Looks back. And adds, "Great game, by the way. Congratulations. I guess you win."

It's like a gut punch. I can't move. I can't say anything. I can't do anything but watch her unlock her door, open it up, step inside, and disappear.

Only then do I find my voice. "But what about Kansas?" I whisper to the cold morning air.

I realize there's a shitload of people on the sidewalk in front of her house. The streets are filled with AM traffic. There's sirens, and sounds of construction, and the whoosh of someone whizzing by on a bicycle.

But here, standing in her front yard, sheltered between these two tall apartment buildings, I go unnoticed. I am ignored. I am alone.

No one sees me. No one heard us fight. No one cares. "Murphy."

I turn at the both familiar and unfamiliar voice and see him over near the side of the house. He walks out from a tangle of bare bushes, his face familiar, his blue eyes narrow, his head shaved, his body bigger than I remember. Hardened from years of prison-yard workouts.

"Kelly," I say back.

"It's good to see ya again."

And that hangs there in the air like a poisonous cloud. I can't say it back. Won't say it back.

But he doesn't notice. He just walks towards me, smiling, hand held out, like we're gonna shake. "I just called ya. Ya didn't answer."

And then his hand is in mine, and he's clapping me on the back, and I'm dying inside. He called me?

He. Called. *Me*?

A scream from inside the house. I hear things crashing. I hear things breaking. But the worst thing I hear is silence when all that is over.

I look at Caleb Kelly.

I've known him since I was four years old and he was ten. His father and my father were friends when they were kids. We almost grew up together. If we'd lived in the same city and were closer in age, we'd probably be like brothers now.

I shake my head at him. "No," I say.

Because we didn't live in the same city. They moved away when I was ten and he was sixteen. He was in and out of juvie while I was doing my homework and planning for a future that never let me catch up with it.

I never saw him again. I swear to God I never saw him again.

But she's never going to believe me.

Caleb smiles. "Yes. And, uh… thank you. For delivering her right into my hands."

I open my mouth to protest, but the pain in my skull sends me reeling to the ground. Blackness, then blurry light, then blackness again.

I feel the blood trickling down my face as my head spins from the blow that came from behind. And it's only then I realize… I *was* playing a game.

Different than the one I thought.

Caleb's Game.

CHAPTER THIRTY

*ISSY

I slam the door to my house, looking around at the mess. My eyes immediately go to the floor where the broken frame was, and find it missing.

What the fuck? Did I put it somewhere last night?

I walk over to the kitchen counter, looking. Sift through the debris of scattered papers, and old mail, and some shards of cheap dishes and canned string beans that should be in my cupboards.

"Ow!" I slap my hand to my neck. There's a stinging, burning pain in the fleshy muscle that stretches from the base of my neck to my shoulder. I grab a—dart?—and pull it out of my skin.

I look at it. At the fuzzy red stabilizer protruding off the end. The chamber, empty now, but presumably once filled with drugs.

And then a man steps out from the hallway.

A man I know. A man I saw on TV this morning. Declan Ivers.

"I will fucking kill you," I say.

"You can fucking try," he snaps back.

My hand is on the canned beans and it sails through the air, hitting him in the side of the head before he can even register what's happening.

I storm him.

One chance. That's what I teach my students in their self-defense classes. One chance to take them down when you have the element of surprise. I drill it into their heads. I make them practice the moves. And then I make them do it again, and again, and again until they no longer have to think about it.

It's just instinct.

I chop him in the throat, releasing all the air in my lungs as I scream. He goes down, but someone else has my arms, then another has my legs, and the room is spinning, and my wrists and ankles are bound with zip ties, and the only thing I can think as they carry me through my house, out into the small backyard, into my detached garage, and place me in the trunk of a car is...

How ironic.

CHAPTER THIRTY-ONE

FINN*

Consciousness comes slowly, but there is a rhythm that keeps time for me.

My head throbbing. My heart pounding. The ticking of a clock somewhere in the darkness, the sound of footsteps, the ring of a phone.

Where the fuck am I?

"Issy," I whisper. I remember that much. They got her.

No. I brought her to them.

To Caleb, through this stupid fucking game I'm not even fuckin' playing.

"Oh, don't worry about her," Caleb says.

I try to open my eyes. Fail. Then try again and see a sliver of blurry light.

"I'm gonna take real good care of Izett, Finn Murphy. Don't you worry."

"Issy," I say.

"What?"

"Her name is Issy, not Izett."

"Right. Issy Grey. So powerful. So special. So tough."

"She could kick your ass." I get a boot to the face for that, and spit out blood. "I could kick your ass too," I say. Because fuck it. If this asshole is gonna kill me, let's get on with it. I've been a dead man walking ever since I shot my father a few months ago.

"Not like this you can't," he says.

"No shit. So why don't you cut these ties off and make it fair."

He kicks me in the back of the head this time. My ears begin to ring. "No one ever said the fight was fair, Finn. You know that better than anyone."

I don't answer. Why bother?

"You know what I don't understand?"

I don't answer that either.

"Why you didn't just step into his boots when it was all said and done."

Now I'm curious. "Who?"

"Your old man. He was handing this over to you on a fuckin' silver platter. And you walked away."

I close my eyes, trying to figure out what he's talking about.

"You came to Denver. You gave it all up to start over, and where did it get ya? Right here, under Declan's thumb."

"Obviously," I croak. "I didn't realize Declan and my father were basically the same fuckin' guy."

"They are? Is that right?" His enunciation is sloppy. *They ahhh. Iz zat right.* He's got a prison drawl, I realize. More commonly known as... thug. "You sure about that?" Caleb asks. "Are you really sure about that? Because you sure as fuck came here lookin' for something, Murphy."

I sure as fuck did.

"Does it have anything to do with this?" Caleb holds up a phone. My phone. The burner phone. "You don't need to answer that. I already know. Did it ever occur to ya, Murphy, that you're not the only one playing this game from both ends?"

What?

He's lying. This is a trap. Don't answer him. He's lying.

"Yeah, I knew," he says. "I always knew you was dirty, Finn. I always knew you and your old man were playing for the other side."

What?

"You never fooled me," he says, tapping the phone to his shaved skull. "I had you pegged as a double the minute I met you back when you was four."

"What the fuck are you talking about?" I wheeze.

"Little fuckin' do-gooder. That's what you were."

I laugh. And it hurts. My head, my ribs, my heart.

"Always telling me, 'Not supposed to lie, Caleb. Not supposed to steal, Caleb. Not supposed to hit people.' Well, fuck you," he says, spit coming out of his mouth with his words. "Just fuck you. You think you're better than me?"

"Honestly?" I manage to croak out.

"What's that?" he asks, bending down, like he wants to hear me better. "You got somethin' to say?"

"It don't take much," I whisper.

"What?"

"To be better than you."

He stands back up. Grits his teeth. Sets his jaw. Draws his leg back, the steel toe of his boot aimed right at my teeth when...

Yelling somewhere else—some other room, some other floor, whatever. It's loud, it's shrill. "It's Issy," I manage to moan.

"Yeah," Caleb says. And even though I can't see his face, I can feel his smile. His evil, diabolical smile. "It's Issy. Let's go watch, shall we?"

I want to ask, *Watch what?*

259

He cuts the zip ties around my ankles, pulls me to my feet, and then I have to concentrate on not smashing my face into the wall, or falling down the stairs and breaking my neck.

When we get down there all the fuzziness fades. The world comes back to me in perfect fucking clarity like a wind rushing across my face in the cold, winter night.

Issy is in the center of the room wearing a white gi with a white belt, facing down a huge man who towers over her like a giant. She's bleeding from one eye. Her lip is split, and someone has duct-taped wrist and ankle weights to her arms and legs.

"Come on, Issy," Caleb shouts. He pushes me down onto the floor, steps on the small of my back, pinning me underneath his boot, and yells, "Fight for your life! Fight for your future! Fight for your man!" And then he drops his voice several octaves. "Because if you lose—" Everyone goes silent. It's like a fuckin' movie or something. A cross between *Children of the Corn* and *Fight Club*. They are desperate to hear his threat. "I'm gonna kill him right in front of you."

Which is pretty uninspiring if you ask me. How he ever got these assholes to do his bidding, I'll never know.

But he's not done. Because he adds to that. "And then you and I will have a little private time together."

I look over at Issy. Meet her eyes as she meets mine. We touch each other's souls.

But then we diverge.

Because she nods yes and I shake no, and...

CHAPTER THIRTY-TWO

*ISSY

My body is spinning in the air the moment after I nod my head yes. Because you know what? I'm fucking sick of this goddamned game. I'm gonna end it. But not only will I end it… I'm gonna win it.

I grab Gargantuan by the neck, slide my body—leg extended—around his back, and push down on his head with all one hundred and fifteen pounds of girl power.

He drops to the floor and even though the weights on my ankles and wrists were supposed to make this difficult, they sure do come in handy when they connect with his ribs and his face.

I get his nose first. To make the blood flow, clog his breathing, and make him weak. Then the eye, because the eyes swell up so pretty if you hit them hard enough. Then the teeth. Just because I want him to remember what I did every time he looks in the goddamned mirror.

A sick feeling floods my body when I hear the crack of breaking enamel.

Blood spatters everywhere. He's moaning, and rolling over on the ground, and I'm just about to turn and take out the next guy when I'm slammed down onto the hardwood floor, face first—so the mud and melted snow tracked in from outside coats my cheek when they bind my wrists and ankles again.

I turn my head, find Caleb's face, and spit in his direction. "There's your show," I say, smiling at him. "I hope you got a kick out of it."

He doesn't smile back. I don't get the brave face. I don't get the attitude, or the jokes, or the threats.

I just get that look. That look I know so well from my memory. The one that said, *Go to bed, Izett. I'll be up to tuck you in later.*

The look that would make me go directly to the upstairs hall bathroom, sit in front of the open toilet, and throw up.

Every. Single. Time.

And it takes every fuckin' ounce of strength I've built up over the past eight years not to puke right now.

I think he's going to rape me.

"Aw, come on now, baby. Don't be afraid." Caleb bends down right next to me to grab my hair and pull my head up off the floor so I can look him in the eyes. He strokes my cheek. "Izett," he whispers. "Don't worry. We know just how you like it. Did you know that your boy here sent his boss a text last night? And do you have any idea what he said in that text?"

My heart skips. Remembering Finn, sitting in his car outside my house, texting on his phone.

"It said you thought you were playing a game. And do you know what kind of game he told his boss you thought you were playing?"

I close my eyes to shut him out, but he yanks my head back so far, I can't breathe.

"Open your eyes and look at me, bitch!" And then his other hand is wrapped around my throat, squeezing until I have to. I have to obey and do what he says because I want to breathe again.

"He said you had a fantasy. You wanted to be fucked in front of other people. Well, baby girl"—I close my eyes and whimper a little—"I'm gonna make your fantasy come true. Right here. Right now."

While all this is happening, Finn was picked up, walked over to where I am, and he's thrown down next to me. His face bloody, just like mine. One eye almost swollen shut.

But one eye is fully open.

And it winks.

"What?" I breathe, not even making a sound. Just lips moving.

He winks again.

I squint back at him. Tilt my head. Is he fucking with me right now? Is he trying to tell me this is all part of the game?

But he's not smiling. This is no joke.

Before I can fully imagine what is happening here, the door bursts open and a man walks in.

A man I recognize. A man who should not be here, but is.

He's older. He has short, white hair. Clean-shaven—in fact, I can smell his aftershave as he walks past me on the floor. I turn my head to follow him. Take in his expensive suit, black trench coat, and American flag pin on his lapel.

Senator Walcott. Chella's father.

And this is how I know we're not playing a game.

This is how I know Finn's wink—blink, whatever it was—wasn't saying, *Be cool, Issy. You're fine.*

It was saying, *See you on the other side, babe.*

"What in the ever-loving fuck is going on here?" the senator bellows, looking around from face to face until his intent gaze rests on Caleb's.

Caleb is still kneeling down, holding my hair, hand squeezing my neck, his threat of rape still echoing in my head. But he lets go now. My face falls, hitting the floor, my eyes on Finn and his on mine.

He doesn't wink again.

CHAPTER THIRTY-THREE

FINN*

I know this man. Walcott. Senator Walcott. A part of me is relieved to see him. It puts things in perspective. It all adds up. It almost makes sense.

"Do you know how fuckin' close you came to being arrested tonight, Senator?" Caleb says.

"What are you talking about? I told you to keep your fuckin' head down after you got out and what did you do on your first day of freedom? You go and kidnap a girl."

"Is that what I did?" Caleb says. He starts pacing the floor, making a wide circle around the senator. "Is that what you think this is about? This girl? I didn't take her," he sneers. "She was just there when I took him."

He points at me.

The senator's gaze lands on me. He squints, confused.

I sigh. Close my eyes. Open them and look at Issy. She's confused too.

"Who the fuck is this?"

"This?" Caleb says, kicking me in the ribs. "This is Special Agent Finn Murphy, Senator. The guy they sent here to bring you down, motherfucker!"

I'm still looking at Issy. She's still looking confused, so I shrug, close my eyes, shake my head, and shrug again.

But then the senator comes to stand between us, severing our connection. "What?"

"What?" Caleb mocks. "Jesus fuckin' Christ. Do I need to spell it out for you?"

The senator doesn't answer.

So Caleb continues. "About four months ago there was a raid outside DC, remember that?" He kicks me again. Right in the same place as last time.

"Drugs?" the senator says.

"Good guess, but try again, you goddamned elitist idiot. Payoffs, asshole. You remember what those are, right? Bribes? You should," Caleb says. "You took enough of them."

The senator stays silent.

"And there was a standoff between two federal agents. Both named Murphy."

No, no, no. This asshole does not get to tell my fucking story.

"And they drew on each other." He leans down to grab my hair the same way he was grabbing Issy. "Isn't that right, Finn? But you, being younger, got there first and pulled that trigger."

I close my eyes, wanting to make this all go away.

"At least you thought you did. Maybe." He stops to lean over to look me in the eyes. "Did you really think you killed him?"

"What?" I croak.

"That wasn't a trick question, son. Did you really think he died?"

"Of course he fuckin' died!" I say. "I went to his goddamned funeral!"

"Are you sure about that?"

"I'm—" But I stop. Think about that day. I caught him taking bribes. I confronted him. He pleaded with me to see it his way. Tried to give me some of the money. And I said no, and I said a lot of other shit too, and then we drew. Him first, but really, me first. And we fired.

I shot him in the chest, but he didn't have armor on. He shot me in the chest too, but I did have armor on.

Then there were sirens and flashing lights, and I was in the ambulance, and he was in another ambulance, and a few hours later, his boss, Deputy Assistant Director Kenner, came into my hospital room—I had two broken ribs because his bullet didn't hit me center mass—and he broke the news.

"Your father didn't die, Finn. They *all* lied to you. They've been lying to you your whole life and you ate it up. And so when they pulled you aside after he died"— Caleb does air quotes for that—"they offered you a deal, right? 'Go spy on someone for us. Go get those bad guys. Go bring them in, Finnegan. And we will forgive you for killing one of our own. For killing your father? No. Just one of our own.'"

"What?" Issy whispers. "This is all about you?" she asks.

"And then I found this," Caleb continues. Out of the corner of my eye, I see that he's holding up my burner phone.

He throws it at me, hitting me in the head. It bounces off me, then it bounces off Issy's cheek, leaving a red mark. Just like it left a red mark on mine when she threw it at my cheek in the car.

It spins, like a top, between us.

Caleb and the senator argue back and forth about who is about to go down, walking into the kitchen to look for a drink.

I realize this is the fucking safe house Declan sent me to with Issy. And just as that thought manifests in my head, he's there. Standing in the doorway, looking down at me with pure malice.

He looks at me, then Issy, and I close my eyes and pray, *Don't, please don't… please don't…*

Then he says, "Go get rid of that fuckin' car," to the group of thugs waiting around for Caleb to give them orders. "Take it somewhere remote and drive it over a cliff."

The goons leave. Even the giant who started this little party fighting a girl. Someone helps him up and he stumbles through the door, probably hoping he can get dropped off at a hospital.

Declan joins Caleb and the senator in the kitchen while I take my attention back to Issy.

Get the phone! I mouth.

Her eyes dart to it, then to me. *How?*

Scoot, I mouth. *Grab. Pass.*

She nods, understanding, as she scoots her body down, turns on her side, grabs the phone between the palms of her bound hands, and then maneuvers herself almost on top of my back to hand it off to me.

My fingertips find all the buttons. Because this is an old phone. It's not a smartphone. Hell, that little bit of clear plastic hardly even counts as a screen. So I find the right button. The one I programmed for my contact when I took this deal and left DC to go undercover in Denver to pay the Bureau back because I killed my father.

As I press it, I wonder if he's gonna be the guy to pick it up on the other end.

"Hello?"

The voice is so loud in this small house.

"Hello?" it says again.

And then the phone is kicked out of my hands. I am kicked, repeatedly. In the ribs, in the face, in the chest…

Issy is screaming as Declan pulls her up from the floor, and drags her down a hallway into a bedroom.

The senator follows Declan, unbuckling his belt as he walks.

And then Caleb grabs my hair once more, forces my head back, and says, "She's gonna pay for that. We're gonna make sure her little sex fantasy comes true."

My heart races, thumping inside my chest as he stands back up, walks down the hallway, and stops. Turning to look at me.

"Don't worry," Caleb says. "I'll leave the door open for ya."

CHAPTER THIRTY-FOUR

*ISSY

Like I said. I have two God-given talents. Martial arts and an ability to make people believe what I tell them. I'm holding on to those two things right now. Because three men are now crowding me. Declan, Finn's partner, the fucking FBI. Senator Walcott, Chella's father, the fucking voice of Washington. And Caleb, my one-time stepfather, the man in my nightmares.

Their hands on my body. Their mouths talking, saying things that don't even register in my brain because they are dark, sick, evil, and none of what they say matters. That's one thing I learned about being a public speaker. My words are only words. It's the people listening who give them power.

I refuse to give these men my power. I refuse to hear their disgusting threats. I refuse to let them crawl inside me and turn me back into the small, scared girl I used to be.

I just stare at them. Face blank. Body motionless. Eyes focused.

Because they have a little problem.

My ankles are bound.

I want to smile, but I force it down and I wait.

They don't need my legs open, Declan is saying. They could rape me any number of ways, Caleb adds. But where's the fun in that? Walcott replies.

Where is the fun in that?

These are some sick, sick people.

There are hands on me. Sliding up my shirt like those hands belong there.

Caleb says something like, "You're about to get your fantasy."

And I'm thinking, *No, you asshole. My fantasy never involved anything nonconsensual.* I won't apologize for a fantasy. I refuse to buy into the notion that my private fantasy gives them permission to do this to me right now.

I don't say that. I say this instead. "There is no traffic jam on the extra mile."

The senator stops fondling me and says, "What?"

"If you aim at nothing you'll hit it every time."

Caleb is holding my legs down as Declan cuts the zip ties around my ankles. He doesn't hear my remarks, he's too busy picturing what he'll be doing next. So by the time it registers in his stupid, pea-sized brain, the tension is gone from my ankles, the senator is looking confused, and Declan is standing up at the foot of the bed, folding knife in hand, right next to Caleb.

Your legs are powerful. When someone is on top of you and you don't want them there, your legs are your best weapon.

The moment that tension releases I kick, thrusting the heel of my foot up, right under Declan's chin. The force is hard enough to break his jaw and the sickening crack that happens simultaneously coincides with Caleb moving forward to grab my bound arms like he's about to take control.

Big mistake, asshole.

Because I've been waiting for this moment my entire adult life.

CHAPTER THIRTY-FIVE

FINN✳

The second Caleb disappears into the bedroom, I'm on my knees. FBI tip number one—zip-tied hands are useless if you don't tie their feet too.

And I'm lucky, I guess. Because Declan knows this. If he was the one in charge of me, my ankles would be bound. But he wasn't. And once I'm on my knees I can get to my feet. And once I'm on my feet it's over, assholes.

Because there are many ways to break out of zip ties. Both with hands in front and hands in back. Some of them easy enough for children, given enough time alone.

But this method is quick.

Thumbs facing each other, bend over, throw your shoulders wide and—*snap*!

It doesn't work the first time, every time. But it does this time. And this time is the only one that matters.

My wrists are burning, the pain in my shoulders searing. But my hands are free.

And that's when I hear Issy say, "If you aim at nothing you'll hit it every time."

Which makes me smile.

I'm down the hall, standing in the doorway, watching as the tiny woman—this little control freak, this crazy cute demon, this woman who feels like my soulmate in a small package—breaks Declan's jaw with a heel to his chin.

Her aim is true and she hits it hard.

273

CHAPTER THIRTY-SIX

*ISSY

My other knee is already pressed into Caleb's stomach, giving me enough time to reposition leg number one as I squirm, bring it in underneath his chest, and kick him back so hard, he knocks Declan backwards into the wall.

I wish my students were here. Because right now I feel like a goddamned role model.

A shadow off to my left makes me look. Finn is standing in the doorway, blood dripping off his wrists where he just broke free of his zip ties.

And that one stupid second is enough time for the senator to pull out a gun from inside his jacket and point it at me.

"Don't move," he snarls, backing up so he can target me, but still keep Finn in view. "I'll fucking shoot her if you move."

And you know what I say back? Still lying there on that bed? My shirt all rumpled from where his disgusting sweaty hands were feeling me up just two seconds ago?

I say, "Go fuck yourself."

Without the asterisk.

CHAPTER THIRTY-SEVEN

FINN✳

She twists, feet flying as she flips herself into a backwards somersault, ending up crouched down on the mattress, balancing on the balls of her feet, bound hands in front of her as she leaps through the air like she's about to choke this motherfucker to death.

And in my head I'm thinking, *No.* And then I'm screaming it. "No! No! No!"

Because the gun goes off. The bullet hits her, blood splattering in all directions. And then I've got that gun in my hand, the old man not quick enough to take a second shot.

But Caleb is back, sucking in air like it's a precious commodity. On his feet, crossing the short distance between us, reaching for me as I pivot and shoot. Hitting him dead center of the chest.

He slams against the wall—eyes open, hands still outstretched—and blood gurgles up and out of his mouth as he crumples to the floor.

I swing the gun back to the senator, hear the door open out in the main room of the safe house, voices shouting—"FBI! FBI!"—while I force myself not to look at Issy lying in a silent heap near his feet.

It's typical shit after that.

"Drop your weapon! Hands in the air! Drop your weapon!"

But I don't drop it. I point it right at the senator.

I have never wanted to kill someone so much in my entire fucking life.

So I shake my head and say, "There's no traffic jam on the extra mile." Because it's the only thing that makes any sense at the moment.

My finger presses against the trigger, squeezing.

"Finn!" a voice calls from behind me. "Don't do it, son." The voice is low now. Somber. Almost soft. "He's not worth it."

And then a hand reaches for my gun as I turn to find my father staring back at me.

"She's still alive." He nods his head to Issy, where two people are already bent over her body, asking her questions and shining lights into her eyes. "Don't let one bad decision take away your entire life, Finn. I already made that mistake enough for both of us."

I watch, feeling helpless, as my father takes the gun from me and hands it over to someone else.

I feel insignificant and small as a medical kit is opened and they lean in closer, blocking Issy from my view, and I wait. I wait for her to say something. Shoot off some smartass remark. Some Zig Ziglar quote like, *Success isn't a destination, it's a journey.*

But she doesn't.

CHAPTER THIRTY-EIGHT

*ISSY

Some people have out-of-body experiences when they're hanging on to life by a thread.

I'm not one of those hippy fuckers. I didn't see a bright light. There was no tunnel to walk through. And there sure as fuck was no sense of peace and wellbeing.

I am in pain.

That's all I think about. The impact of the bullet. The hot blood that splattered across my face as I was thrown backward. Someone slapped me and asked me if I knew my name.

I tried to tell them to go fuck themselves too, but I don't remember actually getting those words out, so… no fun.

Waking up with ceiling lights passing by above in a rush was not what I'd call a welcome interlude, either. Doctors, nurses, all kinds of faces hovering over me.

But one was missing.

Finn.

I'm pretty sure I got that word out, because one nurse, the one holding an IV bag as she jogged alongside the gurney, looked me in the eyes and started to say something, but right now I can't remember any of it.

It could be noon or it could be midnight. I'm not sure. I just know that when I open my eyes, Suzanne is slumped down in a chair at the side of my bed.

There's a lot of beeping machines and lots of plastic tubes. I can't move my right arm because it's secured to my body somehow, and I'm dying of thirst.

"Suzanne," I croak out past cracked lips. But it's barely a whisper and she doesn't wake up. I try again, but breathing hurts right now, and I don't seem to have any extra air to make sounds.

The next time I wake up, she's staring down at me, eyes wide, mouth open as she says my name.

My eyelids flutter. They don't want to stay open, but dropping back into the darkness seems like a bad idea, so I raise my eyebrows as I blink rapidly, hoping that my eyelids will follow the same trajectory, and succeed for about two seconds.

"She's awake!" Suzanne yells.

Which is not quite true, but I think she can tell I'm going the extra mile on that empty highway and optimism is in order.

Then there's nurses—lots of nurses. Lots of questions. A doctor who talks mostly to the nurses, and then everything calms down and they all just look at me.

"Water," I say. Which is probably bad manners because these people did just save my life. But I'm thirsty.

They don't let me drink. There's just a whole lot of medical talk and then I'm pronounced "stable".

Suzanne sighs out a long breath of relief. She holds my hand, the one that's not all bound up in some kind of sling or bandage and won't move, no matter how hard I try.

I'm not in pain and I don't think this is normal, but when I ask, Suzanne points to a bag of liquid attached to a pump, that's feeding me morphine in little drips.

And then exhaustion from looking around the room and trying to make sense of what is actually happening takes over and I fade away, wondering what the hell happened to Finn Murphy.

The next time I wake up I'm in a different room. There's only a few tubes running through my body now, a few beeping noises coming from the machines, and I'm still thirsty.

I'm also alone. Which you wouldn't think would be the one thing I'd fixate on after being shot in the—I look down at my body—upper right chest, but it is.

I think it's night now. The room is dark, my door is open, and there's not much noise in the hallway.

I feel the urge to move, or sit up, or *something*, and immediately regret my slight position change because the pain… holy fucking shit, the pain is overwhelming. I think I might actually pass out for a little bit because when I open my eyes again, there's a nurse in the room with me.

"Good morning," she says brightly. "Are you hungry?"

"Water," I croak.

She holds a cup with one of those bendy straws in it. The straw is yellow and the cup is pink, and I'm thinking this is a nice combination, and that's when I realize I'm fuckin' high as a kite.

But the pain's gone, so I just sip my water and be happy.

"You're not on the TV," the nurse says. Like I should know what this means. She must read the expression on my face as confusion, because once she sets the water down on the little table beside my bed, she clicks a remote and the flatscreen on the wall lights up. "We've all been checking. Mr. Wells asked us to keep an eye on it and so far, so good."

I don't know what that means either. But I don't really care. "Finn?" I ask, my voice stronger now that I've had some water.

She frowns at me. "I'm sorry."

"Oh, my God. Is he dead?"

"No," she says quickly. "No. But the news is saying he was arrested. And now no one is talking about him at all. Well, except for the newscasters."

"Arrested," I repeat. "But what about—"

"Just rest," the nurse says, cutting me off. "There's time to figure everything out later. We're holding all your visitors until you're ready."

"Even Suzanne?"

"Is she the pushy one who keeps telling me about Go Fuck Yourself classes?"

Gotta love Suzanne. "That would be her."

"She stepped out for lunch, but she should be back soon. Would you like to try to use the bathroom?"

I would, so I do. She helps me and then turns her back while I pee with the door open because I might fall over and knock myself out on the sink.

After that I shuffle myself and the IV pole the ten steps back to the bed and decide... I'm not really in the mood to go that extra mile today. But I do need to know what the fuck is happening.

"What happened to me?" I ask.

"You were shot in the chest. Bullet passed right through your upper right quadrant, luckily. There was a lot of blood loss, but the internal damage, while bad, could've been a lot worse. You got really, really lucky, Miss Grey."

I sigh and sink back into the pillows, wincing at the pain leaking past the drugs. "Do I still have a phone?"

"Sorry," she says. "Everything you came in with has already been confiscated as evidence. The FBI is still here. They've been waiting for you to be well enough to talk to them." She eyes me for a moment. "Do you want to talk to them?"

"Do I have a choice?" I ask.

"I can probably buy you another few hours, but after the shift change everyone will know you're awake and they have a court order, so…" She shrugs.

I don't like the sound of this. But I've spent a lot of years hiding from my past and all I want now is the truth. No matter what it is.

So I say, "Yes. Send them in."

There's more to Finn Murphy than he let on. That second phone just confirms the nagging thought in the back of my head the whole time we were together.

The throes of chaos might bring two people closer— the pleasure of panic is real when you're forced to live through something life-altering with a stranger.

But that doesn't mean you know each other.

CHAPTER THIRTY-NINE

FINN✳

"She's awake," the man says as I walk into the small room deep underground at FBI headquarters in DC. He's sitting casually at the solitary table, one foot propped up on one knee, staring at a tablet.

I'm wearing black scrubs, handcuffs, slip-on shoes, and shackles. Before I have a chance to ask anything in return, the man points to the guard—who is built like a tank and towers over my six-foot-three frame by what feels like miles—and says, "Take those off."

The guard complies and I rub my wrists as he deals with the shackles.

"Issy?" I say.

"Take a seat, Murphy." The man eyes me as he points to the only other chair in the room. I know he's FBI, not a lawyer, because he just looks FBI. Dark suit, white shirt, dark tie, dark shoes. He's maybe a little older than me. Dark hair, eye color indistinguishable from this distance, nice haircut if you like the messy look, and stubble casting a shadow across his jawline.

I walk forward and take a seat. "You said she's awake. Does that mean she's out of danger now?" They've given me few updates since I was taken into custody back in Colorado. Issy was put into an ambulance, then Life Flighted down to Denver, and I was put into an unmarked federal car and driven to a private airstrip.

I haven't seen her since. And the last thing I heard she was out of surgery, but that was days ago now.

"Do you know who I am?" the man asks.

"No," I say. "No fuckin' clue."

"Do you know why you're here?"

"Here, as in in custody?" I snort. "Well, I can take a good guess."

"Take a guess," the guy says.

I draw in a deep breath, searching for the words, then let it out and begin. "I shot and killed someone out in Colorado. An exonerated felon who, it turns out, shouldn't have been exonerated."

"Close," the guy says.

He looks familiar but I have no idea why. My head is a cloud of confusion right now. I keep replaying that moment back in my head. When she was shot. The look on her face. The blood, the ambulance… Issy says you don't get a rewind, but that's only in real life. Your brain does rewinds quite well, it turns out. "Why don't you tell me which part I got wrong? And while you're at it, how about a name?"

He reaches into his suit coat pocket, pulls out a badge holder, much like the one I have—had, since they took it away—and flips it open.

"Special Agent Darrel Jameson," I say, squinting as I read his ID.

"That's me. But I'm retired. This," he says, flipping his wallet closed, "is just the one they let me carry when I'm on special assignment. You were my special assignment."

"Me?"

"We're not gonna charge you. In fact, the whole report has been rewritten and your name has now been excluded.

You were never there, Agent Murphy. Do you understand?"

"Uh… I mean, I get it. But no. I don't understand any of this. I thought I killed my father last fall. I saw him take that bullet. And he didn't have a fuckin' vest on, I checked. I was hoping. And—"

"You're getting *waaaaay* ahead of yourself here, Murphy. So just take a breath, sit back, get comfortable, and let me start from the beginning."

So I do.

I listen as he tells his story.

My story, actually.

Except I'm not the one who wrote it.

CHAPTER FORTY

*ISSY

Go F*ck Yourself is where I find myself over the next few weeks. The online class was a hit, but the phone was ringing off the hook looking for the classes. "People want you," Suzanne said. "Not just the information you have."

The FBI interview was as mysterious as the game that precluded it.

Was it a game?

And more importantly, did I win? Or lose?

I can't tell. I have no idea. All I know is that Finn is coming back today. It's been almost five weeks since that night up in the mountains.

Caleb is dead. Sometimes a gunshot wound to the chest kills you, I guess.

Apparently Finn is just a better shot than Senator Walcott.

Speaking of the senator, his name never came up in my interview. Even when I brought it up, it didn't come up. They just moved past it like they had no clue what I was talking about.

Normally I'd be feeling pretty cynical about that, but apparently Senator Walcott is missing. Presumed dead after he went on a hunting trip up in the mountains almost five weeks ago. They think he was either eaten by a mountain lion or mauled by a bear. They're hoping they'll find his body in the spring when the snow melts.

If Chella knows anything about her father's disappearance, she doesn't let on. If she knows it was part of my game, she doesn't say anything. She did look appropriately sad when all the local TV stations were camped outside her tea shop the day after his disappearance. She cried in the interview. Asked people—like hunters and outdoor people and shit—to please be on the lookout for him so she could get closure. If he was dead, she just wanted to know for sure.

But after that… she was just Chella. I don't know her story and I'm not going to ask, because she doesn't know my story and she never asked me either.

Secrets, right? Sometimes you just wanna keep that shit to yourself.

She came over to my hospital room the day I was released, helped me carry all the flowers and stuffed animals out to her car, and then she drove me home, made me tea, and said to call her if I needed anything.

Jordan showed up next. He knocked on my door, then let himself in my house like he belongs there. I think he just came over to feel me out because the conversation went something like this:

ME: Did you fuckin' plan all this?

HIM: Plan all what?

ME: The game.

HIM: What game?

ME: Fuckin' forget it.

HIM: Cool, forgotten.

And then he told me that Finn was fine and handed me a cheap phone. The kind you can buy in the checkout line at Walmart. Told me to keep it charged and someone would be in touch.

Someone was Finn. And that first conversation went like this:

ME: Were you in on it from the beginning?

HIM: In on what?

ME: The game.

HIM: What game?

ME: Fuckin' forget it.

HIM: Cool. I'm gonna be home next week. I'll see ya then.

So I really have no clue what happened last month. The only things I do know are this:

Caleb Kelly might have been unjustly exonerated, but no one in Hell cares.

I met a new man, whom I might be in love with and one day we still might run away to Kansas together.

Izett Gery is gone and Issy Grey isn't.

Was all this my game?

No, I decide.

This was definitely a game, it just wasn't my game.

Did Jordan Wells set all this up? Does he have that kind of power?

And what the fuck happened to Senator Walcott? Did Chella know what kind of man he was? Did she set all this up?

And why was Finn taken back to DC, only to be let go five weeks later, his name scrubbed clean from all reports? Did he set all this up?

I have decided to walk away from it. All of it. Zig says, "Regardless of your past, your tomorrow is a clean slate."

So… bygones, I guess.

Letting it go, I guess.

Oh, no. Not *them*. Not these people who played the game right along with me.

Not Jordan. Not Chella. Not Finn.
These people are dark.
These people are diabolical.
These people are *keepers*.

CHAPTER FORTY-ONE

FINN✳

"You look good, man."

That's Darrel. He glances over at me from behind his sunglasses when I slip into the passenger seat of his BMW in the arrivals lane at Denver International Airport.

"Thanks," I say, shutting the door, and look around at the wide-open sky of Colorado as we pull away and head to the airport exit. "So you're what? Retired again?"

Darrel just nods his head. He's not wearing a suit today. Dark slacks, white button-down—untucked and sleeves rolled up to his elbows—and more than a few days' growth on his face. But the guy still looks *official* somehow. Like you can just tell you don't fuck with him.

And after the story he told me back in DC... I have to admit, I'm glad we're on the same side.

But all that's yesterday's news. Today is new. A fresh start. I'm not an FBI agent anymore, but let's face it. I fucked that shit up a long time ago.

"You decide what to do next?" Darrel asks me. Fuckin' mind-reader too, I guess.

"Maybe," I say. "Sorta? Nah," I finally admit. "I'm just gonna patch things up with Issy and worry about all that other stuff tomorrow."

He doesn't ask any questions about that. He was just feeling me out to see if I was on board with keeping my mouth shut. And it's funny, ya know? How OK I am with keeping my mouth shut.

I shot my father last fall. They told me he died, but they lied. Motherfuckers are always lying. That whole time I was on paid leave for firing my weapon on duty, they were shaking down my old man. Coming up with a plan to weed out the bad seeds and bring some integrity back to this job.

Which is where I come in. They told me, *Just go to Denver. Meet up with your contacts. Feel them out and turn them in. That's all you gotta do and we'll let you go.*

So I did that. Well, I sorta did that. OK, if I'm being honest, I wasn't doing shit until Issy came along. Until she got me involved in her game. Until I woke the fuck up and realized there were things in this world I wanted to be a part of. People I wanted to get to know. Things I wanted to do.

What I didn't know, both back then and the night I began playing the game with Issy, was that my father made a deal with them too. To save me, not himself.

He would hand over all his information—all the dirt he knew and who he knew it on—and in exchange, they'd get me out of the life he forced me into.

Yesterday I escorted him to the minimum-security federal prison camp as my last assignment with the FBI.

He made good, turning in both Declan and Senator Walcott. Caleb Kelly was just a bonus, it turns out. No one's really sure how all that went down.

But that's because none of those assholes know about Jordan Wells. They think Darrel Jameson was running this play.

He's good. I'll give him that. But he's no Jordan. That motherfucker is brutally twisted.

I like him. I like them both, I decide.

Darrel and I don't talk the rest of the way into downtown. Just kinda sit there, satisfied with things.

It was hard to watch my dad go. Real hard. But he kept his head up, told me maybe we'd see each other when he got out, and then turned away and walked into the administration building without looking back.

I have a feeling I'll probably see him again. But I'm gonna let him go for now. Let him find his demons, fight them on his own terms, and figure out his own way forward. A real Zig Ziglar kinda peace washes over me with that thought.

When we get to Issy's office, Darrel pulls into a no-parking zone a few shops up and says, "Good luck, man," as he stares straight ahead.

I might never go out and have a beer with good old Darrel here. But if I ever need a hitman, he's the first guy on my list.

"You too," I say back.

I get out, close the door, but just as I'm about to walk off, I hear a window slide down and look back at him.

"Hey," he says.

"Yeah?" I ask back, leaning down into the window.

"I could use some help. If you need a job and shit."

"What kind of job?" I ask.

"The kind you do."

I smile. The kind of job I do… well, if I wanted to, I could read a lot into that little offer. But I don't feel like reading between the lines today. So I say, "Sure. I'm in."

"Cool," he says. "I'll be in touch." The window starts sliding up, forcing me to step back, and then he pulls away like it never happened.

Go F*ck Yourself has a new sign on the door that says, "Don't count the things you do, do the things that count."

And when I peek through the glass I see a room of women sitting at the various tables in small groups. Suzanne is talking to a few of them. All the tables are filled with black and yellow take-out containers from the Tea Room across the street, and when I go inside, the mood is quiet, but not sad.

Not sad.

Issy is on the other side of the large open area, moderating a class on kickboxing. She looks pretty fuckin' hot in her tight workout pants and halter-top sports bra. I can see her scar. It scares me just to look at it, but I let that feeling go. Because she's still here and that's all that matters.

She doesn't see me at first, but then she's in the middle of explaining some kind spinning jujitsu move thing in slow motion when her eyes meet mine. And when she comes out of the pretend kick and lands on her feet, she's facing me. Like she planned that.

Maybe she planned that? Which makes me smile.

And then *she* smiles. And says, "OK, ladies. Practice that one until I get back."

We walk toward each other. A million questions between us. Serious things to discuss. Major shit to resolve. Demons that should be laid to rest.

But when we finally meet up I say, "You should be resting."

She says, "Go fuck yourself."

And then we laugh.

Like this is funny… when it's not.

It's not funny, it's just… easy. That's all. To let it go. To move on. To start fresh.

She says, "You know, I've done a lot of thinking and I've decided…"

Shit, here it comes. Judgment Day.

"It wasn't the pleasure of panic."

"What?" I ask, confused.

"That brought us together."

"Wasn't it?"

"No," she says, walking towards me. She reaches up to my neck and then she's pulling her legs up to wrap around my middle, and I'm hiking her up, hands under her ass, holding her tight. "It was the serenity of satisfaction."

The kiss that comes after feels like the first kiss. Feels like everything I've ever wanted but was too afraid to ask for. Feels like...

"Yeah," I whisper. "That's exactly right." Satisfaction. "Because pleasure is what you want in the beginning, but satisfaction is what you get at the end."

And then Issy smiles and whispers back in my mouth, "I'm gonna put that on a poster."

J✱RDAN

"So you're probably wondering where the fuck I fit in to all this."

Ixion just looks at me, blank. "Uh… nope."

"I get it, you're confused."

"Why the fuck am I here?" he asks.

"Like I said, confused."

"Jordan," Ix says, looking at his watch. "I got shit to do, OK? So can you get to the fuckin' point already?"

"You remember that day?"

"Nope," he says again. He's pissed. But then again, when isn't Ixion pissed off at me?

We're sitting in my office. Darrel Jameson is in the chair off to my left, Ixion is sitting in front of me, and the new guy, Finn Murphy, is standing at the door, looking out the window, keeping watch in case Wells Senior decides to see what I'm up to.

It's not like I'm hiding this little side business from my father. I'm not. He's well aware of the whole Your Game business.

But he's not aware of *this* game. The one I just played with the FBI.

He has his suspicions though, and I'd like to keep him out of it. Consequently… Finn Murphy takes point at the door.

My phone buzzes and Eileen's voice comes through the speaker. "Jordan? Sorry to bother you, but you have a call on line—"

"Not now, Eileen. Tell whoever it is I'll call them back."

"Sure," Eileen says. "OK."

"That day," I say to Ix. "That day you came in accusing me of playing a game? I'm assuming you were talking about this." I throw my hands wide. "Right?"

"Dude, I have no clue what you're talking about."

"The game, man," I say, leaning forward over my desk like this will make him understand me better. "The FBI, Finn Murphy over there. Issy Grey, and Chella, and Senator"—I whisper the last part—"Walcott."

Now Ixion is squinting at me. "Did you kill that guy?"

"Kill him? Jesus fuck! I'm a goddamned lawyer! Why do people think I'm a criminal?"

Ix kinda laughs at that. And that laugh says, *Where should I start?*

"Well," I say. It's my turn to be confused. "What the fuck were you talking about that day? You seemed pretty pissed off. I assumed it was because Evangeline heard something she shouldn't when she was hanging out with Chella."

"The game you're fucking playing with me and Augustine, asshole."

"You and—Jesus!" I laugh. "Augustine? Shit, I gave up on her."

"You brought her here," Ix says. "You brought me here to get her here."

"Well, that was months ago, man. I'm over her."

"Are you over me yet?"

300

The question lingers in the room. Darrel looks kinda uncomfortable. Finn peeks over his shoulder at me.

My phone buzzes again. "Jordan?" Eileen says through the speaker.

"*What?*" I ask, gritting my teeth.

"She's refusing to be called back."

"Who?" I ask, annoyed behind belief.

"Oaklee Ryan? Do you know her? She's not a client."

I look over at Darrel and he nods, indicating her game is still in play.

"Tell her I'll call her back in ten minutes."

"OK," Eileen says. "But she's a little bit pushy."

Some days I just can't with people, so I take a deep breath and say, "If I were over you, Ixion, and you were over me, then this conversation wouldn't be happening, would it?"

"What the fuck do you want from me?" he asks.

"How about some understanding? How about you flick that fuckin' chip off your shoulder and let the past go? That'd be a great start. How about you fuckin' forgive me? How about you say, 'Hey, Jordan, you're not the asshole I thought you were?' How about that?"

"Because," he says, getting to his feet, "you *are* the asshole I thought you were. That's why."

"I brought down a crooked FBI agent, a pedophile rapist, and a corrupt senator in span of thirty-six hours and that's all you've got to say to me?"

Ixion stares at me. Then he laughs. "Well, that makes me feel a whole lot better about you, Jordan. Thanks."

"Fuck this guy," Darrel says. "We don't need him."

Ix turns, eyes narrow, practically shooting beams of anger at Darrel. "Who. The fuck. Are you?"

Finn isn't watching the door anymore. He's watching Darrel. I'm not watching Ix anymore. I too am watching Darrel.

Darrel says—and I'm pretty sure we're all leaning forward to hear his response—"I'm the truth you never want to hear. I'm the nightmare you never want to have. I'm the goddamned Four Horsemen all wrapped up into one well-dressed ex-FBI-agent who takes down untouchable people as a hobby. That's who the fuck I am. Jordan didn't kill Senator Walcott. I did. And Jordan didn't kill that pedophile rapist, either, *he* did." He points at Finn. "Jordan is the game master. He makes the plans, the rest of us execute them. So do you want to be part of something bigger than yourself? Or do you just want to go through life being some walk-on cut-out character who makes no difference whatsoever?"

Ixion just stares at him. And then he opens his mouth to say—

"Jordan?" Eileen says through my phone speaker.

"Jesus Christ, Eileen. What the fuck is it?"

"Lawton Ayers is here, he's insisting on—Hey!" Eileen yells, but not to me. "Hey, you can't go back there!"

All four of us stare at my phone and then two seconds later we can hear Eileen yelling in the hallway outside my door. Darrel draws his gun, Finn opens the door, and then Lawton Ayers comes rushing in looking like... not himself.

"Dude," Law says. "*Duuuuude*," he says again.

Eileen appears. I look at Darrel, but he's got his gun behind his back. She says, "I'm sorry. He got past me!"

"It's OK, Eileen. I've got this."

"And I'm outta here," Ixion says. And he is. Because he leaves.

I take my attention to Lawton, who is a real cool guy. Fucking loaded real-estate agent. I bought that foreclosed house next to the Botanical Gardens off him last year. He got me a sweet deal. So when I was short a player for Oaklee Ryan's little Boyfriend Experience game, I asked him to fill in.

"What the fuck is going on, Lawton? Oaklee Ryan just called me, seemingly distressed. And why the fuck are you dressed up like a... a..."

"A thug?" Law fills in, his voice a little bit panicked.

"No," I say. "Like a hot dude. Is that a... did you get a *tattoo*?"

"Oh, that's funny," Law says, peeking out my door, looking both ways down the hallway, and then closing and locking it. "Real fucking funny, Jordan. Do you have any idea what kind of game this chick wants me to play with her?"

"Uh, yeah," I say, looking at Darrel, who is laughing. "Little bit of wine, little bit of food, send her flowers at work, maybe some dancing and then cap it all off by taking her to her sister's wedding or something, right?"

"Uh, no," Law says. He's taken up Finn's position at the window, but I'm pretty sure he's not on the lookout for my father.

"Class reunion?" I try again.

"No," Law says. "And when I say no, I mean no to all of that shit. Do you have any idea what she thinks the job of a boyfriend really is?"

I thought I did.

But apparently I don't.

Because when Lawton tells me what Oaklee Ryan wants him to do as her boyfriend... I can only shake my head and laugh.

She might be my biggest rule-bender ever.

But hey, if you obey all the rules, you miss all the fun.

So I look at Law. Sit back in my chair. Steeple my fingers under my chin and say, "Just play, brother. Play your fuckin' heart out. Because winning might not be everything, but it *is* better than losing."

I might have to put that on a poster for Issy Grey.

END *F BOOK SHIT

Welcome to the End of book Shit! This is where I get to reflect back on the story and say whatever I want about it. They are never edited, they are never censored—just 100% Julie in this bad-boy last chapter.

I like the idea of writing about a character who is a self-help speaker. I have a very good friend who kinda does this. Her name is Honoree Corder and she's a business coach and writes books about mindset, and writing, and other magical, badass things. I love her to death. We met in a mastermind group a few years ago and we were sitting next to each other and maybe we got a little bored or whatever, ya know? And like… had our own conversation going on at the end of the table about what the best hand lotion is. It was pretty much love at first sight.

Since then we've seen each other a few times. A couple more times at the mastermind, then at another conference in Vegas last fall, and she was actually one of the four important friends in my life who I introduced to Johnathan when we first started writing books together. (The other three were science fiction writer, Terry Schott, and my assistant Nicole Alexander and her husband Tim).

Honoree has all these cute colloquialisms and funny sayings that feel very Southern. She says the cutest shit in the most badass way and I'm jealous of that because while honesty is something I do well, being friendly and personable feels like a talent I never quite mastered. She

305

can be brutally honest and sweet in the same sentence. And she just does it naturally. She's makes friends everywhere she goes, and when you need help making the hard choices Honoree is the one who will look you in the eye and say, "Bitch, get your shit together!" So I love her for that. She pulls no punches.

So while Issy Grey isn't based on Honoree, Honoree was my inspiration for this character.

Johnathan told me once a few months ago that if I ever stopped writing books I should be a self-help speaker because I have a certain worldview that lends itself to practical, logical answers to difficult, emotional questions.

I think what he means is that I'm Spock. Right? lol I'm logical and practical and see things in a very binary, black and white way. So when I have a problem, the answer to my problem is mostly black and white too. Do it or don't do it. We were emailing back and forth a couple weeks ago and I said that to him. You're Kirk and I'm Spock (because he and I are so very different and Kirk and Spock sum it up pretty well.)

But I do like teaching and I do like helping people so Issy Grey is more of a combination of both me and Honoree together.

I like the idea that helping people can actually help you heal yourself. And I was thinking about this yesterday when I was watching that show Billions on Showtime. Do you watch that? It's really good. It's about this scrappy (pretty unethical) billionaire who bootstrapped his way up from humble beginnings to be one of the most successful stock investors in the world. So in this episode he lost his license to trade stock because the Attorney General (who is his nemesis) found out he did something illegal. And so this "poor" guy is lost. He can't do what he feels like he was meant to do. And he wants to trade stock so bad. Like he sees an opportunity and he wants this so bad, he's almost willing to throw his whole life away to do it.

He just doesn't know how to live any other way.

And I was watching that episode thinking—Dude, just take all that money you have and go help people. Helping people gives you purpose in an immediate way that almost nothing else can. And it heals you at the same time.

So Issy was a woman who took her sadness and loss and turned herself around by helping others. And she did this is a very provocative way that makes people take notice. But her first instinct isn't to fight, it's to run. She's a very good runner. But now… when the past comes back to haunt her, she has a choice to make and it's not so simple. Because helping people is her purpose. And if she leaves her purpose behind, she might leave herself behind too.

Finding one's purpose is a very hard thing to do. Some people struggle their whole lives and never find their purpose so if you've found your purpose you don't turn your back on it. You can't turn your back on it.

Finn is the first character I've written in a long time who isn't good at heart. I don't know if this comes across on the page very well because I am very careful to write a likeable hero, but Finn is the first guy since James Fenici in The Company books, who is probably more of a bad guy than a good one. If you've read the Turning Series you might be thinking… Well, Elias Bricman wasn't good either. Probably true. BUT—Bric wasn't breaking laws. Bric wasn't doing anything illegal. And Jordan is a good guy, regardless of what he appears to be at present.

But I like Finn and that's why he's on Team Jordan now. He's got more to say in the next two books, believe me. And I think it's OK to write a bad guy who doesn't immediately find his good side in a story.

Writing backstory in romance is tricky. Because on the one hand you need just enough of a past to create a good character, but on the other hand, the romance is the whole point of the book. And if you let the backstory overpower the romance, you lose your reader. People don't read my Company books because of the shadow government and the assassins. They read them because of the characters. Not the character's past, but the character's present. So when writing romance you gotta balance this out. Give the reader enough so they can feel like they "know" the character, but not too much that knowing the character overpowers the point. And the point of a romance is the romance.

So Finn hasn't found his purpose yet. He found a person to share his life with, but people need more than romantic love. Yes. That's true. People need to feel complete when they're alone as well as when they're together.

Every time I think about writing a happily ever after book I want to kick myself. lol Because HEA books never make money, only readers who've read through the whole series want them, and when you've got thirty-seven new ideas for books and only so many hours in the day, it's hard to put those aside and revisit a world just for the sake of revisiting it.

So I sneaked something into this book. Chella's HEA. It's still developing and it will play out over the next two books, but I love that her father got what he deserved in this book. And I brought Darrel back from Turning Series to take care of some shit for me. So I'm loving the cross-connection between Turning Series and Jordan's Game. It was always meant to be that way but you never know if you can pull a thing off until you've pulled a thing off. And this series is still developing, so we'll see at the end if I manage it.

But I'm pretty sure there WILL be a HEA book in the future for the Turning and Jordan people. I think that their world is too big to not have one. Which is why I wrote one for Rook & Ronin and the Misters. They all had a big world and they all needed more after their individual stories were over. I'm not sure I'm gonna put this up on Amazon... lol Like... is it book four of Turning Series? Or book five of Jordan's series? I'll have to think on that.

I feel like this EOBS is a little bit all over the place this time. Probably because that's how my life is at the moment. I have so many balls in the air, it's hard to know if I'm coming or going. In fact, I don't think I'm either. I think I'm both coming and going.

Johnathan and I have finished writing our first four-book series, Original Sin. Book three, Flesh Into Fire, will be releasing next week. We have another book planned for July, but we're not announcing it yet. Look for a cover reveal on July 13. I will tell you this – it's a standalone book, it's a romantic comedy, and it's gonna be fucking fantastic! We are staying in Colorado as far as setting goes but we are building an entire new world of characters with their own fictional neighborhood. I'm quite excited about it honestly, and I think it's going to be a lot of fun.

We're also working on our Company TV deal with MGM. Should be signing that contract in the next week or so.

In between all that I'm writing this Jordan series, traveling for book signings, and planning my next solo book outside the Turning/Jordan world which will release in the fall.

So pardon my rambling mind in this EOBS! I have all the things to say and only so many pages at the end to say them!

I hope you continue on with the Jordan books. The stories are standalone but the world is not. The world is just getting started and I think the last two books will leave you totally satisfied and ready for that HEA book that will probably release in December as a little Christmas gift.

Until then, think about what your purpose is. If you haven't found it yet don't worry. It took me forty-three years to find my purpose.

There's no expiration date on your dreams.

Issy might need to put that on a poster. :)

Julie

JA Huss
April 5, 2018

Thank you for reading, thank you for reviewing, and if you want the next book, The Boyfriend Experience, you can find all the links to buy it at:

http://jahuss.com/series/jordans-game

ABO*T THE A*THOR

JA Huss never wanted to be a writer and she still dreams of that elusive career as an astronaut. She originally went to school to become an equine veterinarian but soon figured out they keep horrible hours and decided to go to grad school instead. That Ph.D wasn't all it was cracked up to be (and she really sucked at the whole scientist thing), so she dropped out and got a M.S. in forensic toxicology just to get the whole thing over with as soon as possible.

After graduation she got a job with the state of Colorado as their one and only hog farm inspector and spent her days wandering the Eastern Plains shooting the shit with farmers.

After a few years of that, she got bored. And since she was a homeschool mom and actually does love science, she decided to write science textbooks and make online classes for other homeschool moms.

She wrote more than two hundred of those workbooks and was the number one publisher at the online homeschool store many times, but eventually she covered every science topic she could think of and ran out of shit to say.

So in 2012 she decided to write fiction instead. That year she released her first three books and started a career that would make her a New York Times bestseller and land her on the USA Today Bestseller's List twenty-one times in the next four years.

Her books have sold millions of copies all over the world, the audio version of her semi-autobiographical book, Eighteen, was nominated for an Audie award in 2016, and her audiobook Mr. Perfect was nominated for a Voice Arts Award in 2017.

She also writes book and screenplays with her friend, actor and writer, Johnathan McClain. Their first book, Sin With Me, will release on March 6, 2018. And they are currently working with MGM as producing partners to turn their adaption of her series, The Company, into a TV series.

She lives on a ranch in Central Colorado with her family, two donkeys, four dogs, three birds, and two cats.

If you'd like to learn more about JA Huss or get a look at her schedule of upcoming appearances, visit her website at www.JAHuss.com or www.HussMcClain.com to keep updated on her projects with Johnathan. You can also join her fan group, Shrike Bikes, on Facebook, www.facebook.com/groups/shrikebikes and follow her Twitter handle, @jahuss.

15690949R00182

Printed in Great Britain
by Amazon